PENGUIN BOOKS

AGENT RUNNING IN THE FIELD

John Le Carré was born in 1931 and attended the universities of Bern and Oxford. He taught at Eton and served briefly in British intelligence during the Cold War. For the last fifty-five years, he has lived by his pen. He divides his time between London and Cornwall.

Praise for *Agent Running in the Field*

"Le Carré is one of the best novelists—of any kind—we have."

—*Vanity Fair*

"A word about le Carré's prose: Not only does it hold the coiled energy of a much younger writer, it fits the bitter, angry narrator's voice exceptionally well."

—NPR.org

"Le Carré remains a master at showing us what spies do, wily spiders to the unsuspecting flies they entrap."

—*Booklist* (starred review)

"Deeply pleasurable."

—*Vogue*

"A tragicomic salute to both the recuperative powers of its has-been hero and the remarkable career of its nonpareil author."

—*Kirkus Reviews*

"John le Carré is the great master of the spy story. . . . The constant flow of emotion lifts him not only above all modern suspense novelists, but above most novelists now practicing."

—*Financial Times*

"One of our great writers of moral ambiguity, a tireless explorer of that darkly contradictory no-man's land."

—*Los Angeles Times*

"No other writer has charted—pitilessly for politicians but thrillingly for readers—the public and secret histories of his times."

—*The Guardian* (London)

Agent Running in the Field

JOHN LE CARRÉ

PENGUIN BOOKS

To Jane

PENGUIN BOOKS
An imprint of Penguin Random House LLC
penguinrandomhouse.com

First published in Great Britain by Viking, an imprint of Penguin Books,
a division of Penguin Random House Ltd., 2019
First published in the United States of America by Viking,
an imprint of Penguin Random House LLC, 2019
Published in Penguin Books 2020

ISBN 9781984878892 (paperback)

THE LIBRARY OF CONGRESS HAS CATALOGED THE
HARDCOVER EDITION AS FOLLOWS:
Names: Le Carré, John, 1931– author.
Title: Agent running in the field / John le Carré.
Description: New York : Viking, [2019]
Identifiers: LCCN 2019037844 (print) | LCCN 2019037845 (ebook) |
ISBN 9781984878878 (hardcover) | ISBN 9781984878885 (ebook)
Subjects: GSAFD: Spy stories.
Classification: LCC PR6062.E33 A72 2019 (print) | LCC PR6062.E33 (ebook) |
DDC 823/.914—dc23
LC record available at https://lccn.loc.gov/2019037844
LC ebook record available at https://lccn.loc.gov/2019037845

Printed in the United States of America
1 3 5 7 9 10 8 6 4 2

I

Our meeting was not contrived. Not by me, not by Ed, not by any of the hidden hands supposedly pulling at his strings. I was not targeted. Ed was not put up to it. We were neither covertly nor aggressively observed. He issued a sporting challenge. I accepted it. We played. There was no contrivance, no conspiracy, no collusion. There are events in my life – only a few these days, it's true – that admit of one version only. Our meeting is such an event. My telling of it never wavered in all the times they made me repeat it.

It is a Saturday evening. I am sitting in the Athleticus Club in Battersea, of which I am Honorary Secretary, a largely meaningless title, in an upholstered deckchair beside the indoor swimming pool. The clubroom is cavernous and high-raftered, part of a converted brewery, with the pool at one end and a bar at the other, and a passageway between the two that leads to the segregated changing rooms and shower areas.

In facing the pool I am at an oblique angle to the bar. Beyond the bar lies the entrance to the clubroom, then the lobby, then the doorway to the street. I am thus not in a position to see who is entering the clubroom or who is hanging around in the lobby reading notices, booking courts or putting their names on the Club ladder. The bar is doing brisk trade. Young girls and their swains splash and chatter.

I am wearing my badminton kit: shorts, sweatshirt and a new pair of ankle-friendly trainers. I bought them to fend off a niggling pain in my left ankle incurred on a ramble in the forests of Estonia a month previously. After prolonged back-to-back stints overseas I am savouring a well-deserved spell of home leave. A cloud looms over my professional life that I am doing my best to ignore. On Monday I expect to be declared redundant. Well, so be it, I keep telling myself. I am entering my forty-seventh year, I have had a good run, this was always going to be the deal, so no complaints.

All the greater therefore the consolation of knowing that, despite the advance of age and a troublesome ankle, I continue to reign supreme as Club champion, having only last Saturday secured the singles title against a talented younger field. Singles are generally regarded as the exclusive preserve of fleet-footed twenty-somethings, but thus far I have managed to hold my own. Today, in accordance with Club tradition, as newly crowned champion I have successfully acquitted myself in a friendly match against the champion of our rival club across the river in Chelsea. And here he is sitting beside me now in the afterglow of our combat, pint in hand, an aspiring and sportsmanlike young Indian barrister. I was hard pressed till the last few points, when experience and a bit of luck turned the tables in my favour. Perhaps these simple facts will go some way to explaining my charitable disposition at the moment when Ed threw down his challenge, and my feeling, however temporary, that there was life after redundancy.

My vanquished opponent and I are chatting amiably together. The topic, I remember as if it were yesterday, was our fathers. Both, it turned out, had been enthusiastic badminton players. His had been All-India runner-up. Mine for one halcyon season had been British Army champion in Singapore. As we compare notes in this amusing way I become aware of Alice, our Caribbean-born receptionist and bookkeeper, advancing on me in the company of a very tall and as yet indistinct young man. Alice is sixty years old, whimsical, portly and always a little out of wind. We are two of the longest-standing members of the Club, I as player, she as mainstay. Wherever I was stationed in the world, we never failed to send each other Christmas cards. Mine were saucy, hers were holy. When I say advancing on me, I mean that, since the two of them were attacking me from the rear with Alice leading the march, they had first to advance, then turn to face me, which comically they achieved in unison.

'Mister Sir Nat, sir,' Alice announces with an air of high cere-mony. More often I am Lord Nat to her, but this evening I am a common knight. 'This very handsome and polite young man needs to talk to you *most* privately. But he don't want to *disturb* you in your moment of glory. His name is *Ed. Ed*, say hullo to *Nat*.'

For a long moment in my memory Ed remains standing a couple of paces behind her, this six-foot-something, gawky, bespectacled young man with a sense of solitude about him and an embarrassed half-smile. I remember how two competing sources of light converged on him: the orange strip light from the bar, which endowed him with a celestial glow, and behind him the down lights from the swimming pool, which cast him in oversized silhouette.

He steps forward and becomes real. Two big, ungainly steps, left foot, right foot, halt. Alice bustles off. I wait for him to speak. I adjust my features into a patient smile. Six foot three at least, hair dark and tousled, large brown studious eyes given ethereal status by the spectacles, and the kind of knee-length white sports shorts more commonly found on yachties or sons of the Boston rich. Age around twenty-five, but with those eternal-student features could easily be less or more.

'Sir?' he demands finally, but not entirely respectfully.

'*Nat*, if you don't mind,' I correct him with another smile.

He takes this in. Nat. Thinks about it. Wrinkles his beaky nose.

'Well, I'm *Ed*,' he volunteers, repeating Alice's information for my benefit. In the England I have recently returned to, nobody has a surname.

'Well, hullo, *Ed*,' I reply jauntily. 'What can I be doing for you?'

Another hiatus while he thinks about this. Then the blurt:

'I want to play you, right? You're the champion. Trouble is, I've only just joined the Club. Last week. Yeah. I've put my name on the ladder and all that, but the ladder takes absolutely bloody *months*' – as the words break free of their confinement. Then a pause while he looks at each of us in turn, first my genial opponent, then back to me.

'*Look*,' he goes on, reasoning with me although I have offered no contest. 'I don't know Club protocol, right?' – voice rising in indignation. 'Which is not my fault. Only I asked Alice. And *she* said, ask him yourself, he won't bite. So I'm asking.' And in case further explanation was needed, 'Only I've watched you play, right? And I've beaten a couple of people you've beaten. And one or two who've beaten you. I'm pretty sure I could give you a game. A good one. Yeah. *Quite* a good one, actually.'

And the voice itself, of which by now I have a fair sample? In the time-honoured British parlour game of placing our compatriots on the social ladder by virtue of their diction I am at best a poor contestant, having spent too much of my life in foreign parts. But to the ear of my daughter Stephanie, a sworn leveller, my guess is that Ed's diction would pass as *just about all right*, meaning no direct evidence of a private education.

'May I ask where you play, Ed?' I enquire, a standard question among us.

4

'All over. Wherever I can find a decent opponent. Yeah.' And as an afterthought: 'Then I heard you were a member at this place. Some clubs, they let you play and pay. Not here. This place, you've got to join first. It's a scam in my opinion. So I did. Cost a fucking bomb, but still.'

'Well, sorry you had to fork out, Ed,' I reply as genially as I may, attributing the gratuitous 'fucking' to nervousness. 'But if you want a game, that's fine by me,' I add, noting that the conversation around the bar is drying up and heads are starting to turn. 'Let's fix a date some time. I look forward to it.'

But this doesn't do at all for Ed.

'So when d'you reckon would be all right for you? Like in real terms. Not just *some time*,' he insists, and gets himself a patter of laughter from the bar – which, judging by his scowl, irritates him.

'Well, it can't be for a week or two, Ed,' I reply truthfully enough. 'I have a rather serious bit of business to attend to. A long-overdue family holiday in fact,' I add, hoping for a smile and receiving a wooden stare.

'When d'you get back then?'

'Saturday week, if we haven't broken anything. We're going skiing.'

'Where?'

'In France. Near Megève. Do you ski?'

'Have done. In Bavaria, me. How about the Sunday after?'

'I'm afraid it would have to be a weekday, Ed,' I reply firmly, since family weekends, now that Prue and I can achieve them, are sacrosanct and today is a rare exception.

'So a weekday starting Monday fortnight then, right? Which one? Choose one. Your call. I'm easy.'

'Probably a *Monday* would suit me best,' I suggest, Monday evenings being when Prue conducts her weekly *pro bono* law surgery.

5

'Monday fortnight, then. Six o'clock? Seven? When?'

'Well, tell me what suits *you* best,' I suggest. 'My plans are a bit up in the air' – like, I'll probably be out on the street by then.

'Sometimes they keep me in Mondays,' he says, making it sound like a complaint. 'How about eight? Eight suit you all right?'

'Eight suits me fine.'

'Court one all right by you if I can get it? Alice says they don't like giving courts to singles, but you're different.'

'Any court is fine by me, Ed,' I assure him to more laughter and a smattering of applause from the bar, presumably for persistence.

We trade mobile phone numbers, always a small dilemma. I give him the family one and suggest he text me if there's any problem. He makes the same request of me.

'And hey, Nat?' – with a sudden softening of the overcharged voice.

'What?'

'Mind you have a really good family holiday, okay?' And in case I've forgotten: 'Two weeks Monday then. Eight p.m. Here.'

By now everyone's laughing or clapping as Ed, with a lank, insouciant departing wave of the whole right arm, lopes off for the men's changing room.

'Anyone know him?' I ask, discovering that I have unconsciously turned to observe his departure.

Shakes of the head. Sorry, mate.

'Anyone seen him play?'

Sorry again.

I escort my visiting opponent to the lobby and on my way back to the changing room pop my head round the office door. Alice is bowed over her computer.

'Ed who?' I ask her.

'Shannon,' she intones, not lifting her head. 'Edward Stanley. Single membership. Paid by standing order, town member.'

6

'Occupation?'

'Mr Shannon, he is a *researcher* by occupation. *Who* he research, he don't say. *What* he research, he don't say.'

'Address?'

'Hoxton, in the Borough of Hackney. Same as where my two sisters live and my cousin Amy.'

'Age?'

'Mr Shannon is *not* eligible for junior membership. How much he is not eligible, he don't say. All I know is, that's some hungry boy for you, bicycling all across London just to challenge the Champ of the South. He's heard about you, now he's come to get you, sure as David did Goliath.'

'Did he *say* that?'

'What he didn't say I have divined in my own head. You've been singles champion too long for your age, Nat, same as Goliath. You want his mummy and daddy? How big his mortgage is? How much jail time he done?'

'Goodnight, Alice. And thanks.'

'I wish you goodnight too, Nat. And be sure to give my love to your Prue. And don't you go feeling insecure about that young man, now. You'll put him away, same as you do all them whippersnappers.'

2

If this were an official case history, I would kick off with Ed's full name, parents, date and place of birth, occupation, religion, racial origin, sexual orientation and all the other vital statistics missing from Alice's computer. As it is, I will begin with my own.

I was christened Anatoly, later anglicized to Nathaniel, Nat for short. I am five feet ten inches tall, clean-shaven, tufty hair running to grey, married to Prudence, partner for general legal matters of a compassionate nature at an old-established firm of City of London solicitors, but primarily *pro bono* cases.

In build I am slim, Prue prefers *wiry*. I love all sport. In addition to badminton I jog, run and work out once a week in a gymnasium not open to the general public. I possess a *rugged charm* and the *accessible personality of a man of the world*. I am in appearance and manner *a British archetype*, capable of *fluent and persuasive argument in the short term*. I *adapt to circumstance* and have *no insuperable moral scruples*. I can be *irascible* and am *not by any means immune to female charms*. I am *not naturally suited to deskwork or the sedentary life*, which is the understatement of all time. I can be *headstrong* and *do not respond naturally to discipline*. This can be *both a defect and a virtue*.

I am quoting from my late employers' confidential reports on my performance and general allure over the last twenty-five years. You will also wish to know that in need I can *be relied upon* to exhibit *the required callousness*, though required by whom, and in what degree, is not stated. By contrast I have a *light touch and a welcoming nature that invites trust.*

At a more mundane level, I am a British subject of mixed birth, an only child born in Paris, my late father being at the time of my conception an impecunious major of Scots Guards on attachment to NATO headquarters in Fontainebleau, and my mother the daughter of insignificant White Russian nobility residing in Paris. For *White Russian* read also a good dollop of German blood on her father's side, which she alternately invoked or denied at whim. History has it that the couple first met at a reception held by the last remnants of the self-styled Russian Government-in-Exile at a time when my mother was still calling herself an art student and my father was close on forty. By morning they were engaged to be married: or so my mother told it, and given her life passage in other areas I have little reason to doubt her word. Upon his retirement from the army – swiftly enforced, since at the time of his infatuation my father possessed a wife and other encumbrances – the newlyweds settled in the Paris suburb of Neuilly in a pretty white house supplied by my maternal grandparents where I was soon born, thus enabling my mother to seek other diversions.

I have left till last the stately, all-wise person of my beloved language tutor, minder and de facto governess, Madame Galina, purportedly a dispossessed countess from the Volga region of Russia with claims to Romanov blood. How she ever arrived in our fractious household remains unclear to me, my best guess being that she was the cast-off mistress of a great-uncle on my mother's side who, after fleeing Leningrad, as it then was, and making himself a second fortune as an art dealer, devoted his life to acquiring beautiful women.

Madame Galina was fifty if a day when she first appeared in our household, very plump but with a kittenish smile. She wore long dresses of swishy black silk and made her own hats, and lived in our two attic rooms with everything that she owned in the world: her gramophone, her icons, a pitch-dark painting of the Virgin that she insisted was by Leonardo, box upon box of old letters and photographs of grandparental princelings and princesses surrounded by dogs and servants in the snow.

Second to my personal welfare, Madame Galina's great passion was for languages, of which she spoke several. I had barely mastered the elements of English spelling before she was pressing Cyrillic script on me. Our bedtime readings were a rotation of the same child's story, each night a different language. At gatherings of Paris's fast-dwindling community of White Russian descendants and exiles from the Soviet Union, I performed as her polyglot poster child. It is said I speak Russian with a French intonation, French with a Russian intonation, and such German as I have with a mixture of both. My English on the other hand remains for better or worse my father's. I am told it even has his Scottish cadences, if not the alcoholic roar that accompanied them.

In my twelfth year, my father succumbed to cancer and melancholy and with Madame Galina's help I attended to his dying needs, my mother being otherwise engaged with the wealthiest of her admirers, a Belgian arms dealer for whom I had no regard. In the uneasy triangle that followed my father's demise I was deemed surplus to requirements and packed off to the Scottish Borders, to be billeted in the holidays with a dour paternal aunt, and in term time at a spartan Highlands boarding school. Despite the school's best efforts not to educate me in any indoor subject, I obtained entry to a university in the English industrial Midlands, where I took my first awkward steps with the female sex and scraped a third-class degree in Slavonic Studies.

I have for the last twenty-five years been a serving member of Britain's Secret Intelligence Service – to its initiated, the Office.

*

Even today my recruitment to the secret flag appears preordained, for I don't remember contemplating any other career or wishing for one, except possibly badminton or climbing in the Cairngorms. From the moment my university tutor asked me shyly over a glass of warm white wine whether I had ever considered doing something 'a bit hush-hush for your country' my heart lifted in recognition and my mind went back to a dark apartment in Saint-Germain that Madame Galina and I had frequented every Sunday until my father's death. It was there that I had first thrilled to the buzz of anti-Bolshevik conspiracy as my half-cousins, step-uncles and wild-eyed great-aunts exchanged whispered messages from the homeland that few of them had ever set foot in – before, waking to my presence, requiring me to be sworn to secrecy whether or not I had understood the secret I should not have overheard. There also I acquired my fascination for the Bear whose blood I shared, for his diversity, immensity and unfathomable ways.

A bland letter flutters through my letter box advising me to present myself at a porticoed building close to Buckingham Palace. From behind a desk as big as a gun turret a retired Royal Navy admiral asks me what games I play. I tell him badminton and he is visibly moved.

'D'you know, I played badminton with your dear father in Singapore and he absolutely trounced me?'

No, sir, I say, I didn't know, and wonder whether I should apologize on my father's behalf. We must have talked of other things but I have no memory of them.

'And where's he *buried*, your poor chap?' he enquires, as I rise to leave.

'In Paris, sir.'

'Ah, well. Good luck to you.'

I am ordered to present myself at Bodmin Parkway railway station carrying a copy of last week's *Spectator* magazine. Having established that all unsold copies have been returned to the wholesaler, I steal one from a local library. A man in a green trilby asks me when the next train leaves for Camborne. I reply that I am unable to advise him since I am on my way to Didcot. I follow him at a distance to the car park where a white van is waiting. After three days of inscrutable questions and stilted dinners where my social attributes and head for alcohol are tested, I am summoned before the assembled board.

'And *so*, Nat,' says a grey-haired lady at the centre of the table. 'Now that we've asked you all about yourself, is there something you'd like to ask *us* for a change?'

'Well, as a matter of fact there *is*,' I reply, having first given a show of earnest reflection. 'You've asked me whether you can depend on my loyalty, but can I depend on *yours*?'

She smiles, and soon everyone at the table is smiling with her: the same sad, clever, inward smile that is the closest the Service ever gets to a flag.

Glib under pressure. Latent aggression good. Recommended.

*

In the same month that I completed my basic training course in the dark arts, I had the good fortune to meet Prudence, my future wife. Our first encounter was not auspicious. On my father's death a regiment of skeletons had broken loose from the family cupboard. Half-brothers and half-sisters I had never heard of were laying claim to an estate that over the last fourteen years had been disputed, litigated and picked clean by its Scottish trustees. A friend recommended a City law firm. After five minutes of listening to my woes, the senior partner pressed a bell.

'One of our very best young lawyers,' he assured me.

The door opened and a woman of my own age marched in. She was wearing a daunting black suit of the sort favoured by the legal profession, schoolmarm spectacles and heavy black military boots on very small feet. We shook hands. She gave me no second look. To the clunk of her boots she marched me to a cubicle with Ms P. Stoneway LLB on the frosted glass.

We sit down opposite each other, she sternly tucks her chestnut hair behind her ears and produces a yellow legal pad from a drawer.

'Your profession?' she demands.

'Member, HM Foreign Service,' I reply, and for some unknown reason blush.

After that I remember best her poker back and resolute chin and a stray shaft of sunlight playing on the little hairs of her cheek as I narrate one squalid detail after another of our family saga.

'I may call you Nat?' she asks at the end of our first session. She may.

'People call me *Prue*,' she says, and we set a date for two weeks hence, at which, in the same impassive voice, she gives me the benefit of her researches:

'I have to inform you, Nat, that if all the disputed assets in your late father's estate were placed into your hands tomorrow there would not be sufficient funds even to pay my firm's fees, let alone settle the outstanding claims against you. *However*,' she continues before I am able to protest that I will trouble her no further, 'there *is* provision within the partnership for treating needy and deserving cases on a cost-free basis. And I am happy to inform you that your case has been deemed to fall within that category.'

She needs another meeting in one week's time, but I am obliged to postpone it. A Latvian agent must be infiltrated into a Red Army signals base in Belarus. On my return to British shores I call Prue and invite her to dinner, only to be curtly advised that it is her firm's policy that client relations should remain on an impersonal footing. However, she is pleased to inform me that as a result of her firm's representations all claims against me have been abandoned. I thank her profusely and ask her whether in that case the way is clear for her to have dinner with me. It is.

We go to Bianchi's. She wears a low-cut summer dress, her hair has come out from behind her ears and every man and woman in the room is staring at her. I quickly realize that my usual patter doesn't play. We have barely reached the main course before I am being treated to a dissertation on the gap between law and justice. When the bill comes she takes possession of it, calculates her half to the last penny, adds ten per cent for service and pays me in cash from her handbag. I tell her in simulated outrage that I have never before encountered such barefaced integrity, and she nearly falls off her chair for laughter.

Six months later, with the prior consent of my employers, I ask her whether she will consider marrying a spy. She will. Now it is the Service's turn to take her to dinner. Two weeks later, she informs me that she has decided to put her legal career on hold and undergo the Office's training course for spouses shortly to be posted to hostile environments. She needs me to know that she has taken the decision of her own free will and not for love of me. She was torn, but was persuaded by her sense of national duty.

She completes the course with flying colours. A week later

I am posted to the British Embassy in Moscow as Second Secretary (Commercial), accompanied by my wife Prudence. In the event, Moscow was the only posting that we shared. The reasons for this do Prue no dishonour. I shall come to them shortly.

For more than two decades, first with Prue, and then without her, I have served my Queen under diplomatic or consular cover in Moscow, Prague, Bucharest, Budapest, Tbilisi, Trieste, Helsinki and most recently Tallinn, recruiting and running secret agents of every stripe. I have never been invited to the high tables of policy-making, and am glad of it. The natural-born agent-runner is his own man. He may take his orders from London, but in the field he is the master of his fate and the fate of his agents. And when his active years are done, there aren't going to be many berths waiting for a journeyman spy in his late forties who detests deskwork and has the curriculum vitae of a middle-ranking diplomat who never made the grade.

*

Christmas is approaching. My day of reckoning has come. Deep in the catacombs of my Service's headquarters beside the Thames, I am led to a small, airless interviewing room and received by a smiling, intelligent woman of indeterminate age. She is Moira of Human Resources. There has always been something a little alien about the Moiras of the Service. They know more about you than you know yourself but they're not telling you what it is, or whether they like it.

'Now, your *Prue*,' Moira asks keenly. 'Has she survived her law firm's recent merger? It was upsetting for her, I'm sure.'

Thank you, Moira, it wasn't upsetting at all, and congratulations on doing your homework. I would expect no less.

'And she's *well*, is she? You're *both* well?' – with a note of anxiety I choose to ignore. 'Now that you're safely *home*.'

'Absolutely fine, Moira. Very happily reunited, thanks.'

And now kindly read me my death warrant and let's get this over with. But Moira has her methods. Next on her list comes my daughter Stephanie.

'And no more of those *growing pains*, I trust, now that she's safely at university?'

'None whatever, Moira, thanks. Her tutors are over the moon,' I reply.

But all I'm really thinking is: now tell me that a Thursday evening has been set for my farewell knees-up because nobody likes Fridays, and would I care to take my cup of cold coffee three doors down the corridor to Resettlement section, who will offer me tantalizing openings in the arms industry, private contracting or other laying-out places for old spies such as the National Trust, the Automobile Association and private schools in search of assistant bursars. It therefore comes as a surprise to me when she announces brightly:

'Well, we do have *one* slot for you actually, Nat, assuming you're up for it.'

Up for it? Moira, I am up for it like no one on earth. But only warily up for it, because I think I know what you're about to offer me: a suspicion that turns to certainty when she launches on a child's guide to the current Russian threat.

'I don't have to tell you that Moscow Centre is running us absolutely *ragged* in London, as everywhere else, Nat.'

No, Moira, you don't have to tell me. I've been telling Head Office the same thing for years.

'They're nastier than they ever were, more brazen, more meddlesome and more numerous. Would you say that was fair comment?'

I would, Moira, I would indeed. Read my end-of-tour report from sunny Estonia.

'And ever since we kicked out their *legal* spies in bulk' – meaning spies with diplomatic cover, so my sort – 'they've been flooding our shores with *illegals*,' she goes on indignantly, 'who I think you'll agree are the most troublesome of the species *and* the most difficult to smell out. You have a question.'

Give it a try. Worth a shot. Nothing to lose.

'Well, before you go any further, Moira.'

'Yes?'

'It just occurred to me there might be a slot for me in Russia department. They've got a full complement of upmarket young desk officers, we all know *that*. But what about an experienced visiting fireman, a seasoned, native-grade Russian-speaker such as myself who can fly anywhere at the drop of a hat and take first bite of any potential Russian defector or agent who pops up at a station where nobody speaks a word of the language?'

Moira is already shaking her head.

'No dice, I'm afraid, Nat. I floated you with Bryn. He's adamant.'

There's only one Bryn in the Office: Bryn Sykes-Jordan, to give him his full name, shortened to Bryn Jordan for common usage, ruler-for-life of Russia department and my one-time head of Station in Moscow.

'So no dice *why*?' I insist.

'You know very well why. Because Russia department's average age is thirty-three, even with Bryn's added in. Most have DPhils, *all* have fresh minds, *all* have advanced computer skills. Perfect as you are in every respect, you don't quite meet those criteria. Well, do you, Nat?'

'And Bryn isn't around by any chance?' I ask, a last-ditch appeal.

'Bryn Jordan, even as we speak, is embedded up to his neck in Washington DC, doing what only Bryn can do to salvage our embattled special relationship with President Trump's intelligence community post-Brexit, and *on no account* to be disturbed, thank you, even by you, to whom he sends his affectionate regards and condolences. Clear?'

'Clear.'

'However,' she continues, brightening, 'there is one opening for which you *are* eminently qualified. Even *over*-qualified.'

Here we go. The nightmare offer I've seen coming from the start.

'Sorry, Moira,' I cut in. 'If it's Training section, I'm hanging up my cloak. Very good of you, very thoughtful, all the above.'

I appear to have offended her, so I say sorry again and no disrespect to the fine upstanding men and women of Training section, but it's still thanks but no thanks, upon which her face breaks into an unexpectedly warm if somewhat pitying smile.

'*Not* Training section, actually, Nat, although I'm sure you'd do very well there. Dom is keen to have a word with you. Or should I be telling him you're hanging up your cloak?'

'*Dom?*'

'Dominic Trench, our recently appointed head of London General. Your one-time head of Station in Budapest. He says the two of you got on like a house on fire. I'm sure you will again. Why are you looking at me like that?'

'Are you seriously telling me Dom Trench is head of London General?'

'I don't think I'd *lie* to you, Nat.'

'When did that happen?'

'A month ago. While you were asleep in Tallinn not reading our newsletters. Dom will see you at ten tomorrow morning prompt. Confirm with Viv first.'

'Viv?'

'His assistant.'

'Of course.'

3

'*Nat!* How splendid you look! The sailor home from the sea
indeed. Fit as a fiddle and half your age!' cries Dominic Trench,
bounding from his directorial desk and seizing my right hand in
both of his. 'All that hard work in the gym, no doubt. Prue well?'

'Fighting fit, Dom, thank you. Rachel?'

'Marvellous. I'm the luckiest man on earth. You must meet
her, Nat. You and Prue. We'll make a dinner, the four of us.
You'll love her.'

Rachel. Peeress of the realm, power in the Tory Party, second
wife, recent union.

'And the kids?' I ask gingerly. There had been two by his nice
first wife.

'Superb. Sarah's doing marvellously at South Hampstead.
Oxford squarely in her sights.'

'And Sammy?'

'Twilight time. He'll be out of it soon and following in his
sister's footsteps.'

'And Tabby, may one ask?' Tabitha his first wife and, by the
time they broke up, a neurotic wreck.

'Doing nobly. No new man in sight so far as we know, but
one lives in hope.'

It's my guess that there's a Dom somewhere in everyone's
life: the man – it always seems to be a man – who takes you

aside, appoints you his only friend in the world, regales you with details of his private life you'd rather not hear, begs your advice, you give him none, he swears to follow it and next morning cuts you dead. Five years ago in Budapest he was turning thirty, and he's turning thirty now: the same croupier's good looks, striped shirt, yellow braces more befitting a twenty-five-year-old, white cuffs, gold links and all-purpose smile; the same infuriating habit of placing his fingertips together in a wedding arch, leaning back and smiling judiciously at you over the top of them.

*

'Well, congratulations, Dom,' I say, gesturing at the executive armchairs and Office ceramic coffee table for grade threes and above.

'Thank you, Nat. You're most kind. Took me by surprise, but when the call comes, we rally. Coffee at all? Tea?'

'Coffee, please.'

'Milk? Sugar? The milk's soy, I should add.'

'Just black, thank you, Dom. No soy.'

Does he mean *soya*? Is *soy* the smart man's version these days? He puts his head round the stippled-glass door, engages in stage banter with Viv, sits again.

'And London General still has the same old remit?' I enquire lightly, recalling that Bryn Jordan had once described it in my hearing as the Office's home for lost dogs.

'Indeed, Nat. Indeed. The same.'

'So all London-based substations are nominally under your command.'

'UK-wide. Not only London. The whole of Britain. Excluding Northern Ireland. And still totally autonomous, I'm pleased to say.'

'Administratively autonomous? Or operationally too?'

'In what sense, Nat?' – frowning at me as if I'm out of court.

'Can you, as head of London General, authorize your own operations?'

'It's a blurred line, Nat. As of now, any operation proposed by a substation must notionally be signed off by the regional department concerned. I'm fighting it, practically as we speak.'

He smiles. I smile. Battle joined. In synchronized movements we taste our coffees with no soy and replace our cups on their saucers. Is he about to confide some unwanted intimacy about his new bride? Or explain to me why I'm here? Not yet, apparently. First we must have a jaw about old times: agents we shared, I as their handler, Dom as my useless supervisor. First on his list is Polonius, lately of the Shakespeare network. A few months back, having Office business in Lisbon, I had gone to see old Polonius in the Algarve in an echoing new-build beside an empty golf course that we had bought for him as part of his resettlement package.

'Doing all right, Dom, thank you,' I say heartily. 'No problems with his new identity. Got over his wife's death. He's all right, really. Yes.'

'I hear a *but* in your voice, Nat,' he says reproachfully.

'Well, we promised him a British passport, didn't we, Dom, if you remember. Seems to have got lost in the wash after your return to London.'

'I shall look into it at once' – and a note to himself in ballpoint to prove it.

'He's also a bit cut up that we couldn't get his daughter into Oxbridge. He feels all it needed was a nudge from us and we didn't provide it. Or you didn't. Which is the way he sees it.'

Dom doesn't do guilt. He does injured or he does blank. He opts for injured.

'It's the *colleges*, Nat,' he complains wearily. 'Everyone thinks the old universities are an *entity*. This is wrong. You have to go from one college to the other, cap in hand. I shall chase it' – another ballpoint note.

Second on his list of topics is Delilah, a colourful seventy-something Hungarian woman member of parliament who took the Russian rouble then decided she preferred the British pound before it collapsed.

'Delilah's in great shape, Dom, thanks, just great. A bit fed up to discover my successor was a woman. She said that for as long as I was running her, she could dream that love was round the corner.'

He has a grin and a shake of the shoulders about Delilah and her many lovers, but no laughter comes out. Sip of coffee. Return cup to saucer.

'*Nat*' – plaintively.

'Dom.'

'I'd really thought this was going to be a flashbulb moment for you.'

'And why would that be, Dom?'

'Well, for heaven's sake! I'm offering you a golden opportunity to remodel, single-handed, a home-based Russian outstation that's been in the shade too long. With your expertise you'll put it right in – what? – six months max? It's creative, it's operational, it's you. What more can you want at your time of life?'

'I'm afraid I'm not with you, Dom.'

'You're not?'

'No. I'm not.'

'You mean they didn't *tell* you?'

'They said talk to you. I'm talking to you. That's as far as we've got.'

'You walked in here *blind*? Jesus *Christ*. Sometimes I wonder what those fucking Human Resources people think they're up to. Was it Moira you saw?'

'Maybe she thought it was better coming from you, Dom,

whatever it is. I think you said home-based Russian outstation that's been in the shade too long. There's only one I know of and it's the Haven. It's *not* an outstation, it's a defunct sub-station under the aegis of London General and it's a dumping ground for resettled defectors of nil value and fifth-rate informants on the skids. Last heard of, the Treasury were about to wind it up. They must have forgotten. Is that what you're seriously offering me?'

'The Haven is *not* a dumping ground, Nat – far, far from it. Not on my watch. It's got a couple of officers who are long in the tooth, I grant you. And sources still waiting to realize their potential. But there's first-rate material in there for the man or woman who knows where to look. *And* of course' – as an afterthought – 'it's wide open to anyone who earns their spurs in the Haven to be considered for promotion to Russia department.'

'So is that something you might be considering for yourself, by any chance, Dom?' I enquire.

'Is what, old boy?'

'Making a career move to Russia department. On the back of the Haven.'

He frowns and purses his lips in disapproval. Dom is nothing if not transparent. Russia department, preferably head of it, is his life's dream. Not because he knows the terrain, has the experience or speaks Russian. He doesn't do any of those things. He's a late-entrant City boy, headhunted for reasons I suspect not even he can fathom, with no linguistic qualifications worth a damn.

'Because if that's what's in your mind, Dom, I'd like to make the same journey with you, if that's all right,' I press on facetiously or playfully or angrily, I'm not sure which. 'Or might you be planning to rip the labels off my reports and stick on your own, the way you did in Budapest? Just asking, Dom.'

Dom thinks about this, which means he first looks at me over his wedding-arch fingers, then into the middle distance, then back at me again to make sure I'm still there.

'Here's my offer to you, Nat, take or leave. In my capacity as head of London General. I am formally offering you the opportunity to succeed Giles Wackford as head of substation Haven. For as long as I engage you on a temporary basis, you're within my gift. You'll be taking over Giles's agents *and* his Station imprest forthwith. Also his entertainment allowance, what's left of it. I'm suggesting you hit the ground running and pick up on the rest of your home leave at a later date. What's your question?'

'Doesn't play for me, Dom.'

'And why would that be, pray?'

'I have to talk this whole thing through with Prue.'

'And when you and Prue have so talked?'

'Our daughter Stephanie is about to celebrate her nineteenth birthday. I've promised to take her and Prue for a week's skiing before she goes back to Bristol.'

He cranes forward, frowning theatrically at a wall calendar.

'Starting when?'

'She's in her second semester.'

'I am asking when you leave on your holiday.'

'At five a.m. from Stansted on Saturday, if you're thinking of joining us.'

'Assuming you and Prue have talked things over by then and come to a satisfactory conclusion, I suppose I can have Giles hold the fort at the Haven till Monday week, if he hasn't rolled off his perch by then. Would you be happy with that, or miserable?'

Good question. Would I be happy? I'll be in the Office, I'll be working on the Russia target, even if I'm living off scraps from Dom's table.

But will Prue be happy?

*

The Prue of today is not the dedicated Office spouse of more than twenty years ago. As selfless, yes, and upright. And as much fun when she lets her hair down. And as determined as ever to be of service to the world at large, just never again in a secret capacity. The impressive junior lawyer who had taken courses in counter-surveillance, safety signals and the filling and clearing of dead letter boxes had indeed accompanied me to Moscow. For fourteen exacting months we had shared the perpetual stress of knowing that our most intimate exchanges were listened to, watched over and analysed for any hint of human weakness or lapse in security. Under the impressive guidance of our head of Station – the same Bryn Jordan who today was huddled in anxious conclave with our intelligence partners in Washington – she had played the starring role in husband-and-wife setpiece charades scripted to deceive the opposition's eavesdroppers.

But it was during our second back-to-back stint in Moscow that Prue discovered she was pregnant, and with pregnancy came an abrupt disenchantment with the Office and its works. A lifetime of deception no longer appealed to her, if it ever had. Neither did a foreign birthplace for our child. We returned to England. Perhaps when the baby is born, she'll think differently, I told myself. But that was not to know Prue. On the day Stephanie was born, Prue's father dropped dead of a heart attack. On the strength of his bequest, she paid cash down for a Victorian house in Battersea with a large garden and an apple tree. If she had stuck a flag in the ground and said 'Here I stay', she could not have made her intentions more clear. Our daughter Steff, as we were soon calling her, would never become the kind of diplomatic brat we had seen too many of, over-nannied and shuffled from country to country and school to school in the wake of their mothers and fathers. She would occupy her natural place in society, attend state schools, never private or boarding schools.

And what would Prue herself do with the rest of her life? She would take it up where she had left it. She would become a human rights lawyer, a legal champion of the oppressed. But her decision implied no sudden separation. She understood my love of Queen, country and the Service. I understood her love of law and human justice. She had given the Service her all, she could give no more. From the earliest days of our marriage she had never been the sort of wife who can't wait for the Chief's Christmas party or the funerals of revered members or At Homes for junior staff and their dependants. And I for my part had never been a natural for get-togethers with Prue's radically minded legal colleagues.

But neither of us could have foreseen that as post-Communist Russia, against all hope and expectation, emerged as a clear and present threat to liberal democracy across the globe, one foreign posting would follow on the heels of the last and I would become a de facto absentee husband and father.

Well, now I was home from the sea, as Dom had kindly said. It hadn't been easy for either of us, Prue particularly, and she had every reason to hope that I was back on dry land for good and looking for a new life in what she referred to, a little too often, as the real world. A former colleague of mine had opened up an outward-bound club for disadvantaged kids in Birmingham and swore he'd never been so happy in his life. Hadn't I once talked of doing just that?

4

For the rest of the week leading up to our crack-of-dawn departure from Stansted I affected for reasons of family harmony to
be mulling over whether to accept the *pretty dreary job* I had
been offered by the Office, or make the clean break Prue had
long advocated. She was content to wait. Steff professed herself
unbothered either way. As far as she was concerned I was just
a middle-order bureaucrat who was never going to make the
grade whatever he did. She loved me, but from a height.

'Let's face it, sport, they're not going to appoint us ambassador
to Beijing or give us a knighthood, are they?' she reminded me
cheerfully when the question came up over dinner. As usual, I
took it on the chin. For as long as I was a diplomat abroad, I at
least had status. Back in the mother country, I was part of the
grey mass.

It was not till our second evening in the mountains, while
Steff was out gallivanting with a bunch of Italian kids who
were staying in our hotel, and Prue and I were enjoying a quiet
cheese fondue and a couple of glasses of kirsch at Marcel's, that
I was seized with the urge to come clean to Prue about my job
offer at the Office – really clean – not tiptoe around as I had
been planning, not another cover story, but tell it to her from
the heart, which was the least she deserved after all I'd put her
through over the years. Her air of quiet resignation told me she

had already sensed that I was a long way from opening that outward-bound club for disadvantaged kids.

'It's one of those run-down London substations that's been resting on its laurels since the glory days of the Cold War and not producing anything worth a damn,' I say grimly. 'It's a Mickey Mouse outfit, light miles from the mainstream, and my job will be either to get it on its feet or speed it on its way to the graveyard.'

With Prue, on the rare occasions we get to talk in relaxed terms about the Office, I never know whether I'm swimming against the tide or with it, so I tend to do a bit of both.

'I thought you always said you didn't want a command post,' she objects lightly. 'You preferred to be second man, not bean-counting and bossing other people around.'

'Well, this isn't really a *command* post, Prue,' I assure her warily. 'I'll still be second man.'

'Well, that's all right then, isn't it?' she says, brightening. 'You'll have Bryn to keep you on the rails. You always admired Bryn. We both did' – gallantly setting aside her own scruples.

We exchange nostalgic smiles as we recall our short-lived honeymoon as Moscow spies, with Station head Bryn our ever-watchful guide and mentor.

'Well, I won't be under Bryn *directly*, Prue. Bryn's Czar of All the Russias these days. A sideshow like the Haven's a bit below his pay grade.'

'So who's the lucky person who's going to be in charge of you?' she enquires.

This is no longer the kind of full disclosure I had in mind. Dom is anathema to Prue. She met him when she came out to visit me in Budapest with Steff, took one look at Dom's distraught wife and children and read the signs.

'Well, officially I'll be under what's called *London General*,' I explain. 'But of course in reality, if it's anything *really* major, it trickles up the pyramid to Bryn. It's just for as long as they need me, Prue. Not a day longer,' I add by way of consolation, though which of us I'm consoling is not clear to either of us.

She takes a forkful of fondue, a sip of wine, a sip of kirsch and, thus fortified, reaches both her hands across the table and grasps mine. Does she *guess* Dom? Does she *intuit* him? Prue's near-psychic insights can verge on the disturbing.

'Well, I'll tell you what, Nat,' she says after due reflection. 'I think it's your good right to do exactly what you want to do, for as long as you want to do it, and bugger the rest. And I'll do the same. And it's my turn to pay the bill, so there. The whole of it this time. I owe it to my barefaced integrity,' she adds, in a joke that never pales.

And it was on this happy note, while we're lying in bed and I'm thanking her for her generosity of spirit over the years and she is telling me sweet things about myself in return, and Steff is dancing the night away, or so we hope, that I come up with the notion that now is the ideal opportunity to make a clean breast to our daughter about the true nature of her father's work, or as clean as Head Office allows. It was high time she knew, I reasoned, and far better she hear it from me than from anyone else. I might have added, but didn't, that since my return to hearth and home I was becoming increasingly irked by her light-hearted disdain for me, and by her practice, left over from adolescence, of either tolerating me as a necessary domestic encumbrance or plonking herself on my lap as if I were some kind of fuddy-duddy in the evening of his life, usually for the benefit of her latest admirer. I was also irked, if I am being cruelly honest, by the way Prue's much deserved eminence as a human rights lawyer encouraged Steff in her belief that I had been left standing.

At first the lawyer-mother in Prue is wary. How much *exactly* did I propose to tell her? Presumably there were limits. What were they precisely? Who set them? The Office or me? And how did I intend to handle follow-up questions, should there be any, had I thought about *that*? And how could I be sure of not getting carried away? We both knew Steff's reactions were never predictable, and Steff and I wound each other up too easily. We had form in this respect. And so on.

And Prue's warning words were, as ever, eminently sound and well founded. Steff's early adolescence had been a bit of a living nightmare, as Prue didn't need to remind me. Boys, drugs, screaming matches – all the usual modern-age problems, you might say, but Steff had turned them into an art form. While I was gravitating between overseas stations, Prue had spent every spare hour reasoning with head teachers and form teachers, attending parents' evenings, ploughing through books and newspaper articles and trawling advisory services on the internet for guidance on how best to handle your hell-bent daughter, and blaming herself for all of it.

And I for my part had done my humble best to share the load, flying home for weekends, sitting in conclave with psychiatrists and psychologists and every other kind of *ist*. The only thing they seemed to agree on was that Steff was hyper-intelligent – no great surprise to us – was bored stiff by her peer group, rejected discipline as an existential threat, found her teachers insufferably tedious, and what she really needed was a challenging intellectual environment that was up to her speed: a statement, as far as I was concerned, of the blindingly obvious, but not so to Prue, who has rather more faith than I have in expert opinion.

Well, now Steff had her challenging intellectual environment. At Bristol University. Mathematics and Philosophy. And she was entering her second semester of it.

So tell her.

'You don't think you'd make a better job of it, darling?' I

suggest to Prue, keeper of the family wisdom, in a weak moment.

'No, darling. Since you're determined to do it, it will be *far* better coming from you. Just remember you *are* quick-tempered, and don't on any account do self-deprecation. Self-deprecation will drive her straight round the bend.'

★

Having run my eye over possible locations, rather in the way I'd calculate a risky approach to a potential source, I concluded that the best setting and the most natural must surely be the little-used ski-lift for slalom practice running up the north slope of the Grand Terrain. It had a T-bar of the old type: you went up side by side, no need for eye contact, nobody within earshot, pine forest to the left, steep drop to the valley on the right. A short sharp descent to the bottom of the one and only lift, so no fear of losing touch, obligatory cut-off point at the top, any follow-up questions to be dealt with on the next ascent.

It's a sparkling winter's morning, perfect snow. Prue has pleaded fictional tummy trouble and taken herself shopping. Steff had been out on the tiles with her young Italians till God knows what hour, but seemed none the worse for it, and pleased to be getting some alone-time with Dad. Obviously there was no way I could go into detail about my shady past beyond explaining that I'd never been a real diplomat, just a pretend one, which was the reason why I'd never landed a knighthood or an ambassadorship to Beijing, so maybe she could leave that one out now that I'd come home because it was seriously getting on my nerves.

I'd *like* to have told her why I'd failed to phone her on her fourteenth birthday, because I knew it still rankled. I'd *like* to have explained that I had been sitting on the Estonian side of the Russian border in thick snow praying to God my agent would make it through the lines under a pile of sawn timber. I'd *like* to have given her some idea of how it had felt for her mother and me to live together under non-stop surveillance as members of the Office's Station in Moscow where it could take ten days to clear or fill a dead letter box, knowing that, if you put a foot out of place, your agent is likely to die in hell. But Prue had insisted that our Moscow tour was the part of her life she did not want revisited, adding in her usual forthright way:

'And I don't think she needs to know we fucked for the Russian cameras either, darling' – relishing our rediscovered sex life.

*

Steff and I grab a T-bar and away we go. First time up, we chat about my homecoming and how little I know of the old country I've been serving half my life, so a lot to learn, Steff, a lot to get used to, as I'm sure you understand.

'Like no more lovely tax-free booze when we come to visit you!' she wails, and we share a hearty father–daughter laugh.

Time to uncouple, and down the mountain we sail, Steff leading. So a really good soft opening to our tête-à-tête.

'And there's *no* disgrace to serving your country in *any* capacity, darling' – Prue's counsel ringing in my memory's ear – 'you and I may have differing views on patriotism, but Steff sees it as a curse on mankind, second only to religion. And keep the humour down. Humour at serious moments is simply an escape route as far as Steff's concerned.'

We hook up a second time and set off up the hill. *Now*. No jokes, no self-deprecation, no apology. And stick to the brief that Prue and I thrashed out together, no deviations. Staring hard ahead of me, I select a serious but not portentous tone.

'Steff, there's something about me that your mother and I feel it's time you knew.'

'I'm illegitimate,' she says eagerly.

'No, but I'm a spy.'

She too is staring ahead of her. This wasn't quite how I meant it to begin. Never mind. I say my piece as drafted, she listens. No eye contact so no stress. I keep it short and cool. So there you are, Steff, now you have it. I've been living a necessary lie, and that's all I'm allowed to tell you. I may look like a failure, but I do have a certain status in my own Service. She doesn't say anything. We reach the top, uncouple and set off down the hill, still nothing said. She's faster than I am, or likes to think she is, so I let her have her head. We meet up again at the bottom of the lift.

Standing in the queue we don't speak to each other and she doesn't look in my direction, but that doesn't disconcert me. Steff lives in her world, well now she knows I live in mine too, and it's not some knacker's yard for Foreign Office low-flyers. She's in front of me so she grabs the T-bar first. We have barely set off before she asks in a matter-of-fact voice whether I've ever killed anyone. I chuckle, say no, Steff, absolutely not, thank God, which is true. Others have, if only indirectly, but I haven't. Not even arm's length or third flag, not even as the Office calls it, *deniable authorship*.

'Well if you *haven't* killed anyone, what's the *next*-worst thing you've done as a spy?' – in the same casual tone.

'Well, Steff, I suppose the *next* worst I've done is persuade chaps to do things they might not have done if I hadn't talked them into it, so to speak.'

'Bad things?'

'Arguably. Depends which side of the fence you're on.'

'Such as what, for instance?'

'Well, betray their country for starters.'

'And you persuaded them to do that?'

33

'If they hadn't persuaded themselves already, yes.'

'Just *chaps*, or did you persuade *female* chaps too?' – which if you'd heard Steff on the subject of feminism is not as light-hearted as it might otherwise sound.

'Largely male chaps, Steff. Yes, men, overwhelmingly men,' I assure her.

We have reached the top. We again uncouple and descend, Steff streaking ahead. Once more we meet at the bottom of the lift. No queue. Until now she has pushed her goggles up on to her forehead for the ride. This time she leaves them in place. They're the mirrored kind that you can't see into.

'Persuade *how* exactly?' she resumes as soon as we set off.

'Well, we're not talking *thumbscrews*, Steff,' I reply, which is pilot error on my part: *Humour at serious moments is simply an escape route as far as Steff's concerned.*

'So how?' she persists, gnawing at the subject of persuasion.

'Well, Steff, a lot of people will do a lot of things for *money* and a lot of people will do things for *spite* or *ego*. There are also people who do things for an *ideal*, and wouldn't take your money if you shoved it down their throats.'

'And what ideal would that be exactly, *Dad*?' – from behind the shiny goggles. It's the first time for weeks that she's called me Dad. Also I notice that she is not swearing, which with Steff can be a bit of a red warning light.

'Well, let's say, just for instance, somebody has an idealistic vision of England as the mother of all democracies. Or they love our dear Queen with an unexplained fervour. It may not be an England that exists for *us* any more, if it ever did, but they think it does, so go with it.'

'Do *you* think it does?'

'With reservations.'

'Serious reservations?'

'Well, who wouldn't have, for Christ's sake?' I reply, stung by the suggestion that I've somehow failed to notice that the country's in free fall. 'A minority Tory cabinet of tenth-raters. A pig-ignorant foreign secretary who I'm supposed to be serving. Labour no better. The sheer bloody lunacy of Brexit' – I break off. I have feelings too. Let my indignant silence say the rest.

'Then you *do* have serious reservations?' she insists in her purest tone. 'Even very serious. Yes?'

Too late I realize I have left myself wide open, but perhaps that was what I wanted to achieve all along: to give her the victory, acknowledge I'm not up to the standards of her brilliant professors, and then we can all go back to being who we were.

'So if I've got this right,' she resumes, as we embark on our next ascent, 'for the sake of a country that you have serious reservations about, even *very* serious, you persuade *other* nationals to betray their *own* countries.' And as an afterthought: 'The reason being that *they* don't share the same reservations that *you* have about *your* country, whereas they *do* have reservations about their own country. Yes?'

At which I let out a merry exclamation that accepts honourable defeat while simultaneously asking for mitigation:

'But they're not innocent lambs, Steff! They *volunteer*. Or most of them do. And we look after them. We welfare them. If it's money they're after, we give them a pot of it. If they're into God, we do God with them. It's whatever works, Steff. We're their friends. They trust us. We provide for their needs. They provide for ours. It's the way of the world.'

But she's not interested in the way of the world. She's interested in mine, as becomes apparent on the next ride up:

'When you were telling *other* people who to be, did you ever consider who *you* were?'

'I just knew I was on the right side, Steff,' I reply, as my gall begins to rise despite Prue's best injunctions.

35

'And what side's that?'

'My Service. My country. And yours too, actually.'

And on our absolutely last ride up, after I have composed myself:

'Dad?'

'Fire away.'

'Did you have *affairs* while you were abroad?'

'Affairs?'

'Love affairs.'

'Did your mother say I did?'

'No.'

'Then why the hell don't you mind your own bloody business?' I snap before I can stop myself.

'Because I'm not my bloody mother,' she yells back with equal force.

On which unhappy note we uncouple for the last time and make our separate ways down to the village. Come evening, she declines all offers to blow the walls out with her Italian buddies, insisting that she needs to go to bed. Which she duly does, after drinking a bottle of red burgundy.

And I, after a decent interval, relay our conversation in broadbrush to Prue, omitting for both our sakes Steff's gratuitous parting question. I even try to convince us both that our little talk was mission accomplished, but Prue knows me too well. On the flight back to London next morning Steff seats herself on the other side of the aisle. Next day – the eve of her return to Bristol – she and Prue have the most godawful bust-up. Steff's fury, it emerges, is directed not at her father for being a spy, or even for persuading other chaps to be spies, male or female, but at her own long-suffering mother for keeping such a monumental secret from her own daughter, thereby violating the most sacred trust of womanhood.

And when Prue gently points out that the secret was not hers to divulge but mine, and probably not mine either but the Office's, Steff flounces out of the house, goes to ground at her boyfriend's place and travels alone to Bristol, arriving two days late for the start of term after sending the boyfriend to collect her luggage.

*

Does Ed put in a guest appearance anywhere in this family soap opera? Of course he doesn't. How could he? He never left the island. Yet there was a moment – a mistaken one, but memorable nonetheless – when a young fellow walked in on Prue and myself while we were enjoying a *croûtes au fromage* and carafe of white in the Trois Sommets ski hut that overlooks the whole terrain, and he could have been Ed's double. In the flesh. Not an effigy, but himself.

Steff was having a lie-in. Prue and I had skied early and were planning a gentle teeter down the hill and bed. And lo and behold in walked this Ed-like figure in a bobble hat – same height, same air of being alone, aggrieved and slightly lost – stubbornly stamping the snow off his boots in the doorway while he held everyone up, then yanking off his goggles and blinking round the room as if he'd mislaid his specs. I had even flung up my arm halfway in greeting before stopping myself.

But Prue, quick as ever, intercepted the gesture. And, when for reasons that still elude me I demurred, she demanded a full and frank explanation. So I gave her a capsule version: there was this boy at the Athleticus who wouldn't leave me alone till I'd agreed to give him a game. But Prue needed more. What had struck me so deeply about him on such brief acquaintance? Why had I reacted so spontaneously to his lookalike – not my style at all?

To which it seems I reeled off a string of answers that, being

Prue, she remembers better than I do: an oddball, I seem to have said, something courageous about him; and how, when a rowdy bunch at the bar had tried to take the mickey out of him, he'd gone on hammering away at me till he'd got what he wanted and, implicitly telling them to go screw themselves, pushed off.

*

If you love mountains as much as I do, coming down from them is always going to be depressing, but the sight of a run-down three-storey red-brick eyesore in a Camden back street at nine a.m. on a rain-drenched Monday when you haven't got the least idea of what you'll do with it when you get inside takes some beating.

How any substation came to finish up in this neck of the woods was a mystery in itself. How it had acquired the ironic sobriquet of *the Haven* was another. There was a theory the place had been used as a safe house for captured German spies in the '39–'45 war; another that a former Chief had kept his mistress here; and yet another that Head Office, in one of its endless policy lurches, had decreed that security was best served by scattering its substations across London, and the Haven by its sheer insignificance had got overlooked when the policy was scrapped.

I mount the three cracked steps. The peeling front door opens before I have a chance to insert my aged Yale key. Directly in front of me stands the once redoubtable Giles Wackford, over-weight and leaky-eyed, but in his day one of the smartest agent-runners in the Office stable, and just three years older than myself.

'My dear fellow,' he declares huskily through last night's whisky fumes. 'Punctilious to the minute as ever! My warmest salaams to you, sir. What an honour! Can't think of a better chap to succeed me.'

Then meet his team, which is dispersed in two-man outposts up and down a narrow wooden staircase:

Igor, depressed sixty-five-year-old Lithuanian, one-time controller of the best Cold War Balkan network the Office ever ran, now reduced to handling a stable of tame office cleaners, doormen and typists employed by soft foreign embassies.

Next, *Marika*, Igor's reputed Estonian lover, widow of a retired Office agent who died in Petersburg when it was still Leningrad.

Then *Denise*, a tubby, feisty, Russian-speaking Scottish daughter of part-Norwegian parents.

And last little *Ilya*, a sharp-eyed Russian-speaking Anglo-Finnish boy I had recruited as a double agent in Helsinki five years ago. He had gone on to work for my successor on the promise of resettlement in the UK. At first Head Office wouldn't go near him. It was only after my repeated representations to Bryn Jordan that they agreed to take him on as a member of the lowest form of secret life: junior clerical assistant cleared to Grade C. With cries of Finnish joy, he seizes me in a Russian-style embrace.

And on a top floor condemned to eternal darkness, my ragtag support staff of clerical assistants with bicultural backgrounds and elementary operational training.

Only after we have seemingly completed our grand tour and I am beginning to wonder whether my promised number two exists at all does Giles rap ceremoniously on a stippled-glass door that leads from his own musty office, and there in what I suspect was once a maid's room I have my first sight of the youthful, bold-faced, stately figure of Florence, fluent Russian-speaker, second-year probationer, latest addition to substation Haven and, according to Dom, its white hope.

'Then why hasn't she gone straight to Russia department?' I had asked him.

'Because we deemed her a trifle *callow*, Nat,' Dom had replied loftily in his borrowed speak, implying that he had been at the centre of the decision. 'Talented yes, but we thought we should give her another year to settle.'

Talented but needs to settle. I had asked Moira for a sight of her personal file. True to form, Dom had filched the best line.

*

Suddenly everything the Haven undertakes is Florence-driven. Or so it is in my memory. There may have been other deserving projects, but from the moment my eye lighted on draft *Operation Rosebud* it was the only show in our very small town, and Florence was its only star.

On her own initiative she had recruited the disaffected mistress of a London-based Ukrainian oligarch codenamed Orson who had well-documented links to both Moscow Centre and pro-Putin elements in the Ukrainian Government.

Her ambitious plan, luridly overstated, called for a Head Office stealth team to break into Orson's £75 million Park Lane duplex, bug it to the rafters and make constructive adjustments to a bank of computers installed behind a steel door halfway up the marble staircase leading to the panoramic lounge.

As currently presented, Rosebud's chances of getting the green light from Operations Directorate were in my judgement zero. Illegal break-ins were a highly competitive field. Stealth teams were gold dust. Rosebud in its present state would be just one more unheard voice in a noisy marketplace. Yet the further I delved into Florence's presentation, the more convinced I became that, with ruthless editing and smart timing, Rosebud could deliver actionable high-grade intelligence. And in Florence, as Giles was at pains to inform me over a nocturnal bottle of Talisker whisky in the back kitchen of the Haven, Rosebud had found an implacable if obsessive champion:

'Girl's done *all* her own shoe-leather work, *all* her own

40

paperwork. From the day she dug Orson out of the files she's been living and dreaming the bugger. I said to her: you got a vendetta against this fellow? Didn't even laugh. Said he was a blight on humanity and needed flushing out.'

Long pull of whisky.

'Girl doesn't just cosy up to Astra and make her a friend for life' – *Astra* being the codename of Orson's disenchanted mistress – 'she stitches up the night porter of the target building into the bargain. Spins the fellow this yarn that she's working undercover for the *Daily Mail* doing a feature on the lifestyle of London's oligarchs. Night porter falls in love with her, believes every word she says. Any time she wants to take a look inside the lion's cage, five thousand quid out of the *Daily Mail*'s reptile fund and it's hers for the asking. *Immature*, my arse. Balls like an elephant's.'

*

I organize a quiet lunch with Percy Price, all-powerful head of Surveillance, an empire to itself. Protocol requires that I invite Dom along. It is quickly evident that Percy and Dom are not made for each other, but Percy and I go back a long way. He is a gaunt and taciturn ex-policeman in his fifties. Ten years ago, with the assistance of one of his stealth teams and an agent I was running, we stole a prototype missile from the Russian exhibition stand at an international arms fair.

'My boys and girls keep bumping into this Orson fellow,' he complains thoughtfully. 'Every time we turn over a shifty billionaire with his finger in the Russian pie, Orson pops up. We're not case officers, we're watchers. We watch what we're told to watch. But I'm very glad somebody's decided to go after him at last, because him and his lot have been bothering me for a very long time.'

Percy will see if he can give us a window. It will be touch-and-go, mind, Nat. If Ops Directorate decide at the eleventh hour that another bid is stronger, there's nothing Percy or anyone else can do about it.

'And of course everything goes through me, Percy,' says Dom, and we both say, yes, Dom, of course.

Three days later, Percy calls me on my Office mobile. Looks like there's a bit of slack coming up, Nat. Could be worth a punt. Thanks, Percy, I say, I'll pass the word on to Dom as appropriate, by which I mean as late as possible or not at all.

Florence's cubbyhole is one step from my office. From now on, I inform her, she will spend as much quality time as needed with Orson's disenchanted mistress, codename Astra. She will take her for country drives, escort her on her shopping expeditions and have girly lunches with her at Fortnum's, Astra's favourite. She will also up her cultivation of the night porter at the target building. Disregarding Dom, I authorize a sweetener of five hundred pounds to that end. Under my guidance Florence will also draft a formal application for a first covert reconnaissance of the interior of Orson's duplex to be conducted by a stealth team from Operations Directorate. By involving the Directorate at this early stage, we are signalling serious intent.

*

My initial instinct has been to enjoy Florence with caution: one of those upper-class girls who've grown up with ponies and you never quite know what's going on inside. Steff would loathe her on sight, Prue would worry. Her eyes are large, brown and unsmiling. To cover her shape in the workplace she favours baggy woollen skirts, flat shoes, no make-up. According to her file, she lives with her parents in Pimlico and has no designated partner. Her sexual orientation is by her own wish *undeclared*.

As what I take to be a keep-out sign, she sports a man's gold signet ring on her wedding finger. She has a long stride and a slight lilt with every step. The same lilt is replicated in her voice, which is pure Cheltenham Ladies' College laced with bricklayers' expletives. My first experience of this unlikely pairing occurs during a discussion of Operation Rosebud. We are five: Dom, Percy Price and myself, a pompous Office burglar named Eric and Florence, probationer. The issue of the moment is whether a power cut might usefully be staged as a diversion while Eric's boys and girls are conducting their reconnaissance inside Orson's duplex. Florence, who until now has remained quiescent, springs to life:

'But *Eric*,' she objects. 'Whatever do we think Orson's computers run on? Fucking torch batteries?'

An urgent problem awaiting me is to excise the note of moral outrage that permeates her draft submission to Operations Directorate. I may not be the Office's uncrowned king of paperwork – my personal reports suggest the opposite – but I do know what raises the hackles of our dear planners. When I tell her this in plain English she flares. Is this Steff I'm dealing with, or my number two?

'Oh *Jesus*,' she sighs. 'You're about to tell me you've got a thing about adverbs.'

'I'm telling you nothing of the kind. I'm telling you that it's a matter of embuggerance, as you would say, to Ops Directorate *and* Russia department whether Orson is the most debased man on the planet or a paragon of the virtues. We therefore delete all references to just causes and obscene sums of money stolen from the world's oppressed. We do intent, dividend, risk level and deniability and we make bloody sure the Haven's symbol is watermarked on every page and not mysteriously replaced by anyone else's.'

'Such as Dom's?'

'Such as anybody's.'

She stalks back to her cubbyhole and slams the door. No wonder Giles fell in love with her: he hasn't got a daughter. I call Percy, tell him the Rosebud draft proposal is in the pipeline. When all my excuses for delay have run out, I give Dom a full and frank account of our progress to date – by which I mean, enough to keep him quiet. On the Monday evening, with a pardonable sense of self-satisfaction, I wish goodnight to the Haven and set course for the Athleticus and my long-delayed badminton encounter with Edward Stanley Shannon, researcher.

5

According to my engagements diary, which has never in its life contained information I would not be prepared to leave on a bus or at home, Ed and I played in all fifteen games of badminton at the Athleticus, mainly but not always on Mondays, and sometimes twice weekly, fourteen before the Fall, one after it. My use of *Fall* is arbitrary. It has nothing to do with the autumn season or Adam and Eve. I'm not sure the word covers the case but I have looked in vain for a better.

If I am approaching the Athleticus from the north, it is my pleasure to cover the last lap with a crisp walk across Battersea Park. If I am coming directly from my house, I have only a five-hundred-yard walk. The Athleticus has been my unlikely club and away-from-it-all for a large chunk of my adult life. Prue calls it my playpen. When I was abroad I kept my membership going and used my spells of home leave to stay on the ladder. Whenever the Office hauled me back for an operational meeting, I'd find time to grab a game. In the Athleticus I'm Nat to the world and its brother, nobody gives a hoot what I or anyone else does for a living and nobody asks. Chinese and other Asian members outnumber us Caucasians three to one. Steff has refused to play ever since she learned to say 'no', but there was a time when I'd cart her along for an ice cream and a swim. Prue as a good sport will turn to if asked, but only on sufferance and latterly, what with her *pro bono* work and the class actions her partnership gets embroiled in, not at all.

We have an ageless insomniac Swatownese barman called Fred. We do a junior membership that is wildly uneconomic, but only until age twenty-two. After that it's two hundred and fifty smackers a year and a hefty joining fee. And we'd have had to put up shop or raise the ante still higher if a Chinese member named Arthur hadn't made an anonymous donation of a hundred thousand euros out of the blue, and thereby hangs a tale. As Hon. Club Secretary I was one of the few who were allowed to thank Arthur for his generosity. One evening I was told he was sitting in the bar. He was my age but already white-haired, wearing a smart suit and tie and staring ahead of him. No drink.

'Arthur,' I say, sitting down beside him, 'we don't know how to thank you.'

I wait for him to turn his head, but his gaze stays fixed on the middle distance.

'It's for my boy,' he replies after an age.

'So is your boy with us here tonight?' I ask, observing a group of Chinese kids hanging round the pool.

'No more,' he replies, still without turning his head.

No more? What did that mean?

I mount a discreet search. Chinese names are tricky. There was a junior member who seemed to have the same surname as our donor, but his annual membership was six months overdue and he'd ignored the usual string of reminders. It took Alice to make the connection. Kim, she remembered. That eager, skinny little lad. Sweet as pie, gave his age as sixteen but looked sixty. A Chinese woman, she came along with him, very polite, could have been his mother, or maybe nurse. Bought a six-lesson start-up course for cash outright but that boy, he couldn't connect with the shuttle, not even dolly shots. The coach now, he suggested he give it a try at home, just hand–eye, shuttle on racquet, and come back like in a few weeks. That boy, he never did. The nurse neither. We guessed he'd given up or gone home to China. Oh dear Jesus, don't say it. Well, God bless that poor Kim.

I'm not sure why I recount this episode in such detail except that I love the place and what it has been to me over the years, and it's the place where I played my fifteen games with Ed and enjoyed all but the last one.

*

Our first appointed Monday did not exactly get off to the rollicking start the record suggests. I am a punctual man – Steff says anally so. For our date, made a full three weeks previously, he arrived out of breath with less than three minutes to spare wearing a rumpled town suit and bicycle clips round his ankles. He was armed with a brown imitation-leather briefcase, and he was in a filthy temper.

Bear in mind now that I had seen him only the once in badminton gear. Bear in mind further that he was a good twenty years my junior, had issued me with a challenge under the gaze of my fellow members, and I had accepted his challenge not least to save his face. Further bear in mind that not only was I Club champion, I had spent the morning conducting back-to-back handover meetings with two of Giles's least promising and least productive agents, both women as it happened, and both resenting their change of handler for obvious reasons; my lunch hour soothing Prue's feelings after she had received a hurtful email from Steff demanding that her mobile phone, which she had left on the hall table, be sent by registered mail to an unfamiliar address c/o Juno – who the hell is Juno? – and my afternoon weeding out yet more gratuitous statements about Orson's disgraceful lifestyle, after I had twice instructed Florence to remove them.

Bear in mind finally that by the time Ed charges into the

changing room, giving a good imitation of a man on the run, I have been hanging around fretting in full badminton rig for all of ten minutes watching the clock. Starting to undress himself he grumbles half intelligibly about some 'fucking cycle-hating lorry driver' who did unfriendly things to him at the traffic lights, and his employers who 'kept me late for no fucking reason', to all of which I can only reply 'poor you', then settle down on the bench to observe the rest of his chaotic progress in the mirror.

If I am a less relaxed man than the one he met a couple of weeks back, so the Ed before me bears little resemblance to the shy man-boy who needed Alice's assistance to approach me. Freed of his jacket, he makes a downward swoop of his upper body without bending his knees, slams open his locker, fishes out a tube of shuttles and a couple of racquets, then a rolled-up bundle containing shirt, shorts, socks and sneakers.

Big feet, I'm noting. Could be slow on them. And even while I'm thinking this, he's slung his brown briefcase into the locker and *turned the key on it*. Why? The man's halfway through changing into his badminton kit. In thirty seconds he'll be loading his day clothes into the self-same locker at the same frenzied pace with which he's currently tearing them off. So why lock it *now*, only to have to *unlock* it half a minute later? Is he afraid somebody's going to nick his briefcase while his back's turned?

I don't make a conscious effort to think like this. It's my *déformation professionnelle*. It's what I've been taught to do and have done all my working life, whether the object of my interest is Prue doing her face at her dressing table in Battersea or the middle-aged couple in the corner of a café who've been sitting there too long, who talk to each other with too much earnestness and never look in my direction.

He has hauled his shirt over his head and is displaying his naked torso. Good physique, a bit bony, no tattoos, no scars, no other distinguishing marks, and from where I sit very, very tall.

He removes his spectacles, unlocks the locker, tosses them in and *relocks* it. He pulls on a T-shirt, then the same long shorts he was wearing when he first accosted me, and a pair of ankle socks, originally white.

His knees are now in line with my face. Without spectacles his face is bare and even younger-looking than when he first approached me. Twenty-five at most. He leans over me, peers into the wall mirror. He's fitting his contact lenses. He blinks his eyes clear. I am also noticing that throughout these contortions he has still not once bent his knees. Everything hinges from the waist, whether he's fastening his shoelaces or craning to fix his contacts. So despite his height, maybe problems with reach when it comes to low and wide. Yet again he unlocks his locker, stuffs his suit, shirt and shoes into it, slams the door shut, turns the key, removes it, peers at it as it lies in the palm of his hand, shrugs, unpicks the ribbon attached to it, kicks open the trash bin at his feet, chucks the ribbon in and stows the key in the right-hand pocket of his long shorts.

'All set then?' he demands, as if I, not he, had kept us waiting.

We head for the court, Ed stalking in front of me twiddling his racquet and still fuming to himself, either about his cycle-hating lorry driver or his pea-brained employers or some other irritation yet to be revealed. He knows his way. He's been furtively practising here, I'll bet he has, probably ever since he challenged me. My work requires me to get along with people I wouldn't normally entertain in the woodshed, but this young man is putting a strain on my tolerance and the badminton court is the place to put that right.

*

We played seven bitter games that first evening. Championships included, I don't remember being more stretched or more

49

determined to put a young opponent in his place. I won the four, but only by the skin of my teeth. He was good, but mercifully inconsistent, which gave me the edge. Despite his youth, I reckoned he was as good as he was ever going to be, bearing in mind that he had the reach on me by six or seven inches. And concentration variable, thank God. For a dozen points he'd charge, smash, lunge, lob, drop-shot, retrieve, and force his body into every unlikely angle, and I'd be struggling to keep up. Then for the next three or four rallies he'd switch off and winning didn't seem to matter to him any more. Then he'd come alive again, but by then it was too late.

And from the first to the last rally not a word between us, bar his punctilious enunciation of the score, a responsibility he arrogated to himself from the first point, and the occasional *shit!* when he fluffed. We must have picked up a dozen spectators by the time we'd reached the deciding game and there was even a smattering of applause at the end. And yes, he was heavy on his feet. And yes, his low-angle shots were frenetic, a bit last-minute-ish, despite his superior height.

But, after all that, I had to say he played and lost with unexpected grace, without contesting a single line decision or demanding a replay, not by any means always the case at the Athleticus or anywhere else. And as soon as the game was over he managed a broad grin, the first I'd seen from him since the day he approached me – chagrined, but genuinely sporting and all the better for being unexpected.

'That was a really, really good game, Nat, best ever, yeah,' he assures me sincerely, grabbing my hand and pumping it up and down. 'Got time for a quick snoot? On me?'

Snoot? I've been away from England too long. Or *snort?* The absurd thought crosses my mind that he is offering me cocaine out of his brown briefcase. Then I realize he is simply suggesting we share a civilized drink in the bar, so I say not tonight I'm afraid, Ed, thanks, I'm tied up, which was true: I'd got yet another late-night handover, this time with Giles's one remaining female agent, codename Starlight, an absolute pain of a woman and to my mind patently untrustworthy, but Giles is convinced he has the measure of her.

'How's about a revenge match next week then?' Ed urges with the perseverance I am learning to expect of him. 'No sweat if one of us has to cancel. I'll book anyway. Are you up for that?'

To which I reply, truthfully again, that I'm a bit under the whip so let's take a rain check. And anyway, I'll do the booking, it's my shout. Followed by another of those weird up-and-down handshakes of his. The last I see of him after we've parted, he's bent double with his bicycle clips on, unlocking the chain of his antediluvian bicycle. Somebody is telling him it's blocking the pavement and he's telling them to fuck off.

In the event I had to text him, cancelling next Monday because of Rosebud, which, thanks to Florence's reluctant acquiescence in toning down the moral outrage, and some backstairs lobbying on my part, was acquiring serious legs. He proposed the Wednesday instead, but I had to tell him I was under the whip all week. And when the following Monday came up, we were still hanging by a thread and with due apologies I had to cancel yet again, and the rest of the week didn't look at all good either. I felt badly to have messed him about and was all the more relieved on each occasion to receive a courteous 'no problem'. By the third Friday evening I was still uncertain whether I was going to be able to make the coming Monday or any other day, which would have meant three cancellations on the trot.

It's past closing time. The Haven duty shift is already moving in for the weekend. Little Ilya has again volunteered. He needs the money. My Office line rings. It's Dom. I'm half inclined to let it go on ringing, but relent.

'I have some rather gratifying news for you, Nat,' he announces in his public-meeting voice. 'A certain lady by the name of Rosebud has found favour with our lords of Russia department. They have forwarded our proposal to Operations Directorate for a conclusive determination and action. I wish you a good weekend. You've deserved it, if you'll allow me to say so.'

'*Our* proposal, Dom? Or just London General's proposal?'

'Our *joint* proposal, Nat, as agreed between us. The Haven and London General marching forward side by side.'

'And the accredited author is who precisely?'

'Your intrepid number two is designated as the operation's author despite her status as a probationer, and in that capacity will make her formal presentation in accordance with traditional practice in the Operations room this coming Friday at ten-thirty a.m. sharp. Does that satisfy you?'

Not till I have it in writing, Dom. I call Viv, who is turning out to be an ally. She emails me the formal confirmation. Dom and I to share equal billing. Florence the acknowledged author. Only now do I feel free to text Ed. Sorry for the short notice and all that, is he by any chance still up for this coming Monday?

Ed is.

*

No sweaty grey suit and bicycle clips this time, no grumbling about lorry drivers or pea-brained employers, no imitation-leather briefcase. Just jeans, sneakers, open-necked shirt and a wide, very happy grin under the cyclist's shell hat that he's unbuckling. And I must say that after three solid weeks of day-and-night hard labour, that grin and the up-and-down handshake are a tonic.

'First you chickened, then you scraped up your courage, right?'

'Quivering in my boots,' I agree cheerfully as we set off at light-infantry pace for the changing room.

The game was again needle. But this time no spectators, so tension of the right kind only. As before we were neck and neck till the last few rallies, but to my vexation – but also my relief, because who wants an opponent he can beat every time? – he pipped me fair and square to the post, at which point I was even quicker than he was to insist we move to the bar for that snoot of his. On Mondays you get only a sprinkling of members, but either out of impulse or habit I made for the traditional watcher's corner, a tin-topped table for two set away from the swimming pool and up against the wall with a line of sight to the doorway.

And from then on, without a word from either of us, that isolated tin table became what my mother in her German moments would have called our *Stammtisch* – or, as my *chers collègues* would have it, crime scene – whether for our regular Monday evenings, or stolen weeknights between.

*

I had not expected that first post-badminton beer to be anything more than the usual formality: loser buys first pint, winner the second if anybody wants one, trade pleasantries, fix a return date, shower, go our ways. And since Ed was of an age where life begins at nine p.m., I assumed we'd just do the one pint and I'd cook myself an egg because Prue would be hunkered down in Southwark with her beloved *pro bono* clients.

'You a London man then, Nat?' Ed asks, as we settle to our pints.

I acknowledge that I am indeed such a man.

'What sort then?'

This is further than people normally go at the Club, but never mind.

'Just hunting around really,' I reply. 'Been earning my bread abroad for a while. Now I'm back home and looking for something to get my teeth into.' And for good measure: 'And meanwhile helping an old buddy straighten out his business,' I add, in a well-tried routine. 'How about you, Ed? Alice let slip that you were a *researcher*. Is that about right?'

He ponders my question as if no one's ever asked it before. He seems mildly irritated to be pegged down.

'Researcher, yeah. That's me.' And after a period of reflection: 'Research. Stuff comes in. Sort it. Push it out to the punters. Yeah.'

'So the daily news, basically?'

'Yeah. Whatever. Home, foreign, fake.'

'And corporate, presumably?' I suggest, recalling his invective against his employers.

'Yeah. Very corporate mindset indeed. Toe the line or you're fucked.'

I assume he's said all he wants to say because he has lapsed again into his own thoughts. But he goes on:

'Still. Got a couple of years in Germany out of it, didn't I?' he says, consoling himself. 'Loved the country, didn't like the job a lot. So I came home.'

'To the same sort of job?'

'Yeah, well, same shit, different branch really. I thought it might get better.'

'But it hasn't.'

'Not really. Still, stick it out, I suppose. Make the best of it. Yeah.'

And that was the net sum of our exchanges about our respective occupations, which was fine by me and I assume fine by both of us, because I don't remember either of us ever going there again, however dearly my *chers collègues* wished to believe otherwise. But I do remember as if it were tonight how abruptly our discussion changed course once we had laid the issue of our occupations to rest.

For a while Ed had been scowling into the middle distance and, judging by his rictal grimaces, debating some weighty matter with himself.

'Mind if I ask you a question, Nat?' he enquires in a blurt of sudden resolve.

'Of course I don't,' I say hospitably.

'Only I respect you quite a lot actually. Although it's short acquaintance. It doesn't take long to know a person once you've played them.'

'Go on.'

'Thank you. I will. It is my considered opinion that for Britain and Europe, and for liberal democracy across the entire world as a whole, Britain's departure from the European Union in the time of Donald Trump, and Britain's consequent unqualified dependence on the United States in an era when the US is heading straight down the road to institutional racism and neo-fascism, is an unmitigated clusterfuck bar none. And what I'm asking is: do you in broad principle agree with me, or have I offended you and would it be better if I got up and left now? Yes or no?'

Surprised by this unprompted appeal to my political sympathies from a young man I am barely beginning to know, I preserve what Prue calls my decent silence. For a while he stares sightlessly at the people splashing in the pool, then comes back to me.

'My point being that I would *not* wish to be sitting here with you under false pretences, given that I have admired your play, and you personally. Brexit is the most important decision facing Britain since 1939, in my opinion. People say 1945 but I'm not at all sure why, frankly. So all I'm asking is, do you agree with me? I know I'm over-earnest. I've been told. Plus a lot of people don't like me because I'm outspoken, which I am.'

'In the workplace?' I enquire, still buying time.

'The workplace is a total washout as regards what I would term free speech. In the workplace it is mandatory to have no strongly held opinion on any subject. Otherwise you're a leper. It is therefore my policy to keep my mouth firmly shut at all times in the workplace, hence I am regarded as surly. However, I could name to you many other places where people do not like hearing the hard truth, or not from me. Even if such people profess an admiration for Western democracy, they still prefer the easy life as opposed to recognizing their duty as responsible opponents of the encroaching fascist enemy. But I note you have still not answered my question.'

Let me say here and now, precisely as I repeated the same message *ad nauseam* to my *chers collègues*, that although the word *clusterfuck* had not so far entered my vocabulary, Brexit had long been a red rag to me. I am European born and bred, I have French, German, British and Old Russian blood in my veins and am as much at home on the Continent of Europe as I am in Battersea. As to his larger point about the dominance of white supremacists in Trump's America – well, there too we were not at odds, and neither were many of my *chers collègues*, however much they might later wish themselves into a more neutral posture.

All the same, I had qualms about giving him the answer he was demanding. First question as always: is he setting me up, is he trying to draw me out or compromise me? To which with absolute confidence I could reply no: not this young man, not in a month of Sundays. So next question: do I ignore Old Fred the Swatownese barman's hand-scrawled message stuck to the mirror behind the bar: 'NO BREXIT TALK ALOUD'?

And finally, do I forget that I'm a civil servant, albeit a secret one, pledged to uphold my government's policy, assuming it has one? Or do I rather say to myself: this is a courageous and sincere young fellow – eccentric, yes, not everyone's cup of tea and the better for it in my opinion – whose heart is in the right place, is in need of someone to listen to him, is only seven or eight years older than my daughter – whose radical views on any known topic are a fact of family life – and plays a very decent game of badminton?

Then add another ingredient to the mix, one that only now I am willing to admit to, although I believe it was present in me from our first improbable exchange. I am speaking of an awareness on my part that I was in the presence of something rare in the life I had so far led, and particularly in such a young man: namely true conviction, driven not by motives of gain or envy or revenge or self-aggrandizement, but the real thing, take it or leave it.

Fred the barman pours his chilled lagers slowly and with deliberation into crested flutes, and this was the glass Ed brooded over while he prodded at its frosted sides with the tips of his long fingers, head bowed, waiting for my answer.

'Well, Ed,' I reply, when I have let enough time pass to indicate due consideration. 'Let me put it this way. Yes, Brexit is indeed an unmitigated clusterfuck, though I doubt there is much we can do now to put the clock back. Will that do for you?'

It won't, as both of us knew. My so-called decent quiet is as nothing beside Ed's prolonged silences that, over time, I came to regard as a natural feature of our conversations.

'What about *President Donald Trump* then?' he demands, enunciating the name as if it were the very devil's. 'Do you or do you not regard Trump, which I do, as a threat and incitement to the entire civilized world, plus he is presiding over the systematic no-holds-barred Nazification of the United States?'

I think I must have been smiling by now, but I see no answering light in Ed's lugubrious face which is turned at an angle to me, as if he needs my answer in sound only, without any moderating facial expression.

'Well, if in a less fundamental way, yes, I'm with you there too, Ed, if that's any consolation,' I concede gently. 'But he's not President for ever, is he? And the Constitution is there to inhibit him, not just give him a free rein.'

But this is not enough for him:

'What about all the tunnel-vision fanatics he's got round him? The fundamentalist Christians who think Jesus invented greed? *They're* not going anywhere, are they?'

'Ed,' I say, making a joke of it now. 'When Trump's gone, these people will scatter as ash in the wind. Now for God's sake let's have that other pint.'

By now, I really am expecting the broad grin that washes everything away. It doesn't come. Instead, I get his big bony hand, reached towards me across the table.

'Then we're all right, aren't we?' he says.

And I shake his hand in return and say, yes we are, and only then does he fetch us another lager.

*

For the next dozen-odd Monday-evening games I made not the smallest effort to deny or water down anything he said to me, which meant that from our second encounter onwards – Match No. 2 in my diary – no post-badminton session at our *Stammtisch* was complete without Ed launching himself on a political soliloquy concerning some burning matter of the day.

And he got better over time. Forget his raw opening salvo. Ed was not raw. He was just deeply involved. And – easy to say it now – by being so deeply involved, obsessive. He had also, by Match No. 4 at the latest, revealed himself as a well-informed news junkie with every twist and turn on the world political stage – be it Brexit, Trump, Syria or some other long-running disaster – such a matter of personal concern to him that it would have been downright inconsiderate on my part not to allow him his head. The biggest gift you can give the young is time, and it was always in my mind that I hadn't given Steff enough of it, and perhaps Ed's parents hadn't been any too generous in that respect either.

My *chers collègues* wanted dearly to believe that, by granting him the time of day at all, I led him on. They pointed to our age difference and what they were pleased to call my 'professional charm'. Sheer drivel. Once Ed had established that in his simple bestiary I was broadly a sympathetic ear, I could have been a stranger sitting next to him on the bus. Even now I don't recall a single occasion when my own opinions, even at their most sympathetic, made the least impression on him. He was just grateful to have found himself an audience that didn't do shock, didn't oppose him or simply walk away from him and talk to someone else, because I'm not sure how long he would have sustained an ideological or political argument without losing his rag. The fact that his opinions on any given topic were predictable before he opened his mouth did not disturb me. All right, he was a single-issue man. I knew the breed. I'd recruited a few. He was geopolitically alert. He was young, highly intelligent within the margins of his fixed opinions, and – though I never had occasion to put it to the test – quick to anger when they were opposed.

What did I personally get out of the relationship, apart from our gritty duels on the badminton court? – another question to which my *chers collègues* persistently returned. At the time of my inquisition, I had no formed answer at my fingertips. Only in its aftermath did I recall the sense of moral commitment that Ed imparted, how it acted on me like an appeal to my conscience – followed by the broad, slightly hangdog grin that washed it all away. Added together, they gave me a sense of providing some sort of refuge for an imperilled species. And

I must have said something of this kind to Prue when I suggested I bring him home for a drink, or invite him to Sunday lunch. But Prue in her wisdom was unpersuaded:

'It sounds to me as if you're doing each other a power, darling. Keep him to yourself and don't let me get in the way.'

So I gladly took her advice, and kept him to myself. Our routine never varied, even at the end. We would play our hearts out on the court, collect our jackets, maybe fling a scarf round our necks and set course for our *Stammtisch*, loser makes straight for the bar. We'd exchange a few pleasantries – maybe relive a point or two. He'd ask vaguely after my family, I'd ask him whether he'd had a good weekend, and we'd both give bland answers. Then there'd be a kind of expectant silence on his part which I quickly learned not to fill, and he'd launch on his dissertation of the day. And I'd be agreeing with him, part-agreeing with him or at the most saying woah, Ed, steady now, and giving him the older-wiser man's chuckle. Only rarely, and in the mildest of tones, did I question his more salty assertions – but always with circumspection, because my instinctive knowledge of Ed from the outset was that he was fragile.

Sometimes it was as if someone else was talking out of him. His voice, which was a good one when it was just being itself, would go up an octave, hit a level and stick there on one didactic note, not for long, but long enough for me to think: hullo, I know this register, and Steff's got one too. It's the one you can't argue with because it just rolls on as if you're not there, so best nod him along and wait till it's run its course.

The substance? In a sense, each time the mixture as before. Brexit is self-immolation. The British public is being marched over a cliff by a bunch of rich elitist carpetbaggers posing as men of the people. Trump is Antichrist, Putin another. For Trump, the draft-dodging rich boy brought up in a great if flawed democracy, there is no redemption in this world or the next. For Putin, who has never known democracy, there is a shimmer. Thus Ed, whose Nonconformist background has become by stages a notable feature of these outpourings.

Was there progress, Nat? my *chers collègues* asked me. Did his views *advance*? Did you have a feeling that he was heading for some sort of absolute resolution? Again I could offer them no comfort. Maybe he grew freer and more outspoken once he felt more confident of his audience: me. Maybe I became a more congenial audience for him with time, though I don't remember ever being particularly *un*congenial.

But I'll accept that Ed and I had a few sessions at the *Stammtisch* when I wasn't worrying overmuch – about Steff, or Prue, or some newly acquired agent who was acting up, or the flu epidemic that took half our handlers off the road for a couple of weeks – and I was giving him near enough my full attention. On such occasions I might feel moved to join issue with one or other of his more radical outpourings, not so much to challenge the argument as to temper the assertiveness with which he delivered it. So in that sense: well, if not progress, a growing familiarity on my side, and on Ed's a willingness, if only reluctantly, to laugh at himself now and then.

But bear in mind this simple plea, which is one not of self-exculpation but of fact: I didn't always listen very carefully, and sometimes I switched off altogether. If I was under pressure at the Haven – which happened increasingly to be the case – I would make sure I had my Office mobile in my back pocket before we repaired to the *Stammtisch*, and I would furtively consult it while he banged on.

And from time to time, when his monologues in all their youthful innocence and assertiveness got under my skin, then rather than head straight home to Prue after our final up-and-down handshake, I would take the longer route home through the park in order to give my thoughts a chance to settle.

*

One last word about what the game of badminton meant to Ed and for that matter means to me. For unbelievers, badminton is a namby-pamby version of squash for overweight men afraid of heart attacks. For true believers there is no other sport. Squash is slash and burn. Badminton is stealth, patience, speed and improbable recovery. It's lying in wait to unleash your ambush while the shuttle describes its leisurely arc. Unlike squash, badminton knows no social distinctions. It is not public school. It has nothing of the outdoor allure of tennis or five-a-side football. It does not reward a beautiful swing. It offers no forgiveness, spares the knees, is said to be terrible for hips. Yet, as a matter of proven fact, it requires faster reactions than squash. There is little natural conviviality between us players, who tend on the whole to be a lonely lot. To fellow athletes, we're a bit weird, a bit friendless.

My father played badminton in Singapore when he was stationed there. Singles only. He played it for the army before his decline. He played it with me. In summer holidays on Normandy beaches. In the garden in Neuilly over a washing line for a net, clutching a mahogany tumbler of Scotch in his spare hand. Badminton was the best of him. When I was packed off to Scotland to his godawful school I played badminton there, as he had, and afterwards for my Midlands university. When I was hanging round the Office waiting for my first overseas posting, I rustled up a bunch of my fellow trainees and under the cover name of *the Irregulars* we took on all comers.

And Ed? How did *he* become a convert to the game of games? We're sitting at the *Stammtisch*. He is crystal-gazing into his lager, the way he did when he was solving the world's problems or beating his brains about what was wrong with his backhand, or simply not talking at all but brooding. No question was ever simple once you'd put it to him. Everything needed tracking down to source.

'There was this gym teacher we had at my Grammar,' he says at last. Broad grin. 'Took a couple of us over to her club one evening. That was it really. Her with her short skirt and shiny white thighs. Yeah.'

6

Here, for the edification of my *chers collègues*, is the sum total of whatever I had happened to pick up of Ed's life away from the badminton court by the time of the Fall. Now that I come to write it down, the extent of it would surprise me were it not for the fact that I am a listener and a rememberer by training and habit.

He was one of two children born ten years apart into an old Methodist family of North Country miners. His grandfather had come over from Ireland in his twenties. When the mines closed, his dad became a merchant seaman:

Didn't see a lot of him after that, not really. Came home and got cancer like it was waiting for him – Ed.

His father was also an old-style Communist who had burned his Party card in the wake of the Soviet invasion of Afghanistan in 1979. I suspect Ed nursed him on his deathbed.

After his father's death the family moved to somewhere near Doncaster. Ed won a place at grammar school, don't ask me which one. His mother spent whatever free time she had from work at adult education classes until they were cut:

Mum's got more brain than what she was ever allowed to use, plus she'd got Laura to look after – Ed.

Laura being his younger sister who has learning difficulties and is partially disabled.

At the age of eighteen, he renounced his Christian faith in favour of what he called 'all-inclusive humanism' which I took to be Nonconformism without God, but out of tact I refrained from suggesting this to him.

From grammar school he went to a 'new' university, I am not sure which. Computer Sciences, German an optional extra. Class of degree not specified, so I suspect middling, *new* being his own disparaging term.

As regards girls – always a delicate area where Ed was concerned, and not one I would have entered uninvited – either they didn't like him, or he didn't like them. I suspect that his urgent preoccupation with world affairs and other mild eccentricities made a demanding life-companion of him. I also suspect he didn't know his own attraction.

And of men friends, the people he should be hanging out with in the gym, or sorting the world with, or jogging, cycling, pubbing? Ed never mentioned a single such person to me, and I question whether they existed in his life. Deep down, I suspect, he wore his isolation as a badge of honour.

He had heard about me on the badminton grapevine and had secured me for his regular opponent. I was his prize. He had no wish to share me.

When I had reason to ask him what had prompted him to take a job in the media if he loathed it so much, he was at first evasive:

Saw an ad somewhere, interviewed for it. They set a sort of exam paper, said all right, come on in. That's about it. Yeah – Ed.

But when I asked him whether he had congenial colleagues in his workplace he merely shook his head as if the question were irrelevant.

And the good news in Ed's otherwise solitary universe as far as I could read it? Germany. And again Germany.

Ed had the German bug in a big way. I suppose I have it myself, if only from the reluctant German lurking in my mother. He'd spent a study year in Tübingen and two years in Berlin working for his media outfit. Germany was the cat's whiskers. Its citizens were simply the best Europeans ever. *No other nation holds a candle to Germans, not when it comes to understanding what European union is all about* – Ed on his high horse. He'd considered chucking everything and making a new life there, but it hadn't worked out with the girl, a research student at Berlin University. It was thanks to her, so far as I could gather, that he had made some sort of study of the rise of German nationalism in the nineteen twenties, which seems to have been her subject. What is certain is that on the strength of such arbitrary studies he felt empowered to draw disturbing parallels between the rise of Europe's dictators and the rise of Donald Trump. Get him on this subject, and you got Ed at his most overbearing.

In Ed's world there was no dividing line between Brexit fanatics and Trump fanatics. Both were racist and xenophobic. Both worshipped at the same shrine of nostalgic imperialism. Once embarked on this theme, he lost all objectivity. The Trumpists and the Brexiteers were conspiring to deprive him of his European birthright. Solitary as he might be in other ways, on Europe he showed no compunction in declaring that he spoke for his generation or in pointing the finger at mine.

There was an occasion when we were seated, temporarily exhausted, in the Athleticus changing room after our usual hard-fought game. Diving into his locker to retrieve his smartphone, he insisted on showing me video footage of Trump's inner cabinet gathered round a table as each in turn protests his undying loyalty to his dear leader.

'They're taking the bloody Führer's oath,' he confides to me in a breathless voice. 'It's a replay, Nat. Watch.'

I dutifully watched. And yes, it was emetic.

I never asked him, but I think it was Germany's atonement

for its past sins that spoke most forcefully to his secularized Methodist soul: the thought that a great nation that had run amok should repent its crimes to the world. What other country had ever done such a thing? he demanded to know. Had Turkey apologized for slaughtering the Armenians and Kurds? Had America apologized to the Vietnamese people? Had the Brits atoned for colonizing three-quarters of the globe and enslaving numberless of its citizens?

The up-and-down handshake? He never told me, but my guess was he'd picked it up while he was lodged in Berlin with the girl's Prussian family, and out of some weird sense of loyalty had stuck to the habit.

7

It's ten o'clock on a sun-drenched Friday morning in spring and the birds all know it, as Florence and I, having met for an early coffee, I from Battersea and she, I assume, from Pimlico, step out along the Thames Embankment towards Head Office. In the past, returning from distant outstations for Office parleys or home leave, I have occasionally felt daunted by our over-conspicuous, many-towered Camelot with its whispering lifts, hospital-bright corridors and tourists gawping from the bridge.

Not today.

In half an hour's time Florence will be presenting London General's first full-blown special operation in three years and it will bear the Haven's imprimatur. She sports a smart trouser suit and just a hint of make-up. If she has stage fright she betrays no sign of it. For the last three weeks we have been night owls together, sitting head to head into the small hours at the rickety trestle table in the Haven's windowless Operations room, poring over street maps, surveillance reports, phone and email intercepts, and the latest word from Orson's disenchanted mistress, Astra.

It was Astra who first reported that Orson was about to use his Park Lane duplex to impress a duo of Cyprus-based, Moscow-friendly money-launderers of Slovakian descent with a private bank in Nicosia and an affiliate in the City of London. Both are fully identified members of a Kremlin-approved crime syndicate operating out of Odessa. On receiving word of their arrival, Orson ordered an electronic sweep of his duplex. No devices were discovered. It was now up to Percy Price's intrusion team to remedy that omission.

With the consent of its absent director, Bryn Jordan, Russia department has also taken a couple of its own steps into the water. One of its officers has posed as Florence's *Daily Mail* news editor and clinched the deal with the night porter. The gas company supplying energy to Orson's duplex has been prevailed on to report a leak. A three-man team of burglars under the pompous Eric has reconnoitred the duplex in the guise of the company's engineers and photographed the locks on the re-inforced steel door leading to the computer room. The British lockmakers have provided duplicate keys and guidance on the unscrambling of the combination.

Now all that remains is for Rosebud to be officially green-lit by a plenum of Head Office's big beasts, known collectively as Operations Directorate.

*

If the relationship between Florence and myself is emphatically non-tactile, with each of us going to elaborate lengths not to brush hands or otherwise make physical contact, it is nonetheless close. It turns out that our lives overlap in more ways than we might have expected, given the difference in our ages. Her father the ex-diplomat had done two successive stints at the British Embassy in Moscow, taking with him his wife and three children of whom Florence was the eldest. Prue and I had missed them by six months.

While attending International School in Moscow she had embraced the Russian muse with all the zeal of youth. She even had a Madame Galina in her life: the widow of an 'approved' poet from Soviet times with a tumbledown *dacha* in the old artists' colony of Peredelkino. By the time Florence was ready to attend English boarding school the Service's talent spotters were keeping an eye on her. When she sat her A-level exams, they dispatched their own Russian linguist to assess her language skills. She was awarded the highest grade available to non-Russians, and approached when she was just nineteen.

At university she continued her studies under the Office's supervision and spent part of each vacation on low-grade training runs: Belgrade, Petersburg and most recently Tallinn, where once again we might have met had she not been living her cover as a forestry student and I as a diplomat. She loved to run, as I do: I in Battersea Park, she to my surprise on Hampstead Heath. When I pointed out to her that Hampstead was a long way from Pimlico, she replied without hesitation that there was a bus that took her from door to door. In an idle moment I checked, and it was true: the 24 went all the way.

What more did I know of her? That she had a consuming sense of natural justice that put me in mind of Prue. That she loved the spice of operational work, and had a talent for it that went beyond the normal. That the Office frequently exasperated her. That she was reticent, even guarded, about her private life. And there was an evening, after a long day's work, when I caught sight of her crouched in her cubicle with fists clenched and tears running down her cheeks. One thing I have learned the hard way from Steff: *never* ask what's wrong, just give her space. I gave her space, didn't ask, and the cause of her tears remained her own.

But today she hasn't a care in the world beyond Operation Rosebud.

*

There is a dreamlike quality to my recollection of that morning's gathering of the Office's finest, a sense of what might have been and a remembrance of last things: the top-floor conference room with its sunlit skylights and honey-coloured panelling, the intelligent, listening faces turned to Florence and myself seated shoulder to shoulder at the suitors' end of the table. Every member of our audience was known to me from past lives, and each in his or her different way deserving of my respect: Ghita Marsden, my former head of Station in Trieste and the first woman of colour to make it to the top floor; Percy Price, head of the Service's ever-expanding surveillance arm. The list goes on. Guy Brammel, the portly, wily, fifty-five-year-old head of Russian Requirements presently standing in for Bryn Jordan stranded in Washington. Marion, a senior-ranking member of our sister Service, on attachment. Then two of Guy Brammel's most valued female colleagues, Beth (North Caucasus) and Lizzie (Russian Ukraine). And last and emphatically least, Dom Trench, as head of London General, who makes a point of not entering until everyone else is settled, for fear of being shown to a lesser seat.

'*Florence*,' says Guy Brammel indulgently down the table. 'Let's have your pitch, shall we?'

And suddenly there she is, no longer at my side but standing six feet from me in her trouser suit: Florence, my talented if temperamental second-year probationer, speaking wisdom to her elders while our own little Ilya from the Haven squats elf-like in the projection booth with a cue sheet, accompanying her with his slideshow.

There's no passionate throb to Florence's voice today, no hint of the inner fires that have been raging in her over the last months, or the special place reserved for Orson in her private inferno. I have warned her to keep her emotions down and language clean. Percy Price, our head watcher, is a keen churchman and no friend of Anglo-Saxon expletives. Neither I suspect is Ghita, tolerant though she is of our infidel ways.

And thus far Florence has stayed on message. In reading out Orson's charge sheet she is neither indignant nor declamatory – she can be both at the drop of a hat – but as self-composed as Prue on the occasions when I pop into court for ten minutes just for the pleasure of hearing her tear the opposition into courteous shreds.

First she gives us Orson's unexplained wealth – massive, off-shore, administered from Guernsey and the City of London, where else? – then Orson's other overseas properties, in Madeira, Miami, Zermatt and on the Black Sea, then his unexplained presence at a reception held at the Russian Embassy in London for leading Brexiteers, and his million-pound contribution to an arm's-length fighting fund for Leavers. She describes a covert meeting that Orson attended in Brussels with six Russian cyber experts suspected of wide-scale hacking into Western democratic forums. All this and more without a tremor of emotion.

Only when she comes to the proposed positioning of hidden microphones in the target duplex does her cool desert her. Ilya's slideshow is giving us a dozen of them, each marked with its own red spot. Marion begs to interrupt:

'Florence,' she says severely, 'I fail to understand why you are proposing to deploy special facilities against under-age children.'

I don't think I'd seen Florence struck mute till now. As her substation head I hasten to her assistance.

'I think Marion must be referring to our recommendation that *all* rooms in Orson's duplex should be covered regardless of who occupies them,' I murmur to her in a stage aside.

But Marion is not to be mollified.

'I am questioning the ethics of installing audio *and* visual facilities in a child's nursery. Also in the nanny's bedroom, which

I find equally questionable, if not more so. Or are we to suppose that Orson's children *and* the nanny are of intelligence interest?'

Florence has by now collected herself. Or, if you know her as I do, readied herself for combat. She takes a breath and puts on her sweetest Cheltenham Ladies' College voice.

'The *nursery*, Marion, is where Orson takes his business friends when he's got something especially secret to tell them. The *nanny's* room is where he screws his hookers when the kids are in Sochi having a seaside holiday with Nanny and his wife's out buying jewellery at Cartier's. Source Astra tells us that Orson likes to boast to his women about his clever deals while he screws them. We thought we should hear him do that.'

But it's all right. Everyone's laughing, Guy Brammel loudest; even Marion is laughing. Dom is laughing, which is to say he's shaking and smiling, even if no laughter is coming out. We stand, little groups form at the coffee table. Ghita is offering Florence sisterly congratulations. An unseen hand closes on my upper arm, a thing I don't take kindly to at the best of times.

'Nat. *Such* a good meeting. A credit to London General, a credit to the Haven, a credit to you personally.'

'Glad you enjoyed it, Dom. Florence is a promising officer. Nice to have her authorship recognized. So easy for these things to slip by.'

'And always that moderating voice of yours in the background,' Dom returns, affecting not to hear my little sally. 'I could practically hear it: that fatherly touch of yours.'

'Well, thank you, Dom. Thank you,' I reply handsomely, and wonder what he's got up his sleeve.

*

In the afterglow of a job well done, Florence and I amble back along the river footpath in the sunshine, remarking to each other – but mostly Florence doing the remarking – that if Rosebud yields only a quarter of the dividend we're predicting, one thing we can be reasonably sure of is it will be curtains for Orson's role as Russia's stooge in London and curtains – her most devout wish – for his stockpiles of filthy money stashed around the southern hemisphere by the City of London's ever-rotating laundromat.

Then, because we haven't eaten and time is anyway a little unreal after all the night hours we have invested in this moment, we put off taking the tube, dive into a pub, find an alcove to ourselves and over fish pies and a bottle of red burgundy – also Steff's tipple, as I can't resist telling her, and both of them fish fanatics – we review in suitably oblique language the morning's proceedings, which were actually a lot longer and more technical than I've given here, with contributions from Percy Price and Eric the pompous burglar about such matters as the marking and monitoring of surveillance targets, impregnating the target's shoes or clothing, the use of a helicopter or drone, and what will happen in the event of an unscheduled return by Orson and his entourage to the target duplex while the stealth team is still inside. Answer, they will be politely informed by a uniformed police officer that intruders have been reported in the building, so will the good ladies and gentlemen kindly avail themselves of the police van and enjoy a nice cup of hot tea while investigations proceed?

'So that's really it, is it?' Florence muses over her second or maybe third glass of red. 'We're home and dry. Citizen Kane, your day has finally come.'

'Not till the fat lady sings,' I warn her.

'Who the fuck's she?'

'A Treasury sub-committee has to give its blessing.'

'Consisting of?'

'One mandarin apiece from Treasury, Foreign Office, Home

Office and Defence. Plus a couple of co-opted parliamentarians who can be trusted to do what they're told.'

'Which is what?'

'Rubber-stamp the op and pass it back to Head Office for action.'

'Bloody waste of time, if you ask me.'

We return by tube to the Haven to discover that Ilya has raced ahead of us to report a great victory with Florence as heroine of the hour. Even grumpy Igor, the sixty-five-year-old Lithuanian, emerges from his den to shake her hand and – though he secretly suspects that any replacement of Giles must be a Russian plot – mine also. I escape to my office, sling my tie and jacket over a chair and am in the act of closing down my computer when the family mobile phone croaks at me. Assuming it's Prue and hoping it's Steff at long last, I delve in my jacket pocket. It's Ed, sounding dire.

'That you, Nat?'

'Amazingly, it is. And you must be Ed,' I reply frivolously.

'Yeah, well.' Long pause. 'Only it's about Laura, you see. On Monday.'

Laura, the sister who has learning difficulties.

'That's all right, Ed. If you're tied up with Laura, forget it. We'll play another time. Just say the word and I'll see when I'm free.'

This is not the reason he called, however. There's something else going on. With Ed there always is. Wait long enough, he'll tell you.

'Only she wants a four, you see.'

'Laura does?'

'At badminton. Yeah.'

'Ah. At badminton.'

'She's a demon for it when she's in the mood. No good, mind. I mean, sort of *really* no good. But, you know. Enthusiastic.'

'Of course. That sounds fine. So what kind of four?'

'Well, mixed, you know. With a woman. Maybe your wife.' He knows Prue's name but seems unable to speak it. I say *Prue* for him and he says, 'Yeah, Prue.'

'Prue can't, Ed, I'm afraid. I don't even have to ask her. Mondays are surgery night for hard-luck clients, remember? Haven't you got somebody in your shop?'

'Not really. Not that I can ask. Laura's *really* bad. Yeah.'

By this time my eye has travelled to the stippled-glass door that separates me from Florence's cubbyhole. She's at her desk with her back to me, also closing down her computer. But something gets to her. I've stopped talking but I haven't rung off. She turns, peers at me, then stands, opens the glass door and shoves her head round.

'You needing me?' she asks.

'Yes. Do you play *really bad badminton*?'

8

It's the Sunday evening before the planned Monday foursome with Ed, Laura and Florence. Prue and I are enjoying one of our absolute best weekends since my return from Tallinn. The reality of having me around the house as a permanency is still new to us, and we are both aware that it needs careful work. Prue loves her garden. I am up for the mowing and heavy lifting, but otherwise my finest moment is when I take the gin and tonic out to her on the stroke of six. Her law firm's engagement in a class action against Big Pharma is shaping well and we are both happy about that. I am slightly less happy to find our Sunday mornings given over to 'working brunches' of her dedicated legal team who, from the little I hear of their deliberations, sound more like anarchist plotters than seasoned lawyers. When I say this to Prue, she gives a hoot of laughter and says, 'But that's exactly what we are, darling!'

In the afternoon, we went to a movie – I forget what we saw except that we enjoyed it. When we got home Prue decreed that we should make a cheese soufflé together, which Steff assures us is the gastronomic equivalent of old-time dancing, but we love it. So I grate the cheese and she whizzes the eggs while we listen to Fischer-Dieskau at full volume, which is why neither of us hears the peep-peep of my Office mobile until Prue takes her thumb off the mixer.

'Dom,' I tell her, and she pulls a face.

I remove myself to the living room and close the door because we have an understanding that, if it's Office stuff, Prue prefers not to know about it.

'*Nat*. Forgive my outrageous Sunday intrusion.'

I forgive him, if tersely. I'm assuming from his benign tone that he's about to tell me we've got the Treasury's green light for Rosebud, information that could perfectly well have waited till Monday. But we haven't:

'No, not strictly in yet, I'm afraid, Nat. Any minute now, no doubt.'

Not *strictly*? What does that mean? Like *not strictly* pregnant? But this isn't why he called.

'*Nat*' – this recently developed *Nat* at the start of every other sentence, summoning me to arms – 'can I *possibly* prevail on you for an *enormous* favour? Are you by *any* chance free tomorrow? I know Mondays are always tricky, but just this *once*?'

'To do what?'

'Slip down to Northwood for me. Multinational headquarters. Have you been there before?'

'No.'

'Well, now's your once-in-a-lifetime chance. Our German friends have acquired a hot new live source on Moscow's hybrid warfare programme. They've put together an audience of NATO professionals. I thought it was just up your street.'

'You want me to *contribute* or what?'

'No, no, no. *Far* better not. The wrong climate entirely. It's strictly pan-European so the British voice will not be well received. The good news is, I've authorized a car for you. Grade one, chauffeur-driven. He'll take you there, wait for however long it lasts, and drive you home to Battersea afterwards.'

'This is Russia department stuff, Dom,' I protest irritably, 'not London General. And certainly not the Haven, for Christ's sake. That's like sending the help.'

'*Nat*. Guy Brammel has seen the material and assured me *personally* that Russia department does not see a role for itself at the meeting. Which means in effect you'll be representing not only London General but Russia department in one fell swoop. I thought you'd like that. It's a double honour.'

It's not an honour at all; it's a bloody bore. Nevertheless, like it or not, I am Dom's to command, and there comes a point.

'All right, Dom. Don't bother about a car. I'll take my own. I presume they provide parking in Northwood?'

'Utter nonsense, Nat! I insist. This is a class European gathering. The Office must show the flag. I made the point very strongly to the transport pool.'

I go back to the kitchen. Prue is sitting at the table with her glasses on, reading the *Guardian* while she waits for our soufflé to rise.

*

It's Monday evening at last, it's badminton night with Ed, it's our benefit foursome for his sister Laura, which I have to say in my own way I'm rather looking forward to. I have spent a dismal day incarcerated in an underground fortress in Northwood pretending to listen to a string of German statistics. Between sessions I have stood like a flunky at the buffet table apologizing for Brexit to an assortment of European intelligence professionals. Having been deprived of my mobile phone on arrival, it's not till I'm riding home in my chauffeur-driven limousine in pelting rain that I am able to call Viv – Dom himself being 'unavailable', a new trend – to be told that the Treasury sub-committee's decision on Rosebud is 'temporarily on hold'.

In the normal way, I wouldn't have been unduly bothered, but Dom's 'not strictly in yet' won't go away.

It's rush hour in the rain, and there's a hold-up at Battersea Bridge. I tell the driver to take me straight to the Athleticus. We pull up in time to see Florence, shrouded in a plastic cape, disappearing up the porch steps.

I need to log carefully what happened from now on.

*

I leap out of the Office limousine and am about to yell after Florence when I remember that in the flurry of fixing our foursome she and I failed to agree our cover stories. Who were we, how did we meet and how did we happen to be in the same room when Ed rang? All to resolve, so grab a moment as soon as we can.

Ed and Laura are waiting for us in the lobby, Ed is grinning broadly in an antiquated oilskin coat and shallow hat that I attribute to his nautical father. Laura is hiding behind his skirts and tugging at his leg, not willing to come out. She is small and sturdy with a cap of frizzy brown hair, a radiant smile and a blue dirndl dress. I am still deciding how to greet her – stand back and wave cheerfully or reach round Ed's body to shake her hand – when Florence bounces up to her with 'Wow, Laura, love the dress! Is it new?' at which Laura beams and says 'Ed bought it. In *Germany*' – in a deep, husky voice and gazes adoringly up at her brother.

'Only place in the world to buy one,' Florence pronounces and grabbing Laura's hand marches her off to the women's changing room with a 'see you guys shortly' over her shoulder while Ed and I stare after her.

'Where the hell did you find *her*?' Ed grumbles, masking what is evidently a keen interest, and I have no option but to deliver my half of a makeshift cover story yet to be agreed with Florence.

'Somebody's high-powered assistant is all I know,' I reply vaguely, and set course for the men's changing room before he can ply me with more questions.

But in the changing room to my relief he prefers to loose off about Trump's abrogation of Obama's nuclear treaty with Iran.

'America's word is herewith and henceforth officially declared null and void,' he announces. 'Agreed?'

'Agreed,' I reply – and please just keep going until I've had a chance to nobble Florence, which I'm determined to do as soon as possible because the thought that Ed might take it into his head that I'm something other than a semi-employed business-man is beginning to get to me.

'*And* as to what he just did in *Ottawa*' – still on the subject of Trump while he hauls up his long shorts – 'know what?'

'What?'

'He actually made Russia look good on Iran, which must be a first for anybody's bloody money,' he says with grim satisfaction.

'Outrageous,' I agree, thinking the sooner Florence and I are out on court the happier I'll be – and maybe she's heard some-thing about Rosebud that I haven't, so ask her that too.

'*And* us Brits so desperate for free trade with America that we'll be saying *yes* Donald, *no* Donald, kiss-your-arse-please Donald all the way to Armageddon' – raising his head to give me the full, unblinking stare. 'Well, won't we, Nat? Go on.'

So I agree for the second or is it the third time, noting only that he doesn't usually start setting the world to rights until we're sitting over our lagers at the *Stammtisch*. But he isn't done yet, which happens to suit me fine:

'The man's a pure hater. Hates Europe, he's said so. Hates Iran, hates Canada, hates treaties. Who does he love?'

'How about golf?' I suggest.

Court three is draughty and run down. It occupies its own shed at the back of the Club, so no spectators, no passers-by, which I assumed was why Ed had booked it. This was Laura's treat, and he didn't want anyone staring. We hang around waiting for the girls. Here again Ed might have raised the thorny question of how Florence and I came to know each other, but I encourage him to keep on about Iran.

The women's changing-room door is opened from inside. Alone in her finery Laura strides unevenly on to the catwalk: brand-new shorts, spotless chequered trainers, Che Guevara T-shirt, professional-standard racquet still in its wrapping.

Now enter Florence, not in office fatigues, not in presentational trouser suit or rain-drenched leathers: just a liberated, slender, self-assured young woman with short skirt and the shiny white thighs of Ed's adolescence. I steal a look at him. Rather than appear impressed, he has put on his most uninterested face. My own reaction is one of humorous indignation: Florence, you are not supposed to look like that. Then I get hold of myself and become a responsible home-based husband and father again.

We pair off the only way that makes sense. Laura and Ed versus Florence and Nat. In practice this means Laura stands with her nose in the net and whacks at anything that comes her way, and Ed retrieves whatever she doesn't fluff. It also means that between rallies Florence and I have ample opportunity for a covert word.

'You're somebody's high-powered assistant,' I tell her, as she scoops up a shuttle from the back of the court. 'That's all I know about you. I'm a friend of your boss. Fake it from there.'

No response, none expected. Good girl. Ed is doing some repair work on one of Laura's trainers that has come undone, or she says it has, because Ed's attention means everything to her.

'We bumped into each other in a pal of mine's office,' I go on. 'You were sitting at your computer, I walked in. Otherwise we don't know each other from Adam.' And very softly, as an afterthought: 'Have you had anything on Rosebud while I was in Northwood?'

To all of which I get not a flicker of a response.

We have a threesome knock-up, bypassing Laura at the net. Florence is one of God's athletes: effortless timing and reactions, agile as a gazelle and too graceful for her own good. Ed does his usual leaping and lunging but keeps his eyes hard down between rallies. I suspect that his studied lack of interest in Florence is for Laura's benefit: he doesn't want his little sister to get upset.

Another rally between the three of us until Laura wails that she is being left out and it's no fun any more. We pause everything while Ed drops to his knees to console her. This is the ideal moment for Florence and me to stand casually face to face with our hands on our hips and wrap up our cover story.

'My friend your employer is a commodity trader and you're a high-class temporary.'

But instead of acknowledging my story, she decides to become aware of Laura's distress and Ed's attempts to cheer her up. With a cry of 'Hey, you two, break that up at once!' she bounds to the net and decrees that we will change partners forthwith and it will be the men versus the women in mortal combat, the best of three games and she will serve first. She is on her way to the opposite court when I touch her bare arm.

'You're all right with that? You heard me. Yes?'

She swings round and stares at me.

'I don't feel like fucking lying any more,' she snaps full voiced, eyes blazing. 'Not to him or anybody else. Got that?'

I got it, but did Ed? Mercifully he shows no sign of having done so. Striding to the other side of the net, she prises Laura's hand from Ed's and commands him to join me. We play our epic match, the world's men versus the world's women. Florence savages every shuttle that comes her way. With a lot of help from us men, the women achieve their supremacy over us and, racquets held high, process in triumph to their changing room and Ed and I process to ours.

Is it her love life? I am asking myself. Those lonely tears I saw but didn't remark on? Or are we dealing with a case of what the Office shrinks are pleased to call camel's-back syndrome, when the things you're not allowed to talk about suddenly outweigh the things that you are, and you go down temporarily under the strain?

Extracting my Office mobile phone from my locker I step into the corridor, press for Florence and get an electronic voice telling me this line is disconnected. I try a couple of times more, still no joy. I go back to the changing room. Ed has showered and is sitting on the slatted bench with a towel round his neck.

'I was wondering,' he muses grudgingly, unaware that I had left the room and have now returned. 'Well, you know. Only if you're up for it, sort of thing. Maybe we could do a meal somewhere. Not at the bar. Laura doesn't like it. Out somewhere. The four of us. On me.'

'You mean *now*?'

'Yeah. If you're up for it. Why not?'

'With Florence?'

'I said. Us four.'

'How do you know she's free?'

'She is. I asked her. She said yes.'

Quick think, then, yes, I'm up for it. And the moment I get a chance – preferably before the meal rather than after – I'll find out what the devil's got into her head.

'There's the Golden Moon up the road,' I suggest. 'Chinese. They stay open late. You could give them a try.'

I have barely finished saying this when my encrypted Office mobile phone lets out its hee-haw. Florence after all, I think. Thank God. One minute she's not playing Office rules any more, the next we're all off to dinner.

Muttering something about Prue needing me, I step back into the corridor. But it's not Prue and it's not Florence. It's Ilya, tonight's duty officer at the Haven, and I'm assuming he's about to give me the overdue news that we've got the sub-committee's say-so on Rosebud and high bloody time too.

Except that's not why Ilya has called.

'Flash incoming, Nat. Your farmer friend. For Peter.'

For 'farmer friend' read Pitchfork, Russian research student, York University, inherited from Giles. For Peter, read Nat.

'Saying what?' I demand.

'You're please to pay him a visit at your earliest possible. You personally, nobody else. Plus it's top urgent.'

'His own words?'

'I can send them to you if you want.'

I return to the changing room. It's a no-brainer, as Steff would say. Sometimes we're bastards, sometimes we're Samaritans and sometimes we get it plain wrong. But fail an agent in his hour of need and you fail him for ever, as my mentor Bryn Jordan liked to say. Ed is still sitting on the slatted bench, head slumped forward. He has his knees spread and is staring downwards between them while I'm checking railway timetables on my mobile. Last train for York leaves King's Cross in fifty-eight minutes.

'Got to love you and leave you, I'm afraid, Ed,' I say. 'No Chinese for me after all. Bit of business to attend to before it goes sour on me.'

'Tough,' Ed remarks, without lifting his head.

I make for the door.

'Hey, Nat.'

'What is it?'

'Thanks, okay? Very nice of you, that was. Florence too. I told her. Made Laura's day. Just sorry you can't do the Chinese.'

'Me too. Go for the Peking Duck. It comes with pancakes and jam. What the hell's the matter with you?'

Ed has opened his hands in theatrical display, and is rolling his head around as if in despair.

'Want to know something?'

'If it's quick.'

'Either Europe's fucked or somebody with balls has to find an antidote to Trump.'

'And who might that be?' I enquire.

No answer. He has slumped back into his thoughts, and I am on my way to York.

9

I am doing the decent thing. I am answering the cry that every agent-runner the world over takes to his grave. The tunes vary, the lines vary, but in the end it's the same song every time: I can't live with myself, Peter, the stress is killing me, Peter, the burden of my treachery is too great for me, my mistress has left me, my wife is deceiving me, my neighbours suspect me, my dog's been run over and you my trusted handler are the one person in the world who can persuade me not to cut my wrists.

Why do we agent-runners come running every time? Because we owe.

But I don't feel I owe much to the notably quiescent agent Pitchfork, neither is he my first concern as I take my seat on a delayed train to York in a carriage crammed with screaming kids returning from a London outing. I am thinking about Florence's refusal to join me in a cover story that is as natural to our secret lives as brushing our teeth. I am thinking about the go-ahead for Operation Rosebud that still refuses to materialize. I am thinking of Prue's reply when I called her to tell her I wouldn't be home tonight and asked her whether she has news of Steff:

'Only that she's moved into posh new digs in Clifton and doesn't say who with.'

'*Clifton*. Whatever's the rent?'

'Not ours to ask, I'm afraid. An email. One-way traffic only' – unable for once to hide the note of desperation in her voice.

And when Prue's sad voice isn't sounding in my ear, I have Florence's to regale me: *I don't feel like fucking lying any more. Not to him or anybody else. Got that?* Which in turn leads me back to a question that has been gnawing at me ever since Dom's unctuous phone call with his offer of the chauffeur-driven car, because Dom never does anything without a reason, however twisted. I try Florence on her Office mobile a couple more times, get the same electronic howl. But my mind is still on Dom: why did you want me out of your way today? And are you by any chance the reason why Florence has decided not to lie for her country, which is a pretty massive decision if lying for your country is your chosen profession?

So it's not until Peterborough that, sheltered by a giveaway copy of the *Evening Standard*, I touch in an endless string of digits and apply myself to agent Pitchfork's unsatisfactory case history.

*

His name is Sergei Borisovich Kuznetsov, and henceforth against all known rules of my trade I will call him plain Sergei. He is the Petersburg-born son and grandson of Chekists, his grand-father an honoured general of the NKVD buried in the Kremlin walls, his father an ex-KGB colonel who died of multiple wounds sustained in Chechnya. So far so good. But whether Sergei is the true heir to this noble lineage remains uncertain.

The known facts argue in his favour. But there are a lot of them, some would say too many. At sixteen he was sent to a special school near Perm, which in addition to physics taught 'political strategy', a euphemism for conspiracy and espionage.

At nineteen he entered Moscow State University. On graduating *magna cum laude* in Physics and English he was selected for

88

further training at a special school for sleeper agents. From the first day of his two-year course, according to his testimony, he determined to defect to whichever Western country he was assigned to, which explains why upon arrival at Edinburgh airport at ten at night he asked politely to speak to a 'high officer of British Intelligence'.

His ostensible reasons for doing this were unimpeachable. From an early age he claimed to have secretly worshipped at the feet of such luminaries of physics and humanism as Andrei Sakharov, Niels Bohr, Richard Feynman and our own Stephen Hawking. Always he had dreamed of liberty for all, science for all, humanism for all. How then could he not hate the barbarian autocrat Vladimir Putin and his wicked works?

Sergei was also by his own admission homosexual. This fact of itself, had it become known to his fellow students or instructors, would have had him instantly chucked off the course. But according to Sergei this never happened. Somehow he preserved a heterosexual front, flirting with the girls on the course and even going to bed with a couple – according to himself, purely for cover purposes.

And in substantiation of all the above, just look at the unexpected treasure chest sitting on the table in front of his bemused debriefers: two suitcases and one backpack containing between them an entire toolkit of the authentic spy: carbons for secret writing impregnated with the nearly latest compounds; a fictional girlfriend to write to in Denmark, the covert message to be written in invisible carbon between the lines; a subminiature camera built into a fob for a key ring; three thousand pounds of start-up money in tens and twenties hidden in the base of one suitcase; a wad of one-time pads and for a *bonne bouche* the phone number in Paris that may be called in emergency only.

And everything tallied, right down to his pen portraits of his pseudonymous trainers and fellow trainees, the tricks of the trade he has been taught, the training gigs he has undertaken and his holy mission as a loyal Russian sleeper agent, which he reeled off like a mantra: study hard, earn the respect of your scientific colleagues, espouse their values and philosophy, write papers for their learned journals. In emergency, never under any pretext attempt to contact the depleted *rezidentura* at the Russian Embassy in London because nobody will have heard of you and anyway *rezidenturas* don't service sleeper agents, who are an elite to themselves, hand-raised practically from birth and controlled by their own exclusive team at Moscow Centre. Rise with the tide, contact us every month and dream of Mother Russia every night.

The only point of curiosity – and for his debriefers something more than curiosity – was that there was not one grain of new or marketable intelligence in any of it. Every nugget he revealed had been revealed by previous defectors: the personalities, the teaching methods, the tradecraft, even the spies' toys, two of which were duplicated in the black museum in the distinguished visitors' suite on the ground floor of Head Office.

*

The debriefers' reservations notwithstanding, Russia department under the now absent Bryn Jordan awarded Pitchfork the full defectors' welcome, taking him out to dinners and football matches, co-drafting his monthly reports to his fictional girlfriend in Denmark about the doings of his scientific colleagues, bugging his rooms, hacking his communications and intermittently placing him under covert surveillance. And waiting.

But for what? For six, eight, twelve costly months came not one spark of life from his Moscow Centre handlers: not a letter with or without its secret under-text, not an email, phone call or magic phrase spoken on a predetermined commercial radio broadcast at a predetermined hour. Have they given him up? Have they rumbled him? Have they woken to his covert homosexuality and drawn their conclusions?

As each barren month succeeded the last, Russia department's patience evaporated until a day when Pitchfork was turned over to the Haven for 'maintenance and non-active development' – or, as Giles had it, 'to be handled with a thick pair of rubber gloves and a very long pair of asbestos tongs, because if ever I smelt *triple*, this boy has all the markings and then some'.

The markings maybe, but if so they were yesterday's. Today, if experience told me anything, Sergei Borisovich was just one more poor player in the endless cycle of Russian double-double games who has had his hour and been tossed away. And now he has decided it's time to press his help button.

*

The noisy kids have removed themselves to the buffet car. Alone in my corner seat I call Sergei on the mobile phone we gave him and get the same orderly, expressionless voice I remember from the handover ceremony with Giles back in February. I tell him I am responding to his call. He thanks me. I ask him how he is. He is well, Peter. I say I won't be arriving in York before eleven-thirty and does he need a meeting tonight or can it wait till morning? He is tired, Peter, so maybe tomorrow will be better, thank you. So much for 'top urgent'. I tell him we will be reverting to our 'traditional arrangement' and ask 'Are you comfortable with that?' because the agent in the field, however dubious, must always have the last word on matters of tradecraft. Thank you, Peter, he is comfortable with the traditional arrangement.

From my ill-smelling hotel bedroom I again try Florence's Office mobile phone. It is by now after midnight. More electronic howl. Having no other number for her, I call Ilya at the Haven. Has he received any late word on Rosebud?

'Sorry, Nat, not a dicky bird.'

'Well, you don't need to be so bloody flippant about it,' I snap at him and ring off in a huff.

I might have asked him whether by any chance he has heard from Florence, or happens to know why her Office mobile is cut off, but Ilya is young and volatile and I don't want the whole Haven family in a ferment. It is incumbent on all serving members to provide a landline number where they can be contacted out of hours in case no mobile phone signal is available. The last landline number Florence registered was in Hampstead, where I recall that she also likes to run. Nobody seems to have noticed that Hampstead didn't exactly tally with her claim to live with her parents in Pimlico but then, as Florence assured me, there's always the 24 bus.

I dial the Hampstead number, get the machine and say I am Peter from Customer Security and we have reason to believe her account has been hacked, so for her own protection please to call this number soonest. I drink a lot of whisky and try to sleep.

*

The 'traditional procedure' I am enforcing on Sergei dated from the days when he was being treated as a live double agent with a serious prospect of development. The pick-up point was the forecourt to York city racecourse. He was to arrive by bus, armed with a copy of the previous day's *Yorkshire Post* while his case officer waited in a lay-by in an Office car. Sergei would dawdle with the crowd long enough for Percy Price's surveillance team to decide whether the encounter was being covered by the opposition, a possibility not as far-fetched as it may sound. Once the home team gave the all-clear Sergei would saunter to the bus stop and examine the timetable. Newspaper in his left hand meant abort. Newspaper in his right hand meant all systems go.

The procedure for our handover ceremony as masterminded by Giles had by contrast been rather less traditional. He had insisted it take place in Sergei's own lodgings on the university campus, with smoked salmon sandwiches and a bottle of vodka to wash them down. Our wafer-thin cover if we should have to account for ourselves? Giles was a visiting professor from Oxford on a headhunting expedition and I was his Nubian slave.

Well, now we are back to the traditional procedure, with no smoked salmon. I have hired a clapped-out Vauxhall, the best the rent-a-car company can offer me in the time. I drive with one eye for the mirror and no idea what I'm looking for, but looking all the same. The day is grey, fine rain is falling, more forecast. The road to the racecourse is straight and flat. Perhaps the Romans raced here too. White railings flicker past on my left side. A beflagged gateway appears before me. At pedestrian speed I nose my way through shoppers and wet day pleasure-seekers.

And sure enough there at the bus stop stands Sergei amid a huddle of waiting passengers, examining a yellow timetable. He clutches a copy of the *Yorkshire Post* in his right hand and in his left a music case that isn't in the script with a rolled umbrella threaded through the top. I pull up a few yards past the bus stop, lower the window and yell, 'Hey, Jack! Remember me? Peter!'

At first he pretends not to hear me. It's copybook stuff and so it should be after two years of sleeper school. He turns his head in puzzlement, discovers me, does amazement and delight.

'Peter! My friend! It is you. I truly don't believe my eyes.'

Okay, that's enough, get in the car. He does. We exchange an air-hug for the spectators. He's wearing a new Burberry raincoat, fawn. He takes it off, folds it and lays it reverently on the back seat but keeps the music case between his knees. As we drive away, a man at the bus stop makes a rude face to the woman standing next to him. See what I saw just then? Middle-aged poofter picks up pretty rent boy in broad daylight.

I'm watching for anyone pulling out behind us, car, van or motorbike. Nothing catches the eye. Under the traditional procedure Sergei isn't told in advance where he's going to be taken, and he isn't being told now. He's skinnier and more haunted than I remember him from our handover. He has a tousled mop of black hair and doleful bedroom eyes. His spindly fingers are playing a tattoo on the dashboard. In his rooms in college they played the same tattoo on the wooden arm of his chair. His new Harris Tweed sports jacket is too big for his shoulders.

'What's in the music case?' I demand.

'It is paper, Peter. For you.'

'Only paper?'

'Please. It is very important paper.'

'I'm glad to hear it.'

He is unmoved by my terseness. Perhaps he was expecting it. Perhaps he's always expecting it. Perhaps he despises me, as I suspect he despised Giles.

'Do you have anything on your body, in your clothes or anything else apart from the paper in the music case that I should know about? Nothing that films, records, does anything like that?'

'Please, Peter, I do not. I have excellent news. You will be happy.'

That's enough business till we get there. With the din of the diesel engine and the rattly bodywork I'm scared he's going to come out with stuff I can't hear and my Office smartphone can't record or transmit to the Haven. We're speaking English and we'll speak it until I decide otherwise. Giles had no Russian worth a damn. I see no value in letting Sergei know that I'm any different. I have chosen a hilltop twenty miles out of town allegedly with a fine view over the moors, but all we can see as I heave the Vauxhall to a halt and switch off the engine is grey cloud below us and driven rain whipping across the windscreen. By the laws of tradecraft we should by now have agreed who we are if we're disturbed, when and where we'll meet again, and does he have any pressing anxieties? But he's put the music case flat on his lap and he's already undoing the straps and pulling out a brown A4-size padded envelope, unsealed.

'Moscow Centre has communicated with me at last, Peter. After one whole year,' he declares with something between academic disdain and clotted excitement. 'It is evidently momentous. My Anette in Copenhagen wrote me a beautiful and erotic letter in English and, underneath in our secret carbon, a letter from my Moscow Centre controller which I have translated into English for you' – upon which he affects to make me a presentation of the envelope.

'Hang on a minute, Sergei.' I have taken possession of the padded envelope but haven't looked inside. 'Let me get this straight. You received a love letter from your lady friend in Denmark. You then applied the necessary compound, raised the secret under-text, decoded it and translated the contents into English for my benefit. All by yourself. Single-handed. That right?'

'That is correct, Peter. Our combined patience is rewarded.'

'So *when* did you receive this letter from Denmark exactly?'

'On Friday. At midday. I could not believe my eyes.'

'And today is Tuesday. You waited until yesterday afternoon to contact my office.'

'All weekend while I worked I was thinking only of you. Night and day I was so pleased I was developing and translating all at once in my mind, wishing only that our good friend Norman was with us to enjoy our success.'

Norman for Giles.

'So the letter from your Moscow handlers has been in your possession since Friday. Have you shown it to anyone else in the meantime?'

'No, Peter. I have not. Please look inside the envelope.'

I ignore his request. Does nothing shock him any more? Does his academic standing place him above the ruck of common spies?

'And while you were developing and decoding and translating, did it not occur to you that you are under standing orders to report any letter or other communication you receive from your Russian controllers *instantly* to your handling officer—?'

'But of course. This is what I did exactly, as soon as I had decoded—'

'—before any further action is taken by you, us or anyone else? Which is why your debriefers took the developing compound from you as soon as you arrived in Edinburgh a year ago? So that you *couldn't* do your own developing?'

And when I had waited long enough for my not entirely simulated anger to subside and still received no answer beyond a sigh of forbearance at my ingratitude:

'What did you do for the compound? Pop into the nearest chemist's shop and read out a list of the ingredients so that anyone listening would think, ah great, he's got a secret letter to develop? Maybe there's a chemist's shop on the campus. Is there?'

We sit side by side, listening to the rain.

'Please, Peter. I am not stupid. I took a bus into town. I made purchases at many different chemists. I paid cash, I did not engage in conversations, I was discreet.'

The same self-composure. The same innate superiority. And yes, this man could well be the son and grandson of distinguished Chekists.

*

Only now do I consent to look inside the envelope.

First out, two long letters, the cover letter and the carbon under-text. He had copied or photographed every stage of development and the printouts were there for me to see, neatly ordered and numbered.

Second out, the Danish-stamped envelope with his name and campus address in a girlish Continental hand on the front, and on the back the sender's name and address: Anette Pedersen, who lives in Number Five on the ground floor of an apartment house in a suburb of Copenhagen.

Third out, the surface text in English, running to six closely written sides in the same girlish hand as the envelope, lauding his sexual prowess in puerile terms and claiming that merely thinking about him was enough to give the writer an orgasm.

Then the raised under-text with column after column of four-figure groups. Then the version in Russian, decoded from his one-time pad.

And finally his own translation of the Russian *en clair* text into English for my personal benefit as a non-Russian-speaker. I frown at the Russian version, discard it with a gesture of incomprehension, take up his English translation and read it two or three times while Sergei affects contentment and flattens his hands on the dashboard to ease the tension.

'Moscow say you are to take up residence in London as soon as the summer vacation begins,' I remark casually. 'Why do they want you to do that, do you think?'

'*She* says,' he corrects me in a husky voice.

97

'Who says?'

'Anette.'

'So you're saying Anette is a real woman. Not just some man in Centre signing himself as a woman?'

'I know this woman.'

'The *actual* woman? Anette. You know her, you're saying?'

'Correct, Peter. The same woman who is calling herself Anette for purposes of conspiracy.'

'And how do you arrive at this extraordinary discovery, may I ask?'

He suppresses a sigh to imply that he is about to enter territory where I am unequipped to follow him.

'Each week for one hour this woman lectured us at sleeper school for the class of English only. She *prepared* us for conspiratorial activity in England. She *related* many interesting case histories to us and gave us much advice and courage for our secret work.'

'And you're telling me her name was Anette?'

'Like all instructors and all students, she had only a work name.'

'Which was what?'

'Anastasia.'

'So not Anette?'

'It is immaterial.'

I grit my teeth and say nothing. After a while he resumes in the same patronizing tone.

'*Anastasia* is a woman of considerable intelligence who is capable also of discussing physics without simplicity. I described her in detail to your debriefers. You appear to be ignorant of this information.'

It was true. He had described Anastasia. Just not in such precise or glowing terms and certainly not as a future correspondent calling herself Anette. As far as the debriefers were concerned she was just another Moscow Centre apparatchik dropping in on sleeper school to burnish her image.

'And you think the woman who called herself Anastasia at sleeper school personally wrote this letter to you?'

'I am convinced.'

'Only the under-text, or the surface letter too?'

'Both. Anastasia has become Anette. This is a recognition signal to me. Anastasia our wise instructor from Moscow Centre has become Anette my passionate mistress in Copenhagen who does not exist. Also I am familiar with her handwriting. When Anastasia was lecturing us at sleeper school she advised us on European manners of handwriting without the influence of Cyrillic. Everything she taught us was for one purpose only: to assimilate with the Western enemy: "Over time you will *become* them. You will *think* like them. You will *talk* like them. You will *feel* like them and you will *write* like them. Only in your secret hearts will you remain one of us." Like me, she too was from old Chekist family. Her father, also her grandfather. Of this she was very proud. After her last lecture to us she took me aside and told me: you will never know my name but you and I are of one blood, we are pure, we are old Cheka, we are Russia, I congratulate you with my soul on your great calling. She embraced me.'

Was this where the first faint echoes from my operational past began to ring in my memory's ear? Probably it was, for my immediate instinct was to redirect the conversation:

'What typewriter did you use?'

'Only manual, Peter. I use nothing electronic. This is how we were instructed. Electronic is too dangerous. Anastasia, Anette, she is not electronic. She is traditional and wishes her students to be traditional also.'

Exercising well-honed skills of self-control, I affect to ignore Sergei's obsession with the woman Anette or Anastasia and resume my reading of his decoded and translated under-text.

'You are to rent a room or apartment for July and August in one of three selected districts around North London – yes? – which your controller – you say this former woman lecturer – then proceeds to itemize for you. Do these instructions suggest anything to you?'

'It was how she taught us. In order to prepare a conspiratorial meeting it is essential to have alternative locations. Only in this way can logistical changes be accommodated and security observed. This is also her operational maxim.'

'Have you ever been to any of these North London districts?'

'No, Peter, I have not.'

'When did you last visit London?'

'For one weekend only in May.'

'With whom?'

'It is immaterial, Peter.'

'No, it isn't.'

'A friend.'

'Male or female?'

'It is immaterial.'

'So male. Has the friend got a name?'

No answer. I continue my reading:

'While in London for the months of July and August you will assume the name of Markus Schweizer, a German-speaking Swiss freelance journalist, for which you will be provided with additional documentation. Do you know a Markus Schweizer?'

'Peter, I know no such person.'

'Have you ever used such an alias before?'

'No, Peter.'

'Never heard of one?'

'No, Peter.'

'Was Markus Schweizer the name of the friend you took to London?'

'No, Peter. Also I did not take him. He accompanied me.'

'But you speak German.'

'I am adequate.'

'Your debriefers said more than adequate. They said you were fluent. I'm more interested to know whether you have any explanation for Moscow's instructions?'

I have lost him again. He has lapsed into an Ed-like contemplation, his gaze fixed on the teeming windscreen. Suddenly he has an announcement to make:

'Peter, I regret that I am not able to be this Swiss person. I shall not go to London. It is a provocation. I resign.'

'I'm asking you *why* Moscow should wish you to be the *independent German-speaking freelance journalist* Markus Schweizer for two months of summer in one of three selected districts of North-east London,' I persist, ignoring this outburst.

'It is in order to facilitate my murder. Such a deduction is clear to any mind familiar with Moscow Centre practice. Maybe not you. By providing Centre with an address in London I shall be sending them instructions regarding where and how to liquidate me. That is normal practice in the case of suspected traitors. It will be Moscow's pleasure to select a most painful death for me. I shall not go.'

'Bit of an elaborate way of going about it, isn't it?' I suggest, unmoved. 'Dragging you to London just to kill you. Why not bring you to a deserted place like this, dig a hole, shoot you and put you in it? Then leak it to your friends in York that you're safely home in Moscow and job done? Why aren't you answering me? Is your change of heart in some way connected with the friend you won't tell me about? The one you took to London? I have a feeling I've even met him. Is that possible?'

I am making a leap of intuition. I am putting two and two

together and making five. I am remembering an episode that occurred during the convivial handover with Giles in Sergei's university lodgings. The door opens without a knock, a cheerful youth with an earring and a ponytail pops his head round and starts to say 'Hey, Serge, have you got a—' then sees us and with a suppressed 'whoops' closes the door softly behind him as if to say he was never there.

In another part of my head, the full force of memory has struck home to me. Anastasia alias Anette, and whatever other names she favours, is no longer a fleeting shadow half remembered from my past. She is a solid figure of stature and operational prowess, much as Sergei himself has just described her.

'Sergei,' I say in a gentler tone than I have used so far, 'why else might you not want to be Markus Schweizer in London for the summer? Have you planned a holiday with your friend? It's a stressful life. We understand those things.'

'They wish only to kill me.'

'And if you *have* made holiday plans, and you can tell me who your friend is, then maybe we can come to a mutually acceptable arrangement.'

'I have no such plans, Peter. I think actually you are projecting. Maybe you have plans for yourself. I know nothing about you. Norman was kind to me. You are a wall. You are Peter. You are not my friend.'

'Then who *is* your friend?' I insist. 'Come on, Sergei. We're human. After a year on your own here in England, don't tell me you haven't found somebody to pal up with? All right, maybe you should have notified us. Let's forget that. Let's assume it's not all that serious. Just someone to go on holiday with. A summer partner. Why not?'

He rounds on me in Russian outrage and barks:

'He is not my summer partner! He is the friend of my heart!'

'Well in *that* case,' I say, 'he sounds exactly the sort of friend you need and we must find a way to keep him happy. Not in London, but we'll think of something. Is he a student?'

'He is postgraduate. He is *kulturny*—' and for my better understanding: 'He is cultivated in all artistic subjects.'

'And a fellow physicist perhaps?'

'No. For English literature. For your great poets. For all poets.'

'Does he know you were a Russian agent?'

'He would despise me.'

'Even if you are working for the British?'

'He despises all deception.'

'Then we have nothing to worry about, do we? Just write down his name for me here on this piece of paper.'

He accepts my notepad and pen, turns his back to me and writes.

'And his birthday, which I'm sure you know,' I add.

He writes again, rips off the page, folds it and with an imperious gesture hands it to me. I unfold it, glance at the name, slip it into the padded envelope with his other offerings and recover my notepad.

'So, Sergei,' I say, in an altogether warmer tone. 'We shall resolve the matter of your Barry in the next few days. Positively. Creatively, I'm sure. Then I won't have to tell Her Majesty's Home Office that you've ceased collaborating with us, will I? And by doing so violated the terms of your residence.'

A fresh torrent of rain sweeps across the windscreen.

'Sergei accepts,' he announces.

*

I have driven a distance and parked under a clump of chestnut trees where the wind and rain are not so ferocious. Seated beside me, Sergei has adopted a pose of superior detachment and is pretending to study the scenery.

'So let's talk some more about your Anette,' I suggest, select-
ing my most relaxed tone of voice. 'Or shall we go back to calling
her Anastasia, which is how you knew her when she lectured
you? Tell me more about her talents.'

'She is an accomplished linguist and a woman of great quality
and education and most skilled in conspiracy.'

'Age?'

'I would say, perhaps fifty. Fifty-three maybe. Not beautiful,
but with much dignity and charisma. In the face also. Such a
woman could believe in God.'

Sergei also believes in God, he has told his debriefers. But his
faith must not be mediated. As an intellectual he has no love of
clergy.

'Height?' I enquire.

'I would say, one metre sixty-five.'

'Voice?'

'Anastasia spoke only English with us, in which she was clearly
excellent.'

'You never heard her speak Russian?'

'No, Peter. I did not.'

'Not one word?'

'No.'

'German?'

'Once only she spoke German. It was to recite Heine. This
is a German poet of the Romantic Period, also a Jew.'

'In your mind. Now, or maybe when you were listening to
her speaking. How would you place her geographically? From
what region?'

I had expected him to ponder ostentatiously, but he came
straight back:

'It was my impression that this woman, by her bearing and
dark eyes and complexion, also from the cadence of her speech,
was from Georgia.'

Dull down, I am urging myself. Be your mediocre professional self.

'Sergei?'

'Please, Peter?'

'What is the date of your planned holiday with Barry?'

'It will be for all of August. It will be to visit on foot as pilgrims your historic British places of culture and spiritual freedom.'

'And your university term begins when?'

'September 24th.'

'Then why not postpone your holiday until September? Tell him you have an important research project in London.'

'I cannot do this. Barry will wish only to accompany me.'

But my head is already spinning with alternatives.

'Then consider this. We send you – just for example – an official letter on, say, Harvard University Physics Faculty notepaper congratulating you on your great work in York. We offer you a two-month summer research fellowship on the Harvard campus in July and August, all expenses paid, and an honorarium. You could show that to Barry, and as soon as you've completed your spell in London as Markus Schweizer the two of you can pick up where you left off and have the time of your lives using all those lovely dollars that Harvard will have given you for your research project. Would that play? Well, would it or not?'

'Provided such a letter is plausible and the honorarium is realistic, it is my belief that Barry would be proud for me,' he announces.

Some spies are lightweights pretending to be heavyweights. Some are heavyweights despite themselves. Unless my inflamed memory deceives me, Sergei has just promoted himself to the heavyweight class.

*

Seated in the front of the car, we debate as two professionals the sort of replies we will be sending to Anette in Copenhagen: a first draft of the under-text assuring Centre that Sergei will comply with its instructions, then the cover text, which I propose to leave to his erotic imagination, stipulating only that, together with the under-text, I approve it before it is sent.

Having concluded – not least for my own convenience – that Sergei is likely to be more at ease with a female handler, I inform him that he will henceforth be working to Jennifer, aka Florence, on all matters of routine. I undertake to bring Jennifer to York on a get-to-know-you expedition and discuss what cover best befits their future relationship: perhaps not girlfriend, since Jennifer is tall and good-looking and Barry might take offence. I will remain Sergei's controller, Jennifer will report to me at all stages. And I remember thinking to myself that whatever had got into Florence on the badminton court, here was the gift of a challenging agent operation to restore her morale and test her skills.

At a petrol station on the outskirts of York I invest in two egg-and-cress sandwiches and two bottles of fizzy lemonade. Giles would no doubt have produced a Fortnum's hamper. When we have finished our picnic and cleaned the crumbs out of the car together, I drop Sergei at a bus stop. He attempts to embrace me. I shake his hand instead. To my surprise it is still early afternoon. I return the hire car to the depot and am lucky to catch a fast train that gets me to London in time to take Prue to our local Indian. Since Office matters are off-limits, our dinner conversation turns on the shameful practices of Big Pharma. Back at home, we watch Channel 4 News on catch-up and on this inconclusive note go to bed, but sleep comes slowly to me.

Florence has still not responded to my phone message. The Treasury sub-committee's verdict on Rosebud, according to an enigmatic late email from Viv, is 'due any moment but still pending'. If I do not find these augurs quite as ominous as I might have done, that is because my head is still rejoicing in the improbable chain of connection that Sergei and his Anette have revealed to me. I am reminded of an aphorism of my mentor Bryn Jordan: if you spy for long enough, the show comes round again.

10

Riding on the tube to Camden Town early that Wednesday morning, I took a clear-headed look at the competing tasks awaiting me. How far to take the issue of Florence's insubordination? Report her to Human Resources and instigate a full-blown disciplinary tribunal with Moira in the chair? Heaven forfend. Better to have it out with her one-to-one behind closed doors. And on the positive side, award her the fast-developing case of agent Pitchfork.

Letting myself into the dingy hallway of the Haven, I am struck by the unusual silence. Ilya's bicycle is there, but where is Ilya? Where is anyone? I climb the stairs to the first landing: not a sound. All doors closed. I climb to the second. The door to Florence's cubicle is sealed with masking tape. A red 'No Entry' sign is pasted across it, and the door handle sprayed with wax. But the door to my own office stands wide open. On my desk lie two printouts.

The first an internal memo from Viv informing addressees that after due consideration by the competent Treasury sub-committee Operation Rosebud has been cancelled on grounds of disproportionate risk.

The second is an internal memo from Moira informing all relevant departments that Florence has resigned from the Service as of Monday and that full severance procedure

has been activated in accordance with HO rules of disen-
gagement.

*

Think now, do crisis later.

According to Moira, Florence's resignation occurred a mere
four hours before she showed up for the foursome with Ed and
Laura at the Athleticus, which went a long way to explaining
her aberrant behaviour. What had caused her to resign? On the
face of it, the cancellation of Operation Rosebud, but don't rush
your fences. Having read both documents slowly for a third
time, I stepped back on to the landing, cupped my hands over
my mouth and yelled:

'Everybody out, please. *Now!*'

As my team cautiously emerges from behind closed doors
I piece together the story, or as much of it as anybody knows
or is willing to say. Around eleven on the Monday morning,
while I was safely tucked away in darkest Northwood, Florence
had informed Ilya that she had an appointment with Dom
Trench in his office. According to Ilya, normally a reliable source,
she appeared more worried than excited by the prospect.

At one-fifteenish, while Ilya was upstairs covering the communications desk and the rest of the team were downstairs
having their sandwich lunches and reading their phones,
Florence appeared in the kitchen doorway having returned
from her appointment with Dom. Scottish Denise had always
been closest to Florence in the pecking order and had routinely
taken over her agents when Florence was tied up or on leave.

'She just stood there, Nat, like for minutes, staring at us like
we were all crazy' – Denise, awestruck.

'Had Florence actually *said* anything?'

'Not one single word, Nat. Just looked at us.'

From the kitchen Florence had gone upstairs to her room, locked the door on herself and – back to Ilya – 'five minutes later came out with a Tesco carrier bag containing her flip-flops, the photo of her dead mum she kept on her desk, her cardie for when the heating's off, and girls' stuff from her desk drawer'. How Ilya managed to see all this collection at one glance eludes me, so allow for poetic licence.

Florence then 'kisses me like three times Russian-style' – Ilya, in full flood – 'gives me an extra hug and tells me it's for all of us. The hug is. So I say, what's all this about then, Florence? because we know not to call her Flo. And Florence says, it's nothing really, Ilya, except the ship has been taken over by the rats and I've jumped.'

For want of further testimony, these then were Florence's parting words to the Haven. She had had her parley with Dom, handed in her resignation, returned from Head Office to the Haven, collected her possessions and by approximately 3.05 p.m. was back on the street and unemployed. Within minutes of her departure, two tight-lipped representatives from Domestic Security – not the rats who had taken over the ship, but Ferrets, as they were commonly known – arrived in a green Office van, removed Florence's computer and steel cupboard and demanded to know of each member of my staff in turn whether she had entrusted any article to them for safekeeping or discussed the reasons for her departure. Having received the required assurances on both counts, they sealed her room.

*

Instructing everyone to get on with their work as normal, a forlorn hope, I step back into the street, turn down a side alley and walk hard for ten minutes before settling in a café and ordering myself a double espresso. Breathe slowly. Get your priorities sorted. I try Florence's mobile once more on the off-chance. Dead as a dodo. Her Hampstead phone number has a new message. It is delivered by a young, contemptuous, upper-class male: *'If you're calling for Florence, she's no longer at this number, so get lost.'* I call Dom and get Viv:

'Unfortunately Dom has back-to-back meetings all day, Nat. Can I be of any help at all?'

Oh, I don't think so, thanks, Viv, no. Are his back-to-backs on home ground, would you say, or are they out and about town?

Is she wavering? Yes, she is:

'Dom is not taking calls, Nat,' she says, and rings off.

*

'Nat, my dear fellow,' Dom says in a tone of high surprise, indulging his new habit of using my name as a weapon. 'Always welcome. Do we have an appointment? Would tomorrow suit? I'm a bit snowed under, to be frank.'

And he has the papers strewn across his desk to prove it, which only tells me that he's been expecting me all morning. Dom doesn't do confrontation, which is something we both know. His life is a sideways advance between things he can't face. I drop the latch on his door and sit myself down in a prestige chair. Dom remains at his desk, deep in paperwork.

'You're staying, are you?' he enquires after a while.

'If that's all right with you, Dom.'

He picks another file from his in-tray, opens it, absorbs himself intently in its contents.

'Sad about Rosebud,' I suggest after a suitable silence.

He can't hear me. He's too absorbed.

'Sad about Florence, too,' I reflect. 'One of the best Russian officers the Service ever lost. Can I see the report? Maybe you've got it there?'

The head still down. 'Report? What are you blathering about?'

'The Treasury sub-committee's report. The one about the disproportionate risk. Can I see it please?'

The head up a bit, but not too far. The open file in front of him still matters more.

'Nat, I have to inform you that, as a provisional employee of London General, you are not cleared to anything *like* the appropriate level. Do we have any further questions?'

'Yes, Dom. We do. Why did Florence resign? Why did you pack me off to Northwood on a fool's errand? Were you planning to make a pass at her?'

On the last, the head comes up with a jolt.

'I'd have thought *that* possibility rather more in your line than mine.'

'So why?'

Lean back. Let the fingertips find each other and form their wedding arch. They do. The prepared speech may now begin.

'Nat, as you may suppose, I did receive, on a strictly one-to-one confidential basis, advance warning of the sub-committee's decision.'

'When?'

'That is neither here nor there as far as you are concerned. May I go on?'

'Please do.'

'Florence, we both know, is not what you and I might call a mature person. That is the core reason why she was held back. Talented, nobody contests that, least of all myself. However, it was apparent to me from her presentation of Operation Rosebud that she was emotionally – I dare say *too* emotionally – engaged in its outcome for her own good and ours. I had hoped that by giving her an informal heads-up ahead of the official announcement of the sub-committee's decision I might mitigate her disappointment.'

'So you sent me to Northwood while you dabbed her brow. Very considerate.'

But Dom doesn't do irony, least of all when he is the butt of it.

'However, on the larger issue of her abrupt departure from the Office, we should congratulate ourselves,' he continues. 'Her response to the sub-committee's decision to disallow Rosebud for reasons of national interest was disproportionate and hysterical. The Service may count itself well rid of her. Now tell me about Pitchfork yesterday. A virtuoso performance by the Nat of old, if I may say so. How do you construe his instructions from Moscow?'

Dom's habit of hopping from one subject to another as a means of avoiding unfriendly fire is also familiar to me. However, on this occasion he has done me a favour. I don't think of myself as sly in a general way but Dom raises my game. The only person who is ever going to tell me what took place between him and Florence is Florence, but she's unavailable. So go for goal.

'How do *I* construe his instructions? Better to ask how Russia department would construe them,' I reply, with a loftiness to match his.

'Which is how?'

Lofty, but also firm. I am an old Russia hand pouring cold water on an inexperienced brother officer's ardour.

'Pitchfork is a sleeper agent, Dom. You seem to forget that. He's here for the long haul. He's been sleeping for precisely a year. Time for Moscow Centre to wake him up, blow the dust off him, give him a dummy run and make sure he's still there for them. Once he's proved that he is, it's back to sleep in York.'

He appears about to argue, thinks better of it.

'So our tactic, on the assumption that your premise is correct, which I don't necessarily accept, is *what* exactly?' he demands truculently.

'Watch and wait.'

'And do we, while watching and waiting, alert Russia department that we are so doing?'

'If you want them to take over the case and airbrush London General out of it, now's as good a time as any,' I retort.

He pouts, looks away from me as if to consult a higher authority.

'Very well, Nat' – humouring me – 'we watch and wait as you suggest. I expect you to keep me fully informed of all future developments, however trivial, the moment they occur. And thank you for calling by,' he adds, returning to the papers on his desk.

'However,' I say, not moving from my chair.

'However *what*?'

'There is a subtext to Pitchfork's instructions that suggests to me that we *could* be looking at rather more than just a standard dummy run to keep a sleeper on his toes.'

'You just said the precise opposite.'

'That's because there's an element to Pitchfork's story for which you are in no way cleared.'

'Nonsense. *What* element?'

'And this is no time to be trying to add your name to the indoctrination list, or Russia department will need to know the reason why. Which I assume you wouldn't want any more than I would.'

'*Why* wouldn't I?'

'Because if my hunch is right, what we *could* be looking at – subject to confirmation – is a golden opportunity for the Haven and London General to mount an operation with our two names attached to it and no Treasury sub-committee to spike it. Do I have your ear or shall I come back when it's more convenient?'

He sighs and pushes aside his papers.

'Maybe you're broadly familiar with the case of my former agent Woodpecker? Or are you too young?' I enquire.

'Of course I'm *familiar* with the Woodpecker case. I've read it up. Who hasn't? Trieste. Their *rezident*, former KGB, an old hand, consular cover. You recruited him over badminton, as I recall. He later reverted to type and rejoined the opposition, if he ever left it in the first place. Hardly a feather in your cap, I'd have thought. Why are we talking about Woodpecker suddenly?'

For a latecomer, Dom has done his homework pretty thoroughly.

'Woodpecker was a reliable and valued source until his last year of working for us,' I inform him.

'If you say so. Others might take a different view. May we come to the point, please?'

'I'd like to discuss Moscow Centre's instructions to Pitchfork with him.'

'With *whom*?'

'With Woodpecker. Get his take on them. An insider's view.'

'You're mad.'

'Maybe.'

'Stark staring off-your-head mad. Woodpecker is officially graded toxic. That means nobody from this Service goes there without the written personal consent of the head of Russia department, who happens to be in purdah in Washington DC. Woodpecker is untrustworthy, totally two-faced and an embedded Russian criminal.'

'Is that a no?'

'It's an over-my-dead-body no. As of here and now. I shall put it in writing instantly, copy to the disciplinary committee.'

'Meantime, with your permission I'd like to take a week's golfing leave.'

'You don't play fucking golf.'

'And in the event that Woodpecker agrees to see me, and it turns out that he has an interesting take on Pitchfork's instructions from Moscow Centre, you *may* just decide that you ordered me to pay a call on him after all. And meanwhile I suggest you think twice before you write that rude letter to the disciplinary committee.'

I am at the door when he calls me back. I turn my head but stay at the door.

'Nat?'

'Yes?'

'What do you think you're going to get out of him, anyway?'

'With luck, nothing I don't already know.'

'Then why go?'

'Because nobody calls out Operations Directorate on the strength of a hunch, Dom. Ops Directorate like actionable intelligence, cooked two ways and preferably three. It's called *evidence-based* in case the term is new to you. Which means they are not overly impressed by the self-serving ramblings of a grounded field man stuck in the boondocks of Camden, *or* his somewhat untested head of London General.'

'You're mad,' Dom says again, as he retreats behind his files.

*

I am back at the Haven. Turning the key on the long faces of my team, I go to work drafting a letter to my former agent Woodpecker, alias Arkady. I write in my notional capacity as Secretary of a badminton club in Brighton. I invite him to bring a team of mixed players to our beautiful seaside town. I propose dates and times of play and offer free accommodation. The uses of open word-code are older than the Bible and rest on mutual understandings between writer and recipient. The understanding between Arkady and myself owed nothing to any codebook and everything to the concept that every premise contains its opposite. Thus I was not inviting him, but seeking an invitation from him. The dates on which the notional club was prepared to welcome its guests were the dates on which I hoped to be received by Arkady. My offers of hospitality were a deferential enquiry about whether he would receive me, and where we might meet. The times of play indicated that any time was fine by me.

In a paragraph that came as near to reality as cover allowed, I reminded him of the amicable relations that had long existed between our two clubs in defiance of ever-changing tensions in the larger world, and signed myself Nicola Halliday (Mrs) because Arkady over the five years of our collaboration had known me as Nick, despite the fact that my real name was blazoned on Trieste's official list of consular representatives. Mrs Halliday did not provide her home address. Arkady knew plenty of places to write to if he chose to do so.

Then I sat back and resigned myself to the long wait, because Arkady never took his big decisions in haste.

*

If I was apprehensive about what I had let myself in for with Arkady, my badminton battles with Ed and our political *tours d'horizon* at the *Stammtisch* were becoming ever more precious to me – and this despite the fact that Ed, to my grudging admiration, was beating me hands down.

It seemed to happen overnight. Suddenly he was playing a faster, freer, happier game, and the age gap between us was yawning at me. It took a session or two before I was able to relish his improvement objectively, and as best I could congratulate myself for my part in it. In other circumstances I might have cast round for a younger player to take him on, but when I proposed this to him he was so offended that I backed off.

The larger issues of my life were less easily resolved. Each morning I checked the Office's cover addresses for Arkady's response. Nothing. And if Arkady wasn't my problem, Florence was. She had been friendly with Ilya and Denise but, press them as I might, they knew no more of her whereabouts or doings than any other member of the team. If Moira knew where to get hold of her, I was the last person she was telling. Every time I tried to imagine how Florence, of all people, could have walked out on her beloved agents, I failed. Every time I attempted to reconstruct her seminal encounter with Dom Trench, I failed again.

After much soul searching, I tried my luck with Ed. It was a long shot and I knew it. My makeshift cover story allowed Florence and myself to know nothing of each other beyond the one notional encounter in my notional friend's office and one badminton session with Laura. All I had going for me otherwise was a growing hunch that the two had been mutually attracted on sight, but since I was now aware of Florence's state of mind by the time she showed up at the Athleticus, it was hard to imagine she was in a mood to be attracted to anyone.

We're sitting at the *Stammtisch*. We've finished our first pints and Ed has fetched us a second. He has just trounced me four–one to his understandable satisfaction if not to mine.

'So how was the Chinese?' I ask him, picking my moment.

'Chinese who?' – Ed as usual absorbed elsewhere.

'The Golden Moon restaurant up the road, for God's sake. Where we were all going to have dinner together until I had to rush off to rescue a business deal, remember?'

'Oh yeah, right. Great. She loved the duck. Laura did. Her best thing ever. Waiters spoiled her rotten.'

'And the girl? Whatever her name was? Florence? Was she good value?'

'Oh yeah, well. Florence. She was great too.'

Is he clamming up on me or just being his usual churlish self? I keep trying anyway:

'You don't happen to have a number for her, by any chance? My chum called me up, the one she was temping for. Said she'd been terrific and he had a mind to offer her a full-time job but the agency's not playing ball.'

Ed ponders this for a while. Frowns about it. Searches his mind or makes a show of doing so.

'No, well, they wouldn't, would they?' he agrees. 'Those agency sods would keep her on a string for the rest of her life if they could. Yeah. Can't help you there, I'm afraid. No' – followed by a diatribe against our reigning foreign secretary, 'that fucking Etonian narcissistic elitist without a decent conviction in his body bar his own advancement' et cetera.

*

If there is any consolation to be had from this interminable waiting period, apart from our Monday-evening badminton sessions, it is Sergei, aka Pitchfork. Overnight he has become the Haven's prize agent. From the day his university term ended, Markus Schweizer, Swiss freelance journalist, has taken up residence in the first of his three North London districts. His aim, readily approved by Moscow, is to sample each district in turn and report on it. With no Florence to offer him, I have appointed Denise, state-educated, obsessed from childhood by all things Russian, as his keeper. Sergei has taken to her as if she were his lost sister. To lighten her load, I approve the support of other members of the Haven team. Their cover is not a problem. They can call themselves aspiring reporters, out-of-work actors or nothing at all. If Moscow's London *rezidentura* were to turn out its entire counter-surveillance cavalry, it would come away empty-handed. Moscow's incessant demands for locational details would tax the most diligent sleeper agent, but Sergei is equal to them, and Denise and Ilya are on hand to lend their assistance. The required photographs are taken with Sergei's mobile phone only. No topographical detail is too slight for Anette aka Anastasia. Whenever a fresh set of requirements comes in from Moscow Centre, Sergei drafts his replies in English and I approve them. He translates them into Russian, and covertly I approve the Russian before it is encoded by Sergei using a one-time pad from his collection. By this means Sergei is made notionally answerable for his own errors, and the tetchy correspondence with Centre that follows has the ring of authenticity. Forgery department has made a fine job of the invitation from Harvard University's physics faculty. Sergei's friend Barry is suitably awed. Thanks to Bryn Jordan's ministrations in Washington, a Harvard physics professor will field any stray questions that come in from Barry or anywhere else. I send Bryn a personal note thanking him for his efforts and receive no reply.

Then the waiting again.

Waiting for Moscow Centre to stop dithering and settle for a single location in North London. Waiting for Florence to lift her head above the parapet and tell me what made her walk out on her agents and her career. Waiting for Arkady to come off the fence. Or not.

Then, as things will, everything started happening at once. Arkady has replied; not what you might call enthusiastically but a reply nonetheless. And not to London but to his preferred cover address in Bern: one plain envelope addressed to N. Halliday, Czech stamp, electronic type, and inside it one picture postcard of the Czech spa resort of Karlovy Vary and a brochure in Russian for a hotel ten kilometres outside the same town. And folded inside the hotel brochure a booking form with boxes to tick: dates required, accommodation, estimated time of arrival, allergies. Typed crosses in the boxes inform me that I am expected to check in at ten o'clock this coming Monday night. Given the warmth of our former relationship, it would be hard to imagine a more grudging response, but at least it says 'come'.

Using my uncancelled passport in the alias of Nicholas George Halliday – I was supposed to surrender it on my return to England but nobody asked me for it – I book myself a flight to Prague for the Monday morning and pay for it with my personal credit card. I email Ed regretfully cancelling our badminton fixture. He comes back with 'Chicken'.

On the Friday afternoon I receive a text from Florence on my family mobile. It tells me we can 'talk if you want' and offers me a number that is not the one she is texting from. I ring it from a pay-as-you-go mobile, get the answering service and discover I am relieved not to be talking to her directly. I leave a message saying I will try again in a few days, and come away thinking I sound like somebody I don't know.

At six the same evening I send an 'all eyes' to the Haven, copy to Human Resources, informing them that I am taking a week's leave of absence for family reasons from 25 June to 2 July. If I am wondering what family reasons I am attending to, I need look no further than Steff who, after weeks of radio silence, has announced that she will be descending on us for Sunday lunch with 'a vegetarian friend'. There are moments that are made for cautious reconciliation. As far as I am concerned, this is not one of them but I know my duty when I see it.

*

I am in our bedroom, packing for Karlovy Vary, sorting through my clothes for laundry marks and anything that shouldn't belong to Nick Halliday. Prue, having conducted a long telephone conversation with Steff, has come upstairs to help me pack and tell me all about it. Her opening question is not designed for harmony.

'Do you *really* need to take badminton gear all the way to Prague?'

'Czech spies play it all the time,' I reply. 'Vegetarian *boy* or vegetarian *girl*?'

'Boy.'

'One we know, or one we have yet to know?'

There have been precisely two of Steff's many boyfriends that I managed to engage with. Both turned out to be gay.

'This one is *Juno*, if you remember the name, and they're on their way to Panama together. Juno being short for Junaid, she tells me, which means *fighter*, apparently. I don't know whether that makes him any more appealing to you?'

'It might.'

'From Luton. At three in the morning. So they won't be staying the night with us, you'll be relieved to hear.'

She is right. A new boyfriend in Steff's bedroom and pot smoke coming out from under the door do not accord with my vision of family bliss, least of all when I am packing for Karlovy Vary.

'Who the hell goes to Panama anyway?' I demand just as irritably.

'Well, I think Steff does. In rather a big way.'

Mistaking her tone, I turn sharply to look at her.

'What d'you mean? She's going there and not coming back?' – only to discover she is smiling.

'Do you know what she said to me?'

'Not yet.'

'We could make a *quiche* together. Steff and me. Between us. Make a quiche for lunch. Juno loves asparagus and we mustn't talk about Islam because he's a Muslim and doesn't drink.'

'Sounds ideal.'

'It must be five years since Steff and I cooked *anything* together. She thought you men should be in the kitchen, remember? And we shouldn't.'

Entering the spirit of the occasion as best I can, I take myself to the supermarket, buy unsalted butter and soda bread, the two staples of Steff's gastronomic regime, and to atone for my boorishness a bottle of ice-cold champagne even if Juno isn't allowed any. And if Juno isn't allowed, then my guess is that Steff won't be either, because by now she is probably well on her way to converting to Islam.

I return from shopping to find the pair of them standing in the hall. Two things then happen at once. A courteous, well-dressed young Indian man steps forward and takes my shopping bag from me. Steff throws her arms round me, tucks her head into the crook of my shoulder and leaves it there, then pulls back and says, 'Dad! *Look*, Juno, isn't he *great*?' The courteous Indian man steps forward again, this time to be formally introduced. By now I have spotted a serious-looking ring on Steff's wedding finger, but I have learned that with Steff it's better to wait till I'm told.

The women go to the kitchen to make quiche. I open the champagne and present each of them with a glass, then walk back to the drawing room and offer Juno one too because I don't always take Steff's guidance about her men literally. He accepts without demur and waits for me to invite him to sit down. This is new territory for me. He says he fears this has all come as a surprise to us. I assure him that with Steff nothing surprises us, and he seems relieved. I ask him, why Panama? He explains that he is a graduate zoologist and the Smithsonian has invited him to conduct a field study of large flying bats on the island of

Barro Colorado on the Panama Canal and Steff is going along for the ride.

'But only if I'm bug-free, Dad,' Steff chimes in, poking her head round the door in her apron. 'I've got to be fumigated and I can't breathe on anything and I can't even wear my new fuck-me shoes, can I, Juno?'

'She can wear her own shoes, but she's got to wear covers over them,' Juno explains to me, 'and nobody gets fumigated. That's pure decoration, Steff.'

'And we've got to look out for crocodiles as we step ashore, but Juno's going to carry me, aren't you, Juno?'

'And deprive the crocodiles of a square meal? Certainly not. We are there to preserve the wildlife.'

Steff gives a hoot of laughter and closes the door on us. Over lunch, she flashes her engagement ring round the table, but it's mostly for my benefit because she has bubbled everything to Prue in the kitchen.

Juno says they are waiting until Steff has graduated, which is going to take longer because she has switched to Medicine. Steff hadn't got around to mentioning this fact to us, but Prue and I have also learned not to over-respond to such life-changing revelations.

Juno had wanted to ask me formally for her hand, but Steff insisted that her hand was nobody's property but her own. He asks me anyway, across the table, and I tell him it's their decision alone, and they should take all the time they need. He promises they will. They want children – 'Six,' Steff cuts in – but only down the line, and meanwhile Juno would like to introduce us to his parents, who are both teachers in Mumbai, and they plan to visit England around Christmas time. And may Juno please enquire what my profession is, because Steff has been vague and his parents are sure to want to know. Was it *civil* service or *social* service? Steff had seemed unsure.

Lounging across the table, one hand for her chin and the other for Juno, Steff waits for my answer. I had not expected her to keep our ski-lift conversation to herself and I hadn't seen fit to ask her to do so. But evidently she has.

'Oh, *civil* all the way,' I protest with a laugh. 'Actually *foreign* civil. Travelling salesman for the Queen with a bit of diplomatic status thrown in about sums it up.'

'So commercial counsellor?' Juno enquires. 'May I tell them British commercial counsellor?'

'Would do fine,' I assure him. 'Commercial counsellor come home and put out to grass.'

To which Prue says: 'Nonsense, darling. Nat always talks himself down.'

And Steff says: 'He's a loyal servant of the Crown, Juno, and a shit-hot one, aren't you, Dad?'

When they're gone Prue and I tell each other that maybe it was all a bit of a fairy tale, but if they split up tomorrow Steff will have turned a corner and become the girl we always knew she was. After washing up, we go to bed early because we need to make love and I have a crack-of-dawn flight.

'So who've you got tucked away in Prague then?' Prue asks me mischievously on the doorstep.

I had told her it was Prague and a conference. I hadn't told her it was Karlovy Vary and a walk in the woods with Arkady.

*

If there is one item of information from this seemingly endless period of waiting that I have left till last, that is because at the time it occurred I attached no significance to it. On the Friday afternoon, just as the Haven was packing up for the weekend, Domestic Research section, a notoriously lethargic body, delivered itself of its findings concerning the three districts of North

London on Sergei's list. After making a number of useless obser-
vations about common watercourses, churches, power lines,
places of historical interest and architectural note, they pointed
out in a footnote that all three 'districts under advisement' were
linked by the same bicycle route, which ran from Hoxton to
Central London. For convenience they attached a large-scale
map with the cycle route painted pink. I have it before me as I
write.

II

Not much has been written, and I hope never will be, about agents who devote the best years of their lives to spying for us, take their salaries and bonuses and golden handshakes, and without fuss, without being exposed or defecting, retire to a peaceful life in the country they have loyally betrayed, or some equally benign environment.

Such a man was Woodpecker, otherwise Arkady, one-time head of Moscow Centre's *rezidentura* in Trieste, my former badminton opponent and British agent. To describe his self-recruitment to the cause of liberal democracy is to trace the turbulent journey of an essentially decent man – my view, not everyone's by any means – strapped from birth to the roller-coaster of contemporary Russian history.

The illegitimate street-child of a Tbilisi prostitute of Jewish origin and a Georgian Orthodox priest is secretly nurtured in the Christian faith, then spotted by his Marxist teachers as an outstanding pupil. He grows a second head and becomes an instant convert to Marxism–Leninism.

At sixteen he is again spotted, this time by the KGB, trained as an undercover agent and tasked with the infiltration of Christian counter-revolutionary elements in northern Ossetia. As a former Christian and perhaps a present one, he is well qualified for the task. Many of those he informs on are shot.

In recognition of his good work he is appointed to the lowest ranks of the KGB where he earns himself a reputation for obedience and 'summary justice'. This does not prevent him from attending night school in higher Marxist dialectic or acquiring foreign languages and thereby making himself eligible for intelligence work overseas.

He is dispatched on foreign missions, lends a hand in 'extra-legal measures', euphemism for assassination. Before he becomes too sullied he is recalled to Moscow to be instructed in the gentler arts of fake diplomacy. As an espionage foot soldier under diplomatic cover he serves in the *rezidenturas* of Brussels, Berlin and Chicago, engages in field reconnaissance and counter-surveillance, services agents he never meets, fills and empties countless dead letter boxes and continues to participate in the 'neutralization' of real or imagined enemies of the Soviet state.

Nonetheless, with the advance of maturity no amount of patriotic zeal can prevent him from embarking on an internal re-evaluation of his life's path, from his Jewish mother to his incomplete renunciation of Christianity to his headlong embrace of Marxism–Leninism. Yet even as the Berlin Wall comes down, his vision of a golden age of Russia-style liberal democracy, popular capitalism and prosperity for all is rising from the rubble.

But what role will Arkady himself play in this long-delayed regeneration of the mother country? He will be what he has always been: her stalwart and protector. He will shield her from saboteurs and carpetbaggers, be they foreign or home-bred. He understands the fickleness of history. Nothing endures that is not fought for. The KGB is no more: good. A new, idealistic spy service will protect all Russia's people, not merely her leaders.

It takes his former comrade-in-arms Vladimir Putin to deliver the final disenchantment, first with the suppression of Chechnya's yearnings for independence, then of his own beloved Georgia's.

Putin had always been a fifth-rate spy. Now he was a spy turned autocrat who interpreted all life in terms of *konspiratsia*. Thanks to Putin and his gang of unredeemed Stalinists, Russia was not going forward to a bright future, but backwards into her dark, delusional past.

'You are London's man?' he bellows into my ear in English.

We are two diplomats – technically consuls – one Russian, one English, sitting out a dance at the annual New Year's Eve party of Trieste's leading sports club, where in the course of three months we have played five games of badminton. It is the winter of 2008. After the events of August, Georgia is having Moscow's gun held to her head. The band is playing sixties hit tunes with brio. No eavesdropper or hidden microphone would stand a chance. Arkady's driver and bodyguard, who in the past has watched our games from the balcony and even accompanied us to the changing room, is tonight carousing with a newfound lady friend on the other side of the dance floor.

I must have said 'yes, I am London's man' but I have not heard myself above the din. Ever since our third badminton session when I made my impromptu pass at him, I have been waiting for this moment. It is clear to me that Arkady has been waiting for it too.

'Then tell London he is willing,' he orders me.

He? He means the man he is about to become.

'He works only to you,' he continues, still in English. 'He will play against you here again in four weeks with great bitterness, same time, singles only. He will challenge you officially by telephone. Tell London he will need matching racquets with hollow handles. These racquets will be exchanged at a convenient moment in the changing room. You will arrange this for him.'

What does he want in return? I ask.

'Liberty for his people. All people. He is not materialist. He is idealistic.'

If ever a man recruited himself more sweetly, I have yet to hear of it. After two years in Trieste we lost him to Moscow Centre while he was number two in their Northern Europe department. For as long as he was in Moscow he refused contact. When he was posted to Belgrade under cultural cover my masters in Russia department didn't want me to be seen following him around so they gave me Trade Consul in Budapest and I ran him from there.

It was not till the final years of his career that our analysts began to spot signs, first of exaggeration, then of outright fabrication in his reports. They made more of this than I did. To me it was a just another case of an agent growing old and tired, losing his nerve a little, but not wanting to cut the cord. It was only after Arkady's two masters – Moscow Centre lavishly and we rather more discreetly – had toasted him and decked him with medals in appreciation of his selfless devotion to our respective causes that we learned from other sources that, as his two careers were approaching their close, he had been diligently laying down the foundations of a third: gathering to himself a slice of his country's criminal wealth on a scale that neither his Russian nor his British paymasters at their most munificent could have dreamed of.

*

The bus from Prague plunges deeper into the darkness. The black hills to either side of us rise steadily higher against the night sky. I am not afraid of heights but dislike depths and I am wondering what I'm doing here, and how I have talked myself into a wildcat journey that I would not willingly have undertaken ten years ago or wished on a fellow officer half my age. On field officer training courses, over a Scotch at the end of a long day, we used to address the fear factor: how to balance the odds and measure your fear against them, except we didn't say fear, we said courage.

The bus fills with light. We enter the main thoroughfare of Karlovy Vary, formerly Carlsbad, beloved spa of Russia's *nomen-klatura* since Peter the Great and today its wholly owned subsidiary. Glistening hotels, bathhouses, casinos and jewellery shops with blazing windows float sedately past on either side. Between them flows a river crossed by a noble footbridge. Twenty years back, when I came here to meet a Chechen agent who was enjoying a well-earned holiday with his mistress, the town was still ridding itself of the drab grey paint of Soviet Communism. The grandest hotel was the Moskva and the only luxury to be found was in secluded former rest homes where a few years previously the Party's chosen and their nymphs had disported themselves safe from the proletarian gaze.

It is ten past nine. The bus has pulled up at the terminal. I alight and begin walking. Never look as though you don't know where to go. Never dawdle with intent. I am a newly arrived tourist. I am a pedestrian, the lowest of the low. I am taking stock of my surroundings as any good tourist may. I have a travel bag slung over my shoulder with the handle of my badminton racquet protruding. I am one of those silly-looking English middle-class walkers except I haven't got a guidebook in a plastic envelope tethered round my neck. I am admiring a poster for the Karlovy Vary film festival. Perhaps I should buy a ticket? The poster next along proclaims the healing virtues of the famous baths. No poster announces that the town is also celebrated as the watering-hole of choice for the better class of Russian organized criminal.

The couple ahead of me are unable to progress at a sensible pace. The woman behind me carries a bulky carpetbag. I have completed one side of the high street. It's time to cross the noble footbridge and saunter down the other side. I am an Englishman abroad who is pretending he can't make up his mind whether to buy his wife a Cartier gold watch or a Dior gown or a diamond necklace or a fifty-thousand-dollar suite of reproduction Imperial Russian furniture.

I have arrived in the floodlit forecourt of the Grand Hotel and Casino Pupp, formerly the Moskva. The illuminated flags of all nations undulate in the evening breeze. I am admiring the brass paving stones engraved with the names of illustrious guests from past and present. Goethe was here! So was Sting! I am thinking it is time I caught a cab, and here is one pulling up not five yards from me.

A family of Germans clambers out. Matching tartan luggage. Two children's bicycles, brand new. The driver nods to me. I hop in beside him and toss my travel bag on to the rear seat. Does he speak Russian? Scowl. *Niet.* English? German? A smile, a shake of the head. I have no Czech. On winding unlit roads we climb into the forested hills, then steeply descend. A lake appears on our right. A car with full headlights comes racing at us on the wrong side. My driver holds his course. The car gives way.

'Russia *rich*,' the driver pronounces in a hiss. 'Czech people *no rich. Yes!*' – and at the word *yes*, jams on the brakes and slews the car into what I take to be a lay-by until a crossfire of security lights freezes us in their beam.

The driver lowers his window, shouts something. A blond boy of twenty-odd with a starfish scar on his cheek sticks his head through, peers at my travel bag with its British Airways label, then at me.

'Your name, please, sir?' he demands in English.

'Halliday. Nick Halliday.'

'Your firm, please?'

'Halliday & Company.'

'Why do you come to Karlovy Vary, please?'

'To play badminton with a friend of mine.'

He gives an order to the driver in Czech. We drive twenty yards, pass a very old woman in a headscarf pushing her wheeler. We draw up in front of a ranch-like building with a porch of Ionic marble columns, gold carpet and grab-ropes of crimson silk. Two men in suits stand on the bottom step. I pay off the driver, collect my bag from the rear seat and under the lifeless gaze of the two men ascend the royal gold stairway to the lobby and breathe in the aroma of human sweat, diesel oil, black tobacco and women's scent that tells every Russian he is home.

I stand under a chandelier while an expressionless girl in a black suit examines my passport below my line of sight. Through a glass partition, in a smoke-filled bar marked 'Fully Booked', an old man in a Kazakh hat is holding forth to an audience of awestruck oriental disciples, all men. The girl at the counter is looking over my shoulder. The blond boy with the scar stands behind me. He must have followed me up the gold carpet. She hands him my passport, he flips it open, compares the photograph with my face, says 'Follow me, please, Mr Halliday' and leads me into a sprawling office with a fresco of naked girls and French windows looking on to the lake. I count three empty chairs at three computers, two dressing mirrors, a stack of cardboard boxes bound in pink string and two fit young men in jeans, sneakers and gold neck chains.

'It is a formality, Mr Halliday,' the boy says as the men move in on me. 'We have endured certain bad experiences. We are very sorry.'

We Arkady? Or we the Azerbaijani Mafia who, according to a Head Office file I have consulted, built the place out of the profits of human trafficking? Thirty-odd years back, according to the same file, Russia's Mafiosi agreed among themselves

133

that Karlovy Vary was too nice a place to kill each other. Better to keep it a safe haven for our money, families and mistresses.

The men want my travel bag. The first is holding out his hands for it, the second stands at the ready. Instinct tells me they are not Czech but Russian, probably ex-special forces. If they smile, look out. I hand over my bag. In the dressing mirror the scarred boy is younger than I thought and I guess he is only acting bold. But the two men who are examining my travel bag don't need to act. They have felt the lining, popped open my electric toothbrush, sniffed my shirts, squeezed the soles of my trainers. They have picked at the handle of my badminton racquet, half unwound the cloth binding, tapped it, shaken it and made a couple of swings with it. Have they been briefed to do this, or is it instinct that tells them: if it's anywhere, it's here, whatever *it* is?

Now they are cramming everything back into my travel bag and the scarred boy is giving them a hand, trying to make a tidier job of it. They want to pat me down. I lift my arms, not all the way, just a signal that I'm ready so come for me. Something about how I do this causes the first man to reconsider me, then step forward again more warily while his friend stands at the ready a step behind him. Arms, armpits, belt, chest area, turn me round, feel my back. Then down on his knees while he does my crotch and inside legs and talks to the boy in Russian, which as a simple British badminton player I affect not to understand. The boy with the starfish scar translates.

'They wish you please to remove your shoes.'

I unlace my shoes, hand them over. They take one each, bend them, feel them, hand them back. I lace them up again.

'They ask please: why do you have no mobile phone?'

'I left it at home.'

'Why, please?'

'I like to travel unaccompanied,' I reply facetiously. The boy translates. Nobody smiles.

'They ask also that I take your wristwatch and pen and wallet and return them to you when you depart,' says the boy.

I hand him my pen and wallet and unbuckle my wristwatch. The men sneer. It's a Japanese cheapo, worth five pounds. The men look at me speculatively, as if they feel they haven't done enough to me.

The boy, with surprising authority, snaps at them in Russian: 'Okay. Done. Finish.'

They shrug, smirk doubt, and disappear through the French windows, leaving me alone with him.

'You are to play badminton with my father, Mr Halliday?' the boy asks.

'Who's your father?'

'Arkady. I am Dimitri.'

'Well, great to meet you, Dimitri.'

We shake hands. Dimitri's is damp and mine should be. I am talking to the living son of the same Arkady who on the very day that I formally recruited him swore blind to me that he'd never bring a child into this lousy rotten world. Is Dimitri adopted? Or did Arkady always have a son tucked away and was ashamed of putting the boy's future life at risk by spying for us? At the counter the girl in the black suit offers me a room key with a brass rhinoceros attached to it but Dimitri tells her in ostentatious English, 'My guest will return later,' then leads me back down the golden carpet to a Mercedes four-track and invites me into the passenger seat.

'My father asks that you will please be inconspicuous,' he says.

A second car is following us. I only ever saw its headlights. I promise to be inconspicuous.

We drove uphill for thirty-six minutes by the Mercedes four-track's clock. The road was again steep and winding. It is a while before Dimitri starts quizzing me.

'Sir, you have known my father many years.'

'Quite a few, yes.'

'Was he with the Organs at that time?' – Russian *Organy*, secret services.

I laugh. 'All I ever knew, he was a diplomat who loved his game of badminton.'

'And you? At that time?'

'I was a diplomat too. On the commercial side.'

'It was in Trieste?'

'And other places. Wherever we could meet up and find a court.'

'But for many years you do not play badminton with him?'

'No. I don't.'

'And now you make business together. You are both business-men.'

'But that's pretty confidential information, Dimitri,' I warn him, as the shape of Arkady's cover story to his son becomes clear to me. I ask him what he's doing with his life.

'Soon I will go to Stanford University in California.'

'To study what?'

'I shall be a marine biologist. I already studied this subject at Moscow State, also Besançon.'

'And before that?'

'My father wished me to go to Eton College but he was not satisfied with the security arrangements. Therefore I attended a gymnasium in Switzerland where security was more conveni-ent. You are an unusual man, Mr Halliday.'

'Why's that?'

'My father respects you very much. This is not normal. Also he says you speak perfect Russian but you do not reveal this to me.'

'But that's because you want to practise your English, Dimitri!' I insist playfully, and have a vision of Steff in her goggles riding beside me on the ski-lift.

*

We have stopped at a checkpoint on the road. Two men wave us down, examine us, then nod us through. No guns visible. Karlovy Vary's Russians are law-abiding citizens. Guns are kept out of sight. We drive as far as a pair of Jugendstil stone gateposts from Imperial Habsburg times. Intruder lights go on, cameras peer down at us as two other men appear from a gatehouse, shine needless torches on us and again wave us through.

'You're well protected,' I remark to Dimitri.

'Unfortunately, this is also necessary,' he replies. 'My father loves peace, but such love is not always returned.'

To left and right high wire fencing is threaded into the trees. A dazzled deer blocks our way. Dimitri hoots and it leaps into the darkness. Ahead of us looms a turreted villa, part hunting lodge, part Bavarian railway station. In its uncurtained ground-floor windows, stately people come and go. But Dimitri is not driving towards the villa. He has turned down a forest track. We pass labourers' cottages and enter a cobbled farmyard with stables one side and a windowless barn of blackened weatherboard on the other. He pulls up, reaches across me and shoves open my door.

'Enjoy your game, Mr Halliday.'

He drives away. I stand alone in the centre of the farmyard. A half-moon appears above the treetops. By its shine I make out two men standing in front of the closed doorway to the barn. The door opens from inside. A powerful beam of torchlight leaves me momentarily sightless as the soft-spoken Russian voice with its Georgian intonation calls to me from the darkness:

137

'Are you going to come in and play or do I have to beat the shit out of you out there?'

I step forward. The two men smile courteously and part to let me through. The door closes behind me. I am alone in a white passageway. Ahead of me a second door, open, leads to an AstroTurfed badminton court. Facing me stands the dapper, compact figure of my sixty-year-old former agent Arkady, code-name WOODPECKER, in a tracksuit. Small feet placed carefully apart, arms half raised for combat. The slight forward lean of the seaman or the fighter. Close-cropped grizzled hair, just less of it. The same unbelieving gaze and clamped jaw, the pain lines deeper. The same taut smile, no more readable than on the night years ago when I strolled up to him at a consular cocktail party in Trieste and challenged him to a game of badminton.

He beckons to me with one jerk of his head then turns his back on me and sets off at a martial pace. I follow him across the court and up an open-tread wooden staircase leading to a viewers' balcony. When we reach the balcony, he unlocks a door, beckons me through, relocks it. We climb a second wooden staircase to a long attic room at the end of which a glazed door is set into the gable. He unlocks it and we step on to a balcony overhung with vine. He relocks the door and speaks one Russian word curtly into a smartphone: 'dismiss'.

Two wooden chairs, a table, a bottle of vodka, glasses, a plate of black bread, a half-moon for light. The turreted villa rising above the trees. On its floodlit lawns, men in suits walk singly. Fountains play on a pond presided over by stone nymphs. In precise movements Arkady pours two shots of vodka, briskly hands me a glass, gestures to the bread. We sit.

'Have you been sent by Interpol?' he demands in his rapid Georgian Russian.

'No.'

'Have you come here to blackmail me? To tell me you will hand me over to Putin unless I resume collaboration with London?'

'No.'

'Why not? The situation is favourable to you. Half the people I employ report on me to Putin's court.'

'I'm afraid London wouldn't trust your information any more.'

Only then does he lift his glass to me in a silent toast. I do the same, reflecting that amid all our ups and downs I have never known him so angry.

'So it's not your beloved Russia after all,' I suggest lightly. 'I thought you always dreamed of that simple *dacha* among the Russian birch trees. Or going back to Georgia, why not? What went wrong?'

'Nothing went wrong. I have houses in Petersburg and Tbilisi. However, as an internationalist I love best my Karlovy Vary. We have an Orthodox cathedral. Pious Russian crooks worship in it once a week. When I am dead I shall join them. I have a trophy wife, very young. All my friends want to fuck her. Mostly she doesn't let them. What more should I want from life?' he demands in low, swift tones.

'How's Ludmilla?'

'Dead.'

'I'm sorry. What did she die of?'

'A military-grade nerve agent called cancer. Four years ago. For two years I mourn her. Then what's the point?'

None of us ever met Ludmilla. According to Arkady she was a lawyer like Prue, practising in Moscow.

'And your young Dimitri – he's Ludmilla's son?' I enquire.

'You like him?'

'He's a fine boy. Seems to have a great future.'

'Nobody has.'

He punches a little fist swiftly across his lips in a gesture that has always signalled tension, then stares sharply over the trees at his villa and its floodlit lawns.

'Does London know you're here?'

'I thought I'd tell London later. Speak to you first.'

'Are you freelance?'

'No.'

'A nationalist?'

'No.'

'So what are you?'

'A patriot, I suppose.'

'What of? Facebook? Dot-coms? Global warming? Corporations so big they can gobble up your broken little country in one bite? Who's paying you?'

'My Office. I hope. When I get back.'

'What do you want?'

'A few answers. From old times. If I can get them out of you. Confirmation, if you're willing.'

'You never lied to me?' – like an accusation.

'Once or twice I did. When I had to.'

'Are you lying now?'

'No. And don't you lie to me, Arkady. The last time you lied to me, you bloody nearly ended my beautiful career.'

'Tough,' he remarks, and we share the night view for a while.

'So tell me this.' He takes another pull of vodka. 'What sort of bullshit are you Brits selling us traitors these days? Liberal democracy as the salvation of mankind? Why did I fall for that crap?'

'Maybe you wanted to.'

'You walk out of Europe with your British noses stuck in the air. "We're special. We're British. We don't *need* Europe. We won all our wars alone. No Americans, no Russians, no anyone. We're supermen." The great freedom-loving President Donald

Trump is going to save your economic arses, I hear. You know what Trump is?'

'Tell me.'

'He's Putin's shithouse cleaner. He does everything for little Vladi that little Vladi can't do for himself: pisses on European unity, pisses on human rights, pisses on NATO. Assures us that Crimea and Ukraine belong to the Holy Russian Empire, the Middle East belongs to the Jews and the Saudis, and to hell with the world order. And you Brits, what do you do? You suck his dick and invite him to tea with your Queen. You take our black money and wash it for us. You welcome us if we're big enough crooks. You sell us half London. You wring your hands when we poison our traitors and you say please, please, dear Russian friends, trade with us. Is this what I risked my life for? I don't believe so. I believe you Brits sold me a cartload of hypocritical horseshit. So don't tell me you've come here to remind me of my liberal conscience and my Christian values and my love of your great big British Empire. That would be an error. Do you understand me?'

'Have you finished?'

'No.'

'I don't think you were ever working for my country, Arkady. I think you were working for your own country and it didn't deliver.'

'I don't give a fuck what you think. I asked you what the fuck you want.'

'What I've always wanted. Do you attend reunions of your old comrades? Get-togethers, medal ceremonies? Celebrations of old times? Funerals of the great and good? An honoured veteran like yourself, it's practically mandatory.'

'What if I do?'

'Then I would congratulate you on living out your cover as a body-and-soul Chekist of the old school.'

'I have no problem with cover. I am a fully established Russian hero. I have no insecurities.'

'Which is why you live in a Czech fortress and keep a stable of bodyguards.'

'I have *competitors*. That is not insecurity. That is normal business practice.'

'According to our records you attended four veterans' reunions in the last eighteen months.'

'So?'

'Do you ever discuss casework with your old colleagues? Even new cases, for that matter?'

'If such topics arise, maybe I do. I never raise a topic, never provoke one, as you well know. But if you think you're going to send me on a fishing expedition to Moscow, you're out of your fucking mind. Get to the point, please.'

'Willingly. I came to ask you whether you are still in touch with Valentina, pride of Moscow Centre.'

He is gazing ahead of him, jaw struck imperiously forward. His back is soldier straight.

'I never heard of this woman.'

'Well, that's a surprise to me, Arkady, because you once told me she was the only woman you ever loved.'

Nothing has changed in his silhouetted features. Nothing ever did. Only the alertness of his body tells me he is hearing me.

'You were going to divorce Ludmilla and sign up with Valentina. But from what you just told me, she's not the woman you're now married to. Valentina was only a few years younger than you. That doesn't quite spell trophy wife to me.'

Still nothing stirs.

'We could have turned her, if you remember. We had the means. You yourself provided them. She had been sent to Trieste on an important mission for Centre. A senior Austrian diplomat wanted to sell his country's secrets but refused to deal with any Russian official. Nobody from a consular or diplomatic community. Moscow sent you Valentina. Centre didn't have many women officers in those days, but Valentina was exceptional: brilliant, beautiful and your life's dream, you told me. As soon as she had got her man, the two of you conspired not to tell Centre for a week and treated yourselves to a romantic holiday on the Adriatic. I seem to remember we assisted you with finding suitably discreet accommodation. We could have blackmailed her but we didn't see how we could do that without compromising you.'

'I told you to leave her alone or I would kill you.'

'Indeed you did, and we were duly impressed. She was a fellow Georgian, old Chekist family as I remember. Ticked all the boxes and you were crazy about her. A perfectionist, you told me. Perfect in work, perfect in love.'

How long do we sit staring into the night?

'Too perfect, maybe,' he mutters scathingly at last.

'What went wrong? Was she married? Did she have another man? That wouldn't have stopped you, surely?'

Another prolonged silence, with Arkady a sure sign that he is mustering seditious thoughts.

'Maybe she was too much married to *little Vladi Putin*,' he says savagely. 'Maybe not in her body but in her soul. Putin is *Russia*, she tells me. Putin is *Peter the Great*. Putin is *purity*, he is *clever*. He *outsmarts* the decadent West. He gives us back our Russian *pride*. Whoever steals from the state is a wicked thief because he steals from *Putin* personally.'

'And you were one of those wicked thieves?'

'*Chekists* do not steal, she tells me. *Georgians* do not *steal*. If she knew I had worked for you she would strangle me with piano wire. So maybe it would not have been such an entirely compatible marriage after all' – followed by a bitter laugh.

'How did it end, if it ever did?'

'A little was too much, more was too little. I offered her *all this*' – a jerk of the head at the forest, the villa, the floodlit lawns, the high wire and the solitary black-suited sentries on their rounds. 'She tells me: Arkady, you are Satan, do not offer me your stolen kingdom. I say to her: Valentina, kindly tell me something, please. Who in this whole fucked-up universe is rich today and not a thief? I tell her that success is not a shame, it is an absolution, it is the proof of God's love. But she has no God. Neither have I.'

'Do you still see her?'

He shrugs. 'Am I addicted to heroin? I am addicted to Valentina.'

'And she to you?'

This is how we used to be, tiptoeing together along the brink of his divided loyalties, he as my unpredictable, high-value agent, I as the only person in the world he could safely confide in.

'But you see her now and then?'

Does he stiffen, or is it only my imagination?

'Sometimes in Petersburg when she is willing,' he replies tersely.

'What's her job these days?'

'What was always her job. She was never consular, never diplomatic, never cultural, never press. She is Valentina, the great veteran cleanskin.'

'Doing what?'

'The same as ever. Running illegals out of Moscow Centre. Western Europe only. My old department.'

'Would her work include sleeper agents?'

'Sleeper agents like dig yourself into the shit for ten years, then dig yourself out for twenty? Sure. Valentina runs sleeper agents. Sleep with her, you never wake up.'

'Would she risk her sleeper agents to service a major source outside the network?'

'If the stakes are high enough, sure. If Centre thinks the local *rezidentura* is a nest of arseholes, which it usually is, then the use of her illegals would be authorized.'

'Even her sleeper agents?'

'If they haven't gone to sleep on her, why not?'

'And even today, after all those years, she's a cleanskin,' I suggest.

'Sure. The best.'

'Clean enough to go into the field under natural cover?'

'Whatever she wants. Anywhere. No problem. She's a genius. Ask her.'

'So might she, just for instance, go to a Western country in order to service or recruit an important source, say?'

'If it's a big enough fish, sure.'

'What sort of fish?'

'Big. I told you. Got to be big.'

'As big as you?'

'Maybe bigger. Who gives a shit?'

Today, what follows looks like prescience. It was nothing of the kind. It was about being the man I used to be. It was about knowing my agent better than I knew myself; about sensing the weather signs as they gather in him before he recognized them himself. It was the fruit of stolen nights sitting in a rented car in a back street of some godforsaken Communist city listening to him pour out the story of a life too full of history for one man to bear alone. But the saddest story of them all is the one I'm telling myself now: the recurrent tragedy of his lonely love life, as this man of supposedly unassailable virility becomes at the decisive moment the lost child he once had been, impotent, rejected and humiliated, as desire turns to shame and the anger banks up in him. Of his many ill-chosen partners, Valentina was the archetype, carelessly affecting to return his passion, preening herself against him; and once she had dominated him, tossing him back into the street he came from.

And she is with us now, I can feel it: in the over-careless voice he uses to dismiss her, in the exaggerated body language that is not natural to him.

'Male fish or female fish?' I enquire.

'How the fuck should I know?'

'You know because Valentina told you. How's that?' I suggest. 'Not everything. Just little hints, whispered in your ear, the way she used to. To tantalize you. To impress you. To goad you. This great big fish that's swum into her net. Did she say *British* fish, by any chance? Is that what you're not telling me?'

The sweat is running down his hollowed, tragic face in the moonlight. He is talking as he used to talk, rapidly from his inner self, betraying as he used to betray, hating himself, hating the object of his betrayal, relishing his love for her, despising himself, punishing her for his inadequacies. Yes, a big fish. Yes, British. Yes, a man. A walk-in. Ideological like Communist times. Middle class. Valentina will develop him personally. He will be her possession, her disciple. Maybe her lover, she will see.

'Have you got enough?' he shouts suddenly, spinning his little body round to challenge me. 'Is this why you came here, you piece of imperialist English shit? So that I could betray my Valentina to you a second time?'

He leaps to his feet.

'You slept with her, you pussy hound!' he shouts wildly. 'You think I don't know you fucked every woman in Trieste? Tell me you slept with her!'

'I'm afraid I never had the pleasure, Arkady,' I reply.

He is marching ahead of me, elbows out, little legs at full stretch. I follow him across the bare attic floor, down the two flights of stairs. As we reach the badminton court he grabs my arm.

'Remember what you said to me that first time?'

146

'Of course I do.'

'Say it now.'

'Excuse me, Consul Arkady. I hear you play good badminton. How about a friendly match between two great wartime allies?'

'Embrace me.'

I embrace him. He clutches me hungrily in return, then shoves me away.

'Price one million US payable in gold bars to my numbered Swiss account,' he announces. 'Sterling is shit, hear me? If you don't pay me, I tell Putin!'

'Sorry, Arkady. I'm afraid we're dead broke,' I say, and somehow we are both smiling.

'Don't come back, Nick. Nobody dreams any more, hear me? I love you. Next time you come I kill you. That's a promise.'

Again he shoves me away. The door closes behind me. I am back in the moonlit farmyard. There is a breeze. I feel his tears on my cheeks. Dimitri in the Mercedes four-track is flashing his lights.

'Did you beat my dad?' he asks nervously as we drive away.

'We were about equal,' I tell him.

He hands me back my wristwatch, wallet, passport and ballpoint pen.

*

The two special forces men who searched me are sitting in the lobby with their legs stretched out. Their eyes don't lift as I walk by, but when I reach the top stair and glance back, they are gazing up at me. On the bedhead of my four-poster, a benign Virgin Mary presides over copulating angels. Is Arkady regretting that he allowed me back into his tormented life for thirty minutes? Is he deciding I am better dead after all? He has lived more lives than I ever shall. He has finished up with none. Soft footsteps up and down the corridor. I have an additional room for my bodyguard but no bodyguard to put in it. I have no weapon except my room key, some loose English change and a middle-aged body that is no match for one of theirs.

As big as you? Maybe bigger. Who gives a shit? . . . Sleep with her, you never wake up . . . Nobody dreams any more, hear me?

12

Moscow has spoken. Arkady has spoken. I have spoken and been heard. Dom Trench has torn up his letter to the disciplinary committee. London General has reimbursed my travel expenses, but questioned my use of a taxi to the lakeside hotel in Karlovy Vary. It seems there was a bus I could have taken. Russia department under the temporary leadership of Guy Brammel has declared the Pitchfork case active and immediate. His master, Bryn Jordan, has signalled his assent from Washington and kept to himself whatever thoughts he may have about a certain officer's unscripted visit to a toxic former agent. The notion of a traitor of Arkady's stature in our midst has caused an appropriate fluttering of Whitehall's dovecotes. Agent Pitchfork, installed in a two-room ground-floor apartment in the northern reaches of inner London, has received no fewer than three encoded under-texts from his notional Danish *inamorata* Anette, and their contents send a thrill through the Haven that instantly transmits itself to Dom Trench, Russia department and Operations Directorate in ascending order:

'It is God's vindication, Peter,' Sergei whispers to me in an awestruck voice. 'Maybe it is His wish that I shall be only a very small player in a great operation of which I must be otherwise ignorant. It is immaterial to me. I wish only to prove my good heart.'

Reluctant to shake off old suspicions, nonetheless, Percy Price's watchers maintain counter-surveillance-lite on him on Tuesday and Thursday afternoons, 2.00–6.00 p.m, which is the most Percy can currently afford. Sergei has also asked his minder Denise whether, if he is granted British citizenship, she will accept his hand in marriage. Denise suspects that Barry has found another and that Sergei, rather than admit this to himself, has decided he is straight. The prospects of a union are however slim. Denise is a lesbian and has a wife.

Moscow Centre's carbon under-texts endorse Sergei's choice of lodgings and demand further detailed information on the two remaining selected North London districts, thereby confirming the perfectionist Anette's taste for over-organization. Particular reference is made to public parks, pedestrian and vehicular access, opening and closing times, the presence or otherwise of wardens, rangers and 'vigilant elements'. The location of park benches, gazebos, bandstands and parking availability are also points of great interest. Signals intelligence has confirmed an unusual swell of traffic in and out of Moscow Centre's Northern department.

Since my return from Karlovy Vary my relations with Dom Trench are enjoying a predictable honeymoon, even if Russia department has discreetly relieved him of his authority in all matters relating to Stardust, the random codename thrown up by Head Office's computer to cover the exploitation of data passing between Moscow Centre and Source Pitchfork. But Dom, convinced as ever that rejection is just around the next corner, remains determinedly exalted by the notion that my reports bear our joint symbols. He is aware of his dependence on me and unnerved by it, which I find quietly pleasing.

*

I had promised to get back to Florence but in the euphoria of the moment I had put it off. The enforced lull while we wait for decisive instructions from Moscow Centre offers as good a moment as any to repair my discourtesy. Prue is visiting an ailing sister in the country. She expects to be away for the weekend. I call her to check. Her plans haven't changed. I don't call Florence from the Haven, or on my Office mobile. I go home, eat a cold steak-and-kidney pie, down a couple of Scotches, then, arming myself with small change, stroll up the road to one of Battersea's last-remaining phone boxes and dial the last number she gave me. I am expecting another machine but instead get Florence out of breath.

'Hang on,' she says, clapping her hand over the mouthpiece, and yells at somebody in what sounds like an empty house. I can't hear words but I can hear the echo of them like fogged voices at sea, first Florence's, then a man's. Then back to me, *en clair* and businesslike:

'Yes, Nat?'

'Well, hullo again,' I say.

'Hullo.'

If I am expecting a note of contrition, there is none in the voice and none in the echo.

'I called because I said I would and we seem to have unfinished business,' I say, surprised that I am having to explain myself when the explaining should be all on her side.

'Professional business or personal business?' she demands, and I feel my hackles rise.

'You said in your text that we could *talk if I wanted*,' I remind her. 'Given the manner of your departure, I thought that pretty rich.'

'What *was* the manner of my departure?'

'Sudden to say the least. And remarkably inconsiderate towards certain people in your care, if you want to know,' I snap, and in the long silence that follows regret my harshness.

'How are they?' she asks in a subdued voice.

'The people in your care?'

'Who do you think?'

'They miss you rotten,' I reply more gently.

'Brenda too?' – after yet another long silence.

Brenda, stable name for Astra, Orson's disenchanted mistress, primary source for Operation Rosebud. I am about to tell her with some asperity that *Brenda*, on learning of her departure, has refused further service, but the choke in Florence's voice is all too noticeable so I water my answer down.

'Managing pretty well, all things considered. Asks after you but fully understands that life must go on. You still there?'

'Nat?'

'What?'

'I think you'd better take me out to dinner.'

'When?'

'Soon.'

'Tomorrow?'

'All right.'

'And fish presumably?' I say, remembering our fish pie at the pub after her presentation of Rosebud.

'I don't give a fuck what we eat,' she replies and rings off.

The only fish restaurants I knew were on Finance section's *affordable* list which meant we were liable to bump into Service colleagues dining their contacts, the last thing either of us needed. I plump for a fancy restaurant in the West End and draw a wad of cash from a machine because I don't want the bill featuring on our joint Barclaycard account. Sometimes in life you get caught for sins you haven't committed. I ask for a corner table but needn't have bothered. London is sweltering in the endless heatwave. I arrive, as is my habit, ahead of time and order myself a Scotch. The restaurant is almost deserted and the waiters are sleepy wasps. After ten minutes Florence appears wearing a summer adaptation of her Office fatigues: stern military blouse with long sleeves and high neck, no make-up. At the Haven we had begun with nods and progressed to air kisses. Now we were back to 'hullo' and she's treating me as the ex-lover that I am not.

Under cover of an enormous menu I offer her a glass of house champagne. She reminds me curtly that she drinks red burgundy only. A Dover sole would be fine, she concedes, just a small one. And a crab and avocado to begin with if I'm really having one. I am. I'm interested in her hands. The man's heavy gold signet ring that she wore on her wedding finger has given way to a scruffy silver ring peppered with small red stones. It's loose on her and not a natural fit over the pale imprint of its predecessor.

We get through the business of ordering and return our enormous menus to the waiter. Hitherto she has effectively avoided eye contact. Now she is looking straight at me and there is not a hint of contrition in her stare.

'What did Trench tell you?' she demands.

'About you?'

'Yes. Me.'

I had assumed I would be asking the hard questions, but she has other ideas.

'That you were over-emotional and a mistake, basically,' I reply. 'I said that wasn't the you I recognized. By then you'd flounced out of the Office, so it was all pretty academic. You could have told me during our four at badminton. You could have called me. You didn't.'

'Did *you* think I was over-emotional and a mistake?'

'I just told you. As I said to Trench, this wasn't the Florence I recognized.'

'I asked what you *thought*. Not what you *said*.'

'What was I supposed to *think*? Rosebud was a disappointment

to all of us. But there's nothing exceptional about a special operation being called off at the last minute. So naturally I did *think*
that you had been hot-headed. Also that you must have had
personal issues with Dom. Perhaps they're not my business,' I
add with meaning.

'What else did Dom tell you about our conversation?'

'Nothing of substance.'

'He didn't perhaps refer to his very lovely lady wife *the Baroness
Rachel*, Tory peeress and wealth manager?'

'No. Why should he?'

'You're not a pal of hers by any chance?'

'Never met her.'

She takes a pull of red burgundy, follows it with a pull of
water, measures me with her eyes as if questioning whether I'm
a fit recipient, takes a breath.

'Baroness Rachel is CEO and co-founder, along with her
brother, of an upmarket wealth-management company with
prestige offices in the City. Private clients only need apply. If
you're not talking upwards of fifty million US, don't bother to
call. I assumed you knew that.'

'I didn't.'

'The company's expertise is offshore: Jersey, Gibraltar and
the island of Nevis. Do you know about Nevis?'

'Not yet.'

'Nevis does peak anonymity. Nevis out-obscures the world.
Nobody on Nevis knows who the owners of its numberless
companies are. *Fuck.*'

Her irritation is directed at her knife and fork, which are
trembling out of her control. She lays them down with a crash,
takes another pull of burgundy.

'Want me to go on?'

'Please do.'

'The Baroness Rachel and her brother exercise non-responsible,

unaccountable oversight of four hundred and fifty-three uncon-
nected, no-name, arm's-length offshore companies registered
principally in Nevis. You are listening, right? It's just your face.'

'I'll try and adjust it.'

'In addition to demanding absolute discretion, their clients
demand high returns for their investment. Fifteen, twenty per
cent, or what's the point? The expertise of the Baroness and her
brother is the sovereign state of Ukraine. Some of their biggest
players are Ukrainian oligarchs. One hundred and seventy-six
of the said no-name companies own prime properties in London,
mostly in Knightsbridge and Kensington. However, one such
prime property is a duplex in Park Lane owned by a company
that is owned by a company that is owned by a trust fund that
is owned by Orson. Facts. Non-contestable. Figures also
available.'

I don't do dramatic response, and the Office doesn't invite it.
So no doubt I annoyed her when instead of emitting a cry of
startled outrage I noted that our wine glasses needed filling and
interrupted a long-running dispute between three waiters to
make it happen.

'You want the rest or not?' she demands.

'By all means.'

'When Baroness Rachel is not tending her poor and needy
oligarchs, she sits on a couple of Treasury sub-committees as a
co-opted member of the Upper House. She was in the room
when Rosebud came up. No minutes of the meeting survive.'

Now it's my turn to take a lengthy pull of wine.

'Am I right in thinking that you have been pursuing these
supposed connections for some while?' I enquire.

'You could be.'

'Setting aside for the moment the question of how you think
you know this and whether it's true: how much of it did you
tell Dom at your face-to-face meeting with him?'

'Enough.'

'What's enough?'

'The fact that his lovely lady wife manages Orson's companies while pretending not to, just for starters.'

'*If* she does.'

'I've got friends who are into that stuff.'

'So I'm beginning to gather. How long have you known these friends?'

'What the fuck's that got to do with anything?'

'What about Rachel's membership of the Treasury sub-committee? Is that something you had from your friends?'

'It could be.'

'Is it also something you mentioned to Dom?'

'Why should I? He knew.'

'How d'you know he knew?'

'They're married for fuck's sake!'

Is this a jibe at me? Probably it is, even if the fantasy of our non-existent affair is more deeply rooted in her imagination than in mine.

'Rachel's a great lady,' she goes on sarcastically. 'The glossies adore her. She's got medals for good works. Fundraising dinners at the Savoy. Slums it at Claridge's. The lot.'

'But the glossies don't mention that she sits on top-secret Treasury sub-committees, presumably. Or perhaps the dark web does.'

'How should I know?' – too indignantly.

'That's what I'm asking you. How *do* you know?'

'Don't interrogate me, Nat. I'm not your property any more!'

'I'm surprised you ever thought you were.'

Our first lovers' tiff and we never made love.

'And how did Dom reply to whatever you said to him about his wife?' I ask, after allowing a delay for passions to cool – notably hers, and for the first time I see her waver in her determination to treat me as enemy. She leans forward across the table and lowers her voice:

'One. The highest authorities in the land are conversant with all such connections. They have examined and approved them.'

'Did he say which highest authorities?'

'Two. There is no clash of interests. Full and frank disclosure on all sides. Three, the decision not to proceed with Rosebud was taken in the national interest after due consideration of all aspects of the case. And four, it appears I'm in possession of classified information I'm not entitled to, so keep my fucking mouth shut. Which is what you're about to tell me too.'

She was right, if for different reasons.

'So who else have you told? Apart from Dom and me?' I ask.

'Nobody. Why should I?' – in a return to her earlier hostility.

'Well, keep it that way. I don't want to be vouching for your good character at the Old Bailey. Can I ask you again: how long have you been consorting with these friends of yours?'

No answer.

'Before you joined the Office?'

'It might have been.'

'Who's Hampstead?'

'A shit.'

'What sort?'

'A forty-year-old retired hedge fund manager.'

'Married, I take it.'

'Like you.'

'Is he the same person who told you the Baroness looks after Orson's offshore bank accounts?'

'He said she was the City's go-to investor for rich-shit Ukrainians. He said she could play the financial authorities like a harp. He said he'd used her himself on a couple of occasions and she'd delivered.'

'Used her for what?'

'To get things through. To circumvent regulations that don't regulate. What do you think?'

'And you passed these rumours – this hearsay – to your friends and they took it from there. Is that what you're telling me?'

'Maybe.'

'What am I supposed to do with the story you just gave me? Assuming it's true?'

'Fuck all. That's what everyone does, isn't it?'

She is standing. I stand with her. A waiter brings the exorbitant bill. We all look on while I count twenty-pound notes on to the plate. She follows me into the street and grabs hold of me. We have the embrace we never had, but no kiss.

'And just remember those draconian documents that Human Resources made you sign when you left,' I warn her in parting. 'I'm just sorry it ended badly.'

'Well, maybe it *didn't* end,' she retorts. Then hastily corrects herself as if she has misspoken: 'I just mean, I'll never forget, that's all. All you super people. My agents. The Haven. You were all great,' she goes on too merrily.

Stepping into the road, she waves down a passing cab and slams the door on herself before I can catch her destination.

*

I am alone on the baking-hot pavement. It's ten at night but the day's heat is coming up at my face. Our tryst has ended so swiftly that, what with the wine and the heat, I am tempted to wonder whether it happened at all. What's my next move? Have it out with Dom? She did that already. Call out the Office's praetorian guard and bring down the wrath of God on her *friends*, whom I picture to be a bunch of idealistic angry kids of Steff's age who spend their every waking hour trying to shaft The System? Or take your time, walk home, sleep, see what you think in the morning? I'm about to do all of those things when my Office smartphone peeps an urgent incoming text. Stepping away from the lamplight I tap in the requisite digits.

Source PITCHFORK has received decisive incoming. All Stardusters to assemble in my room 0700 tomorrow.

Signed with the symbol of Guy Brammel, acting head Russia department.

13

Any attempt on my part to set out in neat order the operational, domestic and historic events that crowded the next eleven days is doomed to failure. Footling episodes intrude on others of vast significance. The streets of London may be languishing in the record heatwave, but they are swarming with angry marchers with banners, Prue and her left-leaning lawyer friends among them. Improvised bands pump out protests. Gas-filled effigies sway above the crowds. Police and ambulance sirens scream. The City of Westminster is unapproachable, Trafalgar Square uncrossable. And the reason for this mayhem? Britain is rolling out the red carpet to an American President who has come to sneer at our hard-won ties with Europe and humble the Prime Minister who invited him.

*

The 0700 meeting in Brammel's office is the first in a non-stop string of Stardust war parties. It is attended by the all-important Percy Price, dean of surveillance, and by the elite of Russia department and Operations Directorate. But no Dom, and significantly nobody asks where he is, so I don't. The redoubtable Marion from our sister Service is accompanied by two upstanding male lawyers in dark suits despite the sweltering heat. Brammel himself reads out Sergei's latest instructions from Centre. They are to provide field support for a covert encounter between an important Moscow emissary, gender not provided, and a high-value *British collaborator*, no other details supplied. My own role in Stardust is formally agreed, and simultaneously restricted. Do I detect Bryn Jordan's hand, or am I being more than usually paranoid? As head of substation Haven, I will be 'responsible for the welfare and management of PITCHFORK and his handlers'; all covert communications to and from Moscow Centre will pass through me. But Guy Brammel, as acting head of Russia department, will sign off on all the Haven's communications before they are given circulation.

And there with a jolt my duties officially end: except that they don't because that's not who I am, as the distant Bryn should know better than anyone. Yes, I'll be hunkered down for wearisome sessions with Sergei and his minder Denise in the Haven's decrepit safe flat next door to Camden Town tube station. Yes, I shall be composing Sergei's under-texts and playing chess with him late into the night while we wait for the next obscure East European commercial radio station to confirm by prearranged word-code that our latest love letter to Copenhagen is being processed.

But I'm a field man, not a desk jockey, not a social carer. Haven outcast though I may be, but I am also the natural author of Operation Stardust. Who crucially debriefed Sergei, and scented blood? Who brought him down to London, made the forbidden pilgrimage to Arkady and thus delivered the conclusive evidence that this was not some run-of-the-mill game of Russian musical chairs but a high-end intelligence operation built around a potential or active British source of high value and run personally by Moscow Centre's queen of illegals?

In our time Percy Price and I have stolen a good few horses together, as the saying goes, and not just that prototype Russian ground-to-air missile in Poznań. So it should have come as no great surprise to anyone on the top floor that, within days of the first Stardust war party, Percy and I are crouching in the back of a laundry van fitted out with the latest wonders of modern surveillance, touring the first, then the second, and now the last of the three North London districts Sergei has been instructed to reconnoitre. Percy has christened it Ground Beta and I don't question his choice.

On our tours together, we reminisce about old cases we have shared, old agents, old colleagues, and talk like old men. Thanks to Percy I am also discreetly introduced to his *Grande Armée* of watchers, a privilege that Head Office emphatically does not encourage: after all, one day they may be watching *you*. The venue for this event is a red-brick desanctified tabernacle awaiting demolition on the outskirts of Ground Beta. Our cover is a memorial gathering of souls. Percy has rallied a cool hundred of them.

'Any little boost you can give my boys and girls will be highly welcome and appreciated, Nat,' he tells me in his homely cockney. 'They *are* committed, but the work *can* be on the tedious side, especially with the heat we've got. You look a mite worried, if I may say so. Please remember that my boys and girls like a good face. Only they're watchers, see, so it's natural.'

For love of Percy I press the flesh and pat shoulders, and when he invites me to address a few rallying words of encouragement to his faithful I do not disappoint.

'So what we all hope to be *watching* this coming Friday evening', as I hear my voice ring out pleasingly amid the pitch-pine rafters, '– this 20 July, to be precise – is a highly orchestrated covert encounter between two people who've never met each other. One, codename Gamma, will be a tried-and-tested operative with all the tricks of the trade up his or her sleeve. The other, codename Delta, will be a person of unknown age, profession and gender,' I warn them, protective as ever of my source. 'His or her motives are as much of a mystery to us as I'm sure they will be to you. But what I can tell you is this: if the stack of hard intelligence we are receiving even as I speak means anything at all, the great British public is about to owe you a very considerable debt of thanks, even if it will never know it.'

The thunderous applause, wholly unexpected, touched me.

*

If Percy was uneasy about the effect of my facial expression on his flock, Prue has no such anxiety. We are eating early breakfast.

'It's just lovely to see you all eager for your day,' she tells me, putting down her *Guardian* newspaper. 'Whatever it is you're up to. I'm so very pleased for you, after all the dire thoughts you had about coming home to England and what to do when you got here. I just hope it's not *too* desperately illegal, whatever you're doing. Is it?'

The question, if I read it correctly, marks a substantial advance in our careful journey back to one another. Ever since our Moscow days it has been understood between us that even if I were to bend Office rules and tell her all, her principled objections to the Deep State would not allow her to enjoy my confidences. In return I had made something of a point – perhaps too much of one – of not encroaching on her legal secrets, even when it came to such titanic battles as the one her partnership is currently waging against Big Pharma.

'Well, funnily enough, Prue, just for once, it *isn't* awful at all,' I reply. 'In fact I *think* you might even approve. All the signs are that we're on the verge of exposing a high-level Russian spy' – which isn't just bending Office rules, but trampling on them.

'And you'll bring him or her to court when you've exposed them, whoever they are. Of course you will. *Open* court, I trust.'

'That'll be up to the powers-that-be,' I reply cautiously, since about the last thing the Office would want to do when it has rumbled an enemy agent is turn him over to the forces of justice.

'And have you played an absolutely key role in smoking him or her out?'

'Since you ask, Prue, to be truthful, yes,' I concede.

'Like going to Prague and discussing it all with Czech liaison?'

'There *is* a Czech element. Let me put it that way.'

'Well, I think that's just perfectly brilliant of you, Nat, and I'm very proud of you,' she says, brushing aside years of pained forbearance.

Oh, and her partnership reckons they've got Big Pharma over a barrel. And Steff was very sweet on the phone last night.

*

So it's a bright sunny morning with everything coming together in ways I hadn't dared hope, and Operation Stardust is gathering unstoppable momentum. Sergei's latest instructions from Moscow Centre require him to present himself at a brasserie off Leicester Square at eleven in the morning. He will select a seat in 'the north-west area' and order himself a chocolate latte, a hamburger and a side dish of tomato salad. Between eleven-fifteen and eleven-thirty, with these recognition signals set out before him, he will be approached by a person who will claim to be an old acquaintance, embrace him and depart saying he is late for an appointment. In the course of this embrace Sergei will become the richer by one 'uncontaminated' mobile phone – Moscow's description – containing, in addition to a new SIM card, a slip of microfilm with further instructions.

Braving the same seething crowds and heat that are bedevilling Percy Price's coverage of the encounter, Sergei positions himself in the brasserie as instructed, orders his meal and is delighted to see approaching him with outstretched arms none other than the ebullient and ever-youthful Felix Ivanov – or so his cover name at sleeper school – a fellow student in his same intake and same class.

The covert handover of the mobile phone passes off faultlessly, but acquires unexpected social dimensions. Ivanov is equally surprised and delighted to see his old friend Sergei in such good fettle. Far from pleading an urgent appointment, he sits down beside him and the two sleeper agents enjoy a head-to-head that would have been the despair of their trainers. Despite the clamour, Percy's team has no difficulty hearing them, or for that matter capturing the encounter on camera. As soon as Ivanov – in the meantime randomly christened Tadzio by Russia department's computer – takes his leave, Percy dispatches a team to *house* him, in Tadzio's case to a students' hostel in Golders Green. Unlike his literary namesake, Tadzio is heavily built, husky and cheerful, a little Russian bear much loved by his fellow students, notably the female element.

It also transpires, as Head Office's checkers process the flood of incoming data, that Ivanov is not Ivanov any more, neither is he Russian. On graduating from sleeper school he has been reinvented as a Pole named Strelsky, a technology graduate at the London School of Economics admitted on a student visa. According to his application he speaks Russian, English and perfect German, having studied at the universities of Bonn and Zurich, and his first name is not Felix but Mikhail, defender of mankind. To Russia department he is therefore a creature of great interest, since he belongs to a new wave of spies who, far removed from the clunking methods of the old KGB, speak our Western languages to mother-tongue standards and parrot to perfection our little ways.

In the Haven's decrepit safe house in Camden Town, Sergei and Denise squat side by side on a lumpy sofa. Seated in the one armchair, I open up Tadzio's mobile phone, which technical department has in the meantime made temporarily inactive, fish out the strip of microfilm and lay it under the enlarger. With Sergei's one-time pad to guide us, we decode Moscow's latest instructions. They are in Russian. As usual I prevail on Sergei to translate them into English for me. At this late hour I can't risk letting him discover that I have been deceiving him from the day we met.

As usual the instructions are flawless or, as Arkady would have it, too perfect. Sergei will affix a 'No Nukes' flyer in the top-left corner of the sash window in his basement apartment. He will confirm by return that it is visible to passers-by in both directions, and from what distance. Since no such flyer is available from known protest outlets, the preference these days being for 'No Fracking', Forgery department runs one up for us. Sergei will also purchase an ornamental Victorian pottery Staffordshire dog of between twelve and eighteen inches in height. eBay is awash with them.

*

And didn't Prue and I nip over to Panama a couple of times during these happy, hectic, sun-washed days? Of course we did, in a succession of hilarious nocturnal Skypes, now with Steff alone while Juno is out on bat safari, now with the two of them together, because even when you are surrounded by Stardust, the *real* world, as Prue insists on calling it, has to go on.

The howling monkeys start beating their breasts at two in the morning and wake the entire camp, Steff tells us. And giant bats switch off their radar when they know their flight paths, which is why it's a doddle to catch them in nets stretched between palm trees. But when you disentangle and tag them, you've really, really got to look out, Mum, because they bite and they've got rabies and you have to wear fucking great thick gloves like the sewage man, and their babies are just as bad. Steff's a child again, we tell each other gratefully. And Juno, as far as we dare believe, is a decent, sincere young man who makes a good show of loving our daughter, so world hold still.

But nothing in life is without its consequences. An evening comes – it is now by my shaky reckoning Stardust-night minus eight – when the house phone rings. Prue takes the call. Juno's mother and father have flown to London on a whim. They're staying at an hotel in Bloomsbury owned by a friend of Juno's mother and they've got tickets for Wimbledon and tickets for the one-day England–India cricket international at Lord's. And they would be greatly honoured to meet the parents of their future daughter-in-law 'at any time convenient to the *Commercial Counsellor* and your good self'. Prue collapses in mirth as she struggles to impart this news to me. And well she might since I'm sitting in the back of Percy Price's surveillance van at Ground Beta and Percy is explaining to me where he proposes to position his static posts.

Nevertheless, two days later – S-night minus six – I miraculously contrive to present myself in a smart suit in front of the gas fireplace in our drawing room with Prue at my side, and in my persona of British Commercial Counsellor discuss with our daughter's future parents-in-law such issues as Britain's post-Brexit trade relations with the sub-continent and the tortuous bowling action of India's spin bowler Kuldeep Yadav, while Prue, who has as good a poker face as any lawyer when she needs it, comes as close as she ever did to exploding into giggles behind her hand.

*

As to my essential evening badminton sessions with Ed over these stressful days, I can only say they had never been more essential, or the two of us in better form. For the last three sessions I had been raising my exercise level in the gym and in the park in a desperate effort to contain Ed's newfound mastery of the court, until a day comes when the struggle, for the first time ever, is of no account.

The date, never to be forgotten by either of us, is 16 July. We have played our usual strenuous match. I have lost again, but never mind, get used to it. Casually, towels round our necks, we head for our *Stammtisch* anticipating the usual sporadic Monday-evening clatter of voices and glasses in a largely empty room. Instead we are met by an unnatural, fidgety silence. At the bar, a half-dozen of our Chinese members are staring at a television screen that is routinely given over to sport of any kind from anywhere. But this evening we are not for once watching American football or Icelandic ice hockey but Donald Trump and Vladimir Putin.

The two leaders are in Helsinki giving a joint press conference. They are standing shoulder to shoulder before the flags of both their nations. Trump, speaking as if to order, is disowning the findings of his own intelligence services, which have come up with the inconvenient truth that Russia interfered in the 2016 American presidential election. Putin smiles his proud jailer's smile.

Somehow Ed and I grope our way to our *Stammtisch* and sit. A commentator reminds us, lest we have forgotten, that only yesterday Trump declared Europe to be his enemy and for good measure trashed NATO.

Where am I in my mind, as Prue would say? Part of me is with my former agent Arkady. I am replaying his description of Trump as Putin's shithouse cleaner. I am remembering that Trump 'does everything for little Vladi that little Vladi can't do for himself'. Another part of me is with Bryn Jordan in Washington, cloistered with our American colleagues as they stare incredulously at the same act of presidential treachery.

So where is Ed in *his* mind? He is bone still. He has retreated into himself: just deeper and further than I have seen him go. At first his mouth remains open in disbelief. His lips slowly come together and he licks them, then absentmindedly wipes them with the back of his hand. But even when old Fred the barman, who has his own sense of proprieties, switches us over to a cluster of frenzied women cyclists racing round a bowl, Ed's eyes don't leave the screen.

'It's a replay,' he pronounces at last in a voice throbbing with discovery. 'It's 1939 all over again. Molotov and Ribbentrop, carving up the world.'

This was too rich for my blood and I told him so. Trump might be the worst President America has ever had, I said, but he was no Hitler, much as he might wish to be, and there were plenty of good Americans who weren't going to take this lying down.

At first he didn't seem to hear me.

'Yeah, well,' he agreed in the faraway voice of a man coming round from an anaesthetic. 'There were plenty of good Germans too. And a fat lot of bloody good *they* did.'

14

S-night is upon us. In the Operations room on the top floor of Head Office, all is calm. The time is 1920 hours by the LED clock above the fake-oak double doors. If you're Stardust-cleared, the show will start in fifty-five minutes. If you're not, there are a couple of eagle-eyed janitors at the door who will be pleased to advise you of your mistake.

The mood is leisured and, as the deadline approaches, becoming more so. Already nobody is panicking, everybody has time for everything. Assistants drift in and out bearing open laptops, Thermos flasks, bottled water and sandwiches for the buffet table. A wit asks if there's popcorn. A plump man with a fluorescent lanyard fiddles with two flat screens on the wall. Both show the same lush image of Lake Windermere in autumn. The chatter we are hearing over our earphones belongs to Percy Price's surveillance team. By now his hundred souls will be dispersed as shoppers come home from work, stall-holders, waitresses, cyclists, Uber drivers and innocent bystanders who have nothing better to do than ogle passing girls and murmur into mobile phones. They alone know that the mobile phones they are murmuring into are encrypted; that they are talking, not to their friends, families, lovers and pushers, but to Percy Price's control centre, which this evening is a double-glazed eyrie perched halfway up the wall on my left side. And there sits Percy now, in signature white cricket shirt with sleeves rolled up and earphones on as he silently mouths commands to his scattered crew.

We are sixteen strong and rising. We are the same impressive team that assembled to hear Florence's failed oratorio for Operation Rosebud, with welcome additions. Marion from our sister Service is again attended by her two dark-suited spear carriers, also known as lawyers. Marion means business, we are told. She is smarting from the top floor's refusal to hand her Service Operation Stardust on a platter, arguing that the putative presence of a highly placed traitor in the Whitehall village puts the case squarely in its court. Not so, Marion, say our top-floor mandarins. The sources are ours, ergo the intelligence is ours, ergo the case is ours and goodnight. In Moscow, in the bowels of Lubyanka, formerly Dzerzhinsky, Square, I imagine similar nervous spats breaking out as the denizens of Northern department's illegals section dig themselves in for the same long night.

I have been promoted. In place of Florence at the suitors' end of the table, I have Dom Trench sitting opposite me at the centre of it. We have had no renewal of our discussion about Rosebud. I am therefore puzzled when he leans across the table and says in a low voice:

'I trust we are not at odds regarding your chauffeured trip to Northwood some while back, Nat?'

'Why should we be?'

'I expect you to speak for me if called upon.'

'About what? Don't tell me the car pool is kicking up?'

'Regarding certain associated matters,' he replies darkly, and withdraws into his shell. Is it really only ten minutes ago that I asked him in the most casual of ways what informal offices of state his baroness wife currently adorns?

'She *flits*, Nat,' he had replied, and braced himself as if in the presence of royalty. 'My darling Rachel is an inveterate *flitter*.

If it's not some Westminster quango that you and I have never even heard of, she's off to Cambridge to argue with the great and good about how to rescue the Health Service. Your Prue is no different, I'm sure.'

Well, Dom, Prue thank God *is* different, which is why we've got a bloody great placard in the hall with the unoriginal logo 'TRUMP LIAR' that I trip over every time I walk into the house.

Lake Windermere fades to white, stutters and returns. The lights in the Operations room are going down. Shadowy late arrivals scurry in and take their places at the long table. Lake Windermere bids a lingering farewell. In its place Percy Price's cameras are giving us tracking shots of contented citizens enjoying the sunshine in a North London public park at half past seven on a sweltering summer's evening.

You do not expect, minutes before the consummation of a nail-biting intelligence operation, to be seized by a surge of admiration for your fellow countrymen. But on our screens is London as we love it to be: multi-ethnic kids playing improvised netball, girls in summer dresses basking in rays of the endless sun, old folk sauntering arm in arm, mothers pushing prams, picnickers under spreading trees, outdoor chess, boules. A friendly bobby strolls comfortably among them. How long since we saw a bobby all alone? Somebody is playing a guitar. It takes me a moment to remind myself that many of this happy throng were only thirty-six hours ago members of my congregation in the same desanctified tabernacle whose cumbersome spire this minute dominates the skyline.

The Stardust team has learned Ground Beta by heart and thanks to Percy so have I. The public park boasts six crumbling tarmacadam tennis courts with no nets, a children's playground with a climbing frame, seesaws and a tunnel. There is an ill-smelling boating pond. A bus route, a bicycle route and a busy thoroughfare with no parking form the western border; its eastern side is dominated by a high-rise council estate, its northern by a terrace of gentrified Georgian houses. In one of these, in a semi-basement, Sergei has his Moscow-approved apartment. It has two bedrooms. In one of them, Denise sleeps with her door locked. In the other, Sergei. An iron staircase leads down to it. From the upper half of its sash window you can see into the playground and follow a narrow concrete footpath with six fixed benches placed twenty feet apart, three a side. Each bench is twelve feet long. Sergei has sent photographs of them to Moscow, numbered one to six.

The park also boasts a well-liked self-service café which can be approached either by way of an iron man-gate from the street side or from the park itself. Today the café is under temporary new management, the regular staff having received a full day's pay in lieu, which as Percy says ruefully is where your costs come in. There are sixteen indoor tables and twenty-four outdoor. Outdoor tables have permanent umbrellas against rain or sun. For food and drink there is the indoor self-service counter. On hot days an outdoor ice-cream bar is marked by the sign of a happy cow licking at a double vanilla cone. Attached to the rear premises are public toilets with facilities for baby changing and the disabled. Plastic bags and green waste bins are provided for dog walkers. All this Sergei has dutifully reported in lavish under-texts to his insatiable Danish heart-throb, the perfection-ist Anette.

At Moscow's behest we have also supplied photographs of the café, inside and out, and of the approaches to it. Having twice eaten there at his controller's bidding, once inside, once outside, on both occasions between seven and eight p.m., and reported to Moscow on the density of diners, Sergei is under orders not to show his face there until further notice. He will remain in his semi-basement and wait on an event yet to be advised.

'I will be all things, Peter. I will be one-half safe house keeper and one-half counter-surveillance.'

He says *half* because it transpires that he and his old school friend Tadzio will be sharing operational duties. Should they bump into one another by accident they will ignore each other.

I am scanning the crowd on the off-chance of a familiar face. During her sojourn in Trieste and again on the Adriatic coast, Arkady's Valentina had been comprehensively filmed and photographed as a Moscow Centre emissary and potential double agent. But a woman of regular features can do pretty well anything she wishes with her looks over twenty years. The imagery section has produced a range of possible likenesses. Any one of them could be the new Valentina alias Anette alias you name it. I keep an open mind as a handful of women of mixed age alight at the bus stop, but not one of them advances on the man-gate leading to the café and the open spaces of the park. Percy's cameras settle on an elderly bearded priest with a mauve surplice and dog collar.

'Anyone to do with you at all, Nat?' he calls over my earpiece.

'No, Percy, nothing to do with me, thank you.'

Ripples of laughter. We settle again. A different, shaky camera pans along the benches beside the tarmacadam path. I guess it is attached to our friendly bobby as he acknowledges the smiles of members of the public either side of him. We linger on a middle-aged woman in a tweed skirt and sensible brown brogue shoes reading her free copy of the *Evening Standard*. She wears a wide straw hat and has a shopping bag beside her on the bench. Perhaps she is a member of a ladies' bowling club. Perhaps she is Valentina waiting to be recognized. Perhaps she is just another mature English spinster who doesn't mind the heat.

'Could be, Nat?' Percy enquires.

'Could be, Percy.'

We are in the open-air section of the café. The camera looks down on two ample bosoms and a swaying tea tray. On the tea tray, one teapot small, one cup and saucer, one plastic teaspoon, one sachet of milk. And a cellophane-wrapped slice of Genoa fruitcake on a paper plate. Legs, feet, umbrellas, hands and pieces of face jostle as we pass by with our burden. We pull up. A woman's voice, homely, friendly, Percy-trained, blurts into a neck microphone:

'*Excuse* me, dear. Is anybody sitting in that chair?'

The freckled, cheeky face of Tadzio is looking up at us. He speaks straight into camera. His perfect English is exactly that. If there is a cadence to it, it is German, or – with Zurich University in mind – Swiss:

'This one's taken, I'm afraid. Lady just went to get herself a cup of tea. I promised to keep it for her.'

The camera shifts to the empty seat next to him. It has a denim jacket slung over it, the same jacket Tadzio wore for his encounter with Sergei in the Leicester Square brasserie.

A more sophisticated camera takes over: a sniper-type camera levelled, I suspect, from the upper window of a broken-down double-decker bus with warning triangles that Percy installed this very morning as one of his static posts. No camera shake. We zoom in. Hold Tadzio alone at his table sucking Coca-Cola through a straw while he scrolls his smartphone.

A woman's back enters the frame. It is not a tweedy back. It is not an ample back. It is an elegant female back and tapers at the waist. It has a hint of the gym about it. It wears a long-sleeved white blouse and a lightweight Bavarian-style waistcoat. A slender neck is topped by a man's straw trilby. Its voice – which comes to us from two unsynchronized sources, the one I suspect being the cruet set sitting on the table, the other further away and directional – is forceful, foreign and amusing:

'Excuse me, kind sir. Is this chair actually *occupied*, or is it for your jacket *only*?'

To which Tadzio, as if on command, springs to his feet and exclaims cheerfully, 'All yours, lady, absolutely free!'

Whisking his denim jacket off the chair with showy gallantry, Tadzio drapes it over the back of his own chair and sits down again.

A different angle, a different camera. With a deafening chime the tapered back sets down its tray, transfers a paper mug, tea or coffee presumed, two packets of sugar, a plastic fork and a slice of sponge cake to the table, and deposits the tray on an adjacent trolley before sitting herself beside Tadzio without turning to camera. With no further word passing between them, she picks up the fork, cuts into her sponge cake and takes a sip of tea. The brim of the straw trilby casts a black shadow over her face, which is turned downward. Her head lifts in response to an enquiry we have yet to hear. In the same moment, Tadzio glances at his wristwatch, mutters an inaudible exclamation, leaps to his feet, grabs his denim jacket and, as if remembering an urgent appointment, makes a hasty departure. As he does so, we are treated to a full shot of the woman he has abandoned. She is trim, handsome, dark haired, strong featured and, in her mid to late fifties, well preserved. She wears a long, dark-green cotton skirt. She has more presence than is comfortable in an itinerant female intelligence agent operating under natural cover. She always did have: why else would Arkady have fallen for her? She was his Valentina then, she is our Valentina now. Somewhere in the outer reaches of the building we are sitting in, the face-recognition team must have come to the same conclusion because the pre-awarded codename Gamma is winking at us in red phosphorescent print from our twin screens.

'You wish, sir?' she enquires into camera with heavy playfulness.

'Yeah, well. I wondered whether it was all right to sit here,' Ed explains, plonking his tray on the table with a monumental crash, and sits himself in what, seconds earlier, was Tadzio's chair.

*

If today I boldly write *Ed* as an instantaneous, positive identification, that does not accurately reflect my response. This is *not* Ed. It can't be. It's Delta. An Ed body-type, yes, I grant you. A nearly-Ed, similar to the version of him that appeared in the doorway of the Trois Sommets, covered in snow, while Prue and I were tucking into our *croûtes au fromage* and a bottle of white. Tall, ungainly and the same leftward list of the shoulder, the same refusal to stand up straight: granted. The voice? Yes, well, an Ed-like voice, no question: slurred, northern, graceless till you got to know it, the universal voice of our British young when they wish you to know they're not about to take your bullshit. So an Ed soundalike, yes. And an Ed lookalike. But not your real Ed, no way. Not even on two screens at once.

And it was while I was still in this short-lived state of resolute denial that I either failed – or refused – for ten, twelve seconds by my rough calculation, to take aboard whatever further courtesies passed between Ed and Gamma after Ed plonked himself in the chair beside her. I am assured – since I never saw the footage again – that I missed nothing of substance, and the exchanges were as trivial as they were intended to be. My recollection is further complicated by the fact that, by the time I returned to reality, the digital clock at the foot of our screens had actually *gone back* by twenty-nine seconds, Percy Price having decided that this was the opportune moment to regale us with flashback images of our newfound quarry. Ed is standing in line in the interior of the café, brown briefcase in one hand, tin tray in the other. He shuffles past the sandwiches, cakes and pastries stall. He selects a cheddar-and-pickle baguette. He is at the drinks counter, ordering himself an English breakfast tea. The microphones render his voice in a metallic bellow:

'Yeah, a large one would be great. Cheers.'

He is standing at the cash desk in a ham-fisted muddle, juggling his tea and baguette, beating his pockets for his wallet, briefcase wedged between his big feet. He is Ed codenamed Delta and he is loping over the threshold into the outdoors, tray in one hand, briefcase in the other, blinking around him as if he's wearing the wrong spectacles. I am remembering something I read a hundred years ago in a Chekist handbook: a clandestine meeting appears more authentic if food is taken.

15

I remember taking a reading of my *chers collègues* at around this point, and ascertaining no common reaction beyond a shared fixation with the two flat screens. I remember discovering that my head was the only one looking the wrong way, and hastily readjusting it. I don't recall Dom at all. I recall one or two fidgets round the room like symptoms of restlessness in a boring play, and a few crossings of legs and a clearing of throats here and there, chiefly from our top-floor mandarins, Guy Brammel for one. And the permanently aggrieved Marion from our sister Service: I saw her stalk from the room on tiptoe, which is a kind of anomaly, for how do you take long paces on tiptoe? But she managed it, long skirt and all, to be followed by her two spear-carrier lawyers in their black suits. Then a short-lived blaze of light as their three silhouettes sidle through the doorway before the guards close it in their wake. And I remember having a wish to swallow and not being able to, and a heave of the stomach like a low punch when you haven't braced your muscles in readiness. And then bombarding myself with a scattershot of unanswerable questions that in retrospect are part of the process that any professional intelligence officer goes through when he wakes to the fact he's been hoodwinked all ways up by his agent and is chasing round for excuses, and not finding any.

Surveillance doesn't switch off because you do. The show

goes on. My *chers collègues* went on. I went on. I watched the whole of the rest of the movie in real time, live on screen, without uttering a word or offering the smallest gesture that could in any way inhibit the enjoyment of my fellow members of the audience – even if thirty hours later, when I was standing under the shower, Prue did remark on the bloodied imprint made by my fingernails digging into my left wrist. She also refused to accept my story of a badminton injury, going so far as to suggest in a rare moment of accusation that the fingernails were not my own.

And I wasn't just *watching* Ed as the rest of the show unfolded. I was sharing his every move with a familiarity unmatched by anyone's in the room. I alone knew his body language from badminton court to *Stammtisch*. I knew how it could be skewed by some bit of internal anger he needed to get rid of, how words clogged up at the front of his mouth when he was trying to get them out all at once. And maybe that's why I knew for a certainty, when Percy ran back the archive footage of him blundering out of the restaurant, that his tip of the head in recognition was directed not at Valentina, but at Tadzio.

It was only *after* Ed had spotted Tadzio that he approached Valentina. And the fact that by then Tadzio was already on his way out of the scene merely proves that, as ever in crisis, I continue to make reasoned operational judgements. Ed and Tadzio had previous form together. By introducing Ed to Valentina, Tadzio had completed his mission, hence his abrupt departure from the scene, leaving Ed and Valentina sitting at ease, talking casually to each other like two strangers who find themselves seated beside one another, sipping tea and eating cheddar baguette and sponge cake respectively. So in sum, a classic covert encounter, perfectly orchestrated, or as Arkady would have it, too perfectly, and excellent use of a denim jacket.

With the soundtrack it was no different. Here again I had the edge over every other spectator in the room. Ed and Valentina speak English throughout. Valentina's is good but still not free of the mellifluous Georgian lilt that had so beguiled Arkady a decade ago. There was something else about her voice – timbre, accent – that like a long-forgotten tune kept nagging at me, but the harder I tried to place it, the more elusive it became.

But *Ed's* voice? No mystery there. It's the same mannerless voice that addressed me at our first badminton session: bruised, grouchy, distracted, and here and there plain rude. It will remain with me until the end of my days.

*

Gamma and Ed are leaning forward, talking head-to-head. Gamma the professional is at times barely audible even to the microphones on the table. Ed, by contrast, seems unable to keep his voice below a certain level.

GAMMA: You are comfortable, Ed? You had no worries or problems on your way here?

ED: I'm all right. Apart from somewhere to tie up my bloody bike. No point getting a new one round here. They'd have the wheels off before you chained it up.

GAMMA: You saw nobody you recognized? Nobody who made you uneasy?

ED: Don't think so, no. Haven't looked really. Bit late now, anyway. How about yourself?

GAMMA: Were you surprised when Willi waved you down in the street? [Willi with a hard W, as German] He says you almost fell off your bicycle.

ED: He's bloody right I did. Him just standing there on the pavement, flapping his hand at me. I thought

he was waving for a cab. Never occurred to me
he was your lot. Not after Maria told me to
get lost.

GAMMA: I would say that Maria acted with great discretion
in the circumstances, nevertheless. We have
reason to be a little bit proud of her, would you
not agree?

ED: Yeah, yeah, great. Smart footwork all round. One
minute you're not going to touch me with a
bargepole. The next, Willi's flagging me down in
German and saying he's a friend of Maria's and
you're all up for it and we're back on course and let's
go. Bit unsettling, frankly.

GAMMA: Unsettling maybe, but completely necessary.
Willi needed to catch your ear. If he had called to
you in English you might have dismissed him as a
local drunk and ridden straight past him. However,
I hope that you are still prepared to be of assistance
to us. Yes?

ED: Well, somebody's got to do it, haven't they? You
can't just sit there saying something's all wrong
but it's not your business because it's secret, can
you? Not if you're a halfway decent human being,
can you?

GAMMA: And you yourself are a *very* decent human being,
Ed. We admire your courage, but also your
discretion.

(Long pause. Gamma expecting Ed to speak. Ed taking
his time.)

ED: Yeah, well, I was quite relieved to be honest when
Maria told me to get lost. Quite a considerable

weight off my mind, that was. Didn't last, though. Not when you know you've got to act or you're like the others.

GAMMA: [Bright new voice] I have a suggestion for us, Ed. [Consulting her mobile phone] A nice one, I hope. So far we are two casual strangers exchanging pleasantries over a nice cup of tea. In a minute I shall stand up and wish you an enjoyable evening and thank you for our little conversation. After two minutes you will please finish your baguette, rise slowly, not forgetting your briefcase, and walk towards your bicycle. Willi will find you and escort you to a comfortable place where we can talk freely and privately. Yes? Does my suggestion worry you in any way?

ED: Not really. Long as my bike's okay.

GAMMA: Willi has been keeping an eye on it for you. No vandals have attacked it. Goodbye, then, sir. [Handshake, almost Ed-style] It is always pleasant talking to strangers in your country. Especially when they are young and handsome like you. Please don't get up. Goodbye.

She waves and heads off down the path to the main road. Ed makes a show of waving back, takes a mouthful of baguette, leaves the rest. He sips his tea, scowls at his wristwatch. For one minute and fifty seconds we watch him, head down, toying with his beaker of tea exactly as he likes to toy with his frosted glass of lager at the Athleticus. If I know him at all, he is trying to decide whether to do as she suggests or forget it and hightail home. At one minute fifty-one he makes a grab for his briefcase, stands, ponders and eventually picks up his tray and ambles over to a rubbish bin. He deposits his rubbish like a good citizen, adds his tray to the stack, and after screwing up his face for further reflection, decides to follow Valentina down the concrete path.

*

The second reel, as I will call it for convenience, is set in Sergei's semi-basement, but Sergei himself plays no part in it. His orders, received over his new 'uncontaminated' mobile phone and covertly copied to the Haven and Head Office, are to check the park once more for 'indications of hostile surveillance', then make himself scarce. It is therefore a safe presumption on the surveillance team's part that Sergei has been cast as cut-out and will not be permitted direct contact with Ed. Tadzio on the other hand, being already conscious to Ed and vice versa, will provide for his operational needs. But Tadzio, like Sergei, will not be present for the intimate conversation about to take place between Moscow Centre's distinguished emissary and my Monday badminton and conversation partner Edward Shannon in Sergei's semi-basement flat.

*

GAMMA: So, Ed. Hullo again. We are alone, we are safe and private and we may talk. First I have to thank you on behalf of all of us for your offer of help in our time of need.

ED: That's all right. Long as it really helps.

GAMMA: I have certain obligatory questions for you. Do you allow me? Do you have any like-minded colleagues in your department who are assisting you? Kindred spirits to whom we should also be grateful?

ED: It's just me. And I'm not proposing to bother anyone else for stuff. It's not like I've got accomplices, right?

GAMMA: Then can we please talk a little more about your modus operandi? You said many things to Maria and of course we have them well recorded. Maybe tell me a little more about your special work with the copier. You told Maria you work it alone sometimes.

ED: Yeah, well, that's the point, isn't it? If stuff is sensitive enough, I get to do the handling on my own. I go in, the normal crew has to get out and stay out. They haven't been through the sheep-dip.

GAMMA: Sheep-dip?

ED: Developed vetting. There's only this one other clerk cleared apart from me, so we take turns. Her and me. Nobody trusts electronic any more, do they? Not for the really delicate stuff. It's all paper and hand-carry, like going back in time. If copies have got to be made, it's back to the old steam copier.

GAMMA: Steam?

ED: Old-fashioned. Basic. It's a joke.

GAMMA: And while you were operating the steam copier, you had your first sight of the papers called *Jericho*. Yes?

ED: More than a first sight. Like about a minute's worth. The machine stuck. I just stood there looking at it.

GAMMA: So that was your moment of epiphany, we may say?

ED: Of what?

GAMMA: Of revelation. Of enlightenment. The moment when you decided you must take the heroic step and contact Maria.

ED: Well, I didn't know it was going to be *Maria*, did I? Maria's who they gave me.

GAMMA: Was your decision to come to us instantaneous, would you say, or did it grow on you over the next hours or days?

ED: I saw the stuff and I just thought, Christ, that's it.

GAMMA: And the vital passage you saw was marked Topsecret Jericho. Yes?

ED: I told her all this.

GAMMA: But I am not Maria. The passage you saw had no addressee, you say.

ED: It couldn't have, could it? I only saw a middle bit. No addressee, no signature. Just the header: Topsecret Jericho and the reference.

GAMMA: Nevertheless, you told Maria that the document was addressed to the Treasury.

ED: Seeing there was a Treasury goon standing like a foot away from me waiting for me to run the stuff off, it seemed pretty obvious it was addressed to the Treasury. Are you testing me?

GAMMA: I am confirming that, as Maria reported, you have excellent recall and you do not decorate your information for greater effect. And the reference was—

ED: KIM stroke one.

GAMMA: KIM being the symbol of which entity?

ED: British joint intelligence mission, Washington.

GAMMA: And the figure 1?

ED: The head man or woman of the British team.

GAMMA: Would you know the name of that person?

ED: No.

GAMMA: You are totally brilliant, Ed. Maria was not exaggerating. I thank you for your patience. We are careful people. Are you the proud owner of a smartphone by any chance?

ED: I gave Maria the number, didn't I?

GAMMA: Maybe for safety give it to me again.

(Ed wearily intones a number. Gamma makes a show of writing it in her diary.)

GAMMA: Are you permitted to take your smartphone into your work area?

ED: No way. Check it in at the door. All metal objects. Keys, pens, small change. A couple of days ago they made me take my bloody shoes off.

GAMMA: Because they suspected you?

ED: Because it was clerks' week. The week before it was line managers.

GAMMA: Maybe we can provide you with an inconspicuous device that takes pictures but is not metallic and doesn't look like a smartphone. Would you like that?

ED: No.

GAMMA: No?

ED: That's spy stuff. I'm not into that. I'm helping the cause when I feel like it. That's all I'm doing.

GAMMA: You also gave Maria other incoming materials from your embassies in Europe that were not codeword-protected.

ED: Yeah, well, that was just so that she knew I wasn't some sort of conman.

GAMMA: But classified 'secret' nonetheless.

ED: Yeah, well, it had to be, didn't it? Otherwise I could have been anybody.

GAMMA: And have you brought us material of the same sort today? Is that what you are carrying in your disgraceful briefcase?

ED: Willi said bring whatever you can get, so I did.

(Long silence before Ed with apparent reluctance unfastens the buckles of his briefcase, extracts a plain buff folder, opens it on his lap then passes it to her.)

ED: [While Gamma reads] If it's not useful, I'm not going for it. You can tell them that too.

GAMMA: Obviously the priority for all of us is codeword Jericho material. For these additional possibilities, I shall have to consult my colleagues.

ED: Well, just don't tell them where you got it from, that's all.

GAMMA: And material of *this* classification – plain secret, no codeword – you can bring us copies without too much problem?

ED: Yeah. Well. Over lunch hour's best.

(She extracts a mobile phone from her bag, photographs twelve pages.)

GAMMA: Did Willi tell you who I am?

ED: He said you were high up in the pecking order. Some sort of top cat.

GAMMA: Willi is right. I am a top cat. However, to you I am Anette, I am a Danish teacher of English language to secondary level, resident in Copenhagen. We met when you were studying in Tübingen. We were both on the same summer foundation course for German culture. I am your older woman, I am married, you are my secret lover. From time to time I visit England and this is where we make love. It is a flat that I borrow from my journalist friend, *Markus*. You are listening?

ED: 'Course I am. Jesus.

GAMMA: You do not need to know Markus personally. He is a tenant here. That is all. However, when we cannot meet this will be where we hope you will post your documents or letters to me as you pass by on your bicycle, and Markus as a good friend will make sure our correspondence remains completely private. This is what we call a *legend*. You are happy with this legend or do you wish to discuss a different one?

ED: Sounds all right. Yeah. Go for it.

GAMMA: We would like to reward you, Ed. We would like to express our appreciation. Financially or in any other way you wish. Maybe we make a nest egg for you in another country and one day you claim it. Yes?

ED: I'm all right, thanks. Yeah. They pay me pretty decently. Plus I've got a bit put by. [Awkward grin] Curtains cost a bit. New bath. Good of you all the same, but no thanks. All right? So that's settled. Don't ask again, actually.

GAMMA: Do you have a nice girlfriend?

ED: What's that got to do with anything?

GAMMA: Does she share your sympathies?

ED: Most of them. Sometimes.

GAMMA: Does she know you are in touch with us?

ED: Shouldn't think so.

GAMMA: Perhaps she could help you. Act as your intermediary. Where does she think you are now?

ED: On my way home, I suppose. She's got her own life, same as me.

GAMMA: Is she engaged in similar work to yours?

ED: No. Not. Definitely not. Wouldn't think of it, ever.

GAMMA: What kind of work is she engaged in?

ED: Actually, shut up about her, d'you mind?

GAMMA: Of course. And you have not called attention to yourself?

ED: How am I supposed to have done that?

GAMMA: You haven't stolen your employer's money; you are not conducting a forbidden love affair like ours? [Waits for Ed to get the joke. Eventually he does and manages a stiff grin] You have not argued with your senior staff, they do not regard you as subversive or undisciplined, you are not the subject of an internal investigation as a result of some act you have committed or failed to commit? They are not aware that you object to their policies? No? Yes?

(Ed has again withdrawn into himself. His face is set in a dark frown. If Gamma knew him better she would wait patiently until he emerges.)

GAMMA: [Playful] Are you concealing something embarrassing from me? We are tolerant people, Ed. We have a long tradition of humanism.

ED: [After further reflection] I'm just *ordinary*, right? There's not many of us about, if you want my personal opinion. Everyone else sits with the fence halfway up his arse waiting for someone to do something. I'm doing it. That's all.

*

The pottery Staffordshire dog is the safety signal, she is telling him – or I think she is, because my ears are blurring. If there's no doggie in the window, it means abort, she's telling him. Or maybe she's saying it means come on in. This 'No Nukes' poster means *we have a vital message for you*. Or maybe it says we will

190

have one next time you pass, or alternatively: never pass this way again. Sound tradecraft requires that the agent leaves first. Ed and Valentina stand facing each other. Ed looks dazed, very tired and hangdog, the way he used to look when I was still able to beat him in a do-or-die best of seven games before we settled to our lagers. Valentina takes his hand in both of hers, draws him to her and awards a purposeful kiss to each cheek but abstains from the third Russian kiss. Ed churlishly submits. An exterior camera picks him up as he climbs the iron staircase, briefcase in hand. An aerial camera watches him unchain his bicycle, fit the briefcase into the front basket and ride off in the direction of Hoxton.

*

The double doors to the Operations room open. Marion and her spear-carriers return. Doors close, lights please. Behind the soundproofed glass walls of his eagle's nest Percy Price is apportioning his troops in ways not hard to guess: one team stays on Gamma, another stays on Ed and houses him, remote surveillance only. A female voice from space advises us that subject Gamma has been 'successfully marked', we may only guess what with. So also apparently have Ed and his bicycle. Percy is well satisfied.

The screens flicker and go blank. No Lake Windermere in autumn. Marion stands upright as a Guardsman at the end of the long table. She is wearing spectacles. Her dark-suited spear-carriers stand either side of her. She takes a breath, raises a document from her right side and reads aloud to us in a slow deliberate voice.

'We regret to inform you that the man identified as *Ed* in the surveillance footage you have just witnessed is a full-time member of my Service. His name is Edward Stanley Shannon and he is a qualified Category A clerical officer with clearance to top secret and above. He has a second-class honours degree in Computer Sciences. He is a Grade 1 digital specialist currently earning a basic annual salary of £32,000 with incentive bonuses available to him for overtime, weekends and language skills. He is a Class 3 German linguist on assignment to the European element of a highly classified inter-services department under Whitehall's aegis. From 2015 to 2017 he served in Berlin in his department's liaison office. He is not and never was considered suitable for operational duties. His present duties include the weeding or sanitizing of top-secret materials destined for our European partners. In effect this entails excising, under advisement, intelligence material destined exclusively for the United States. Some of this material may also be construed as contrary to European interests. As Shannon correctly stated in the footage you have just seen, he is one of only two Grade 1 specialists entrusted with the task of copying documents of exceptional sensitivity. Shannon has successfully undergone developed vetting and one subsequent top-up.'

Her lips have stuck. She purses them, discreetly moistens them, and continues:

'In Berlin Shannon was the subject of an episode attributed to drink and the unwanted termination, on his side, of a love affair with a German woman. He received counselling and was judged to have made a full recovery to his mental and physical health. There is no further example of ill-discipline, dissident or suspect behaviour recorded against him. In the workplace he is regarded as a loner. His line manager describes him as "friendless". He is unmarried and listed as heterosexual with no known current partner. He has no known political affiliations.'

Another moistening of the lips.

'An immediate damage assessment is under way, as is an

enquiry into Shannon's past and present contacts. Pending the outcome of such enquiries, Shannon will not, repeat not, be made aware that he is under observation. Given the background and evolving nature of the case I am authorized to state that my Service is amenable to the formation of a joint task force. Thank you.'

'Can I just add a word to that?'

To my surprise I am standing, and Dom is staring up at me as if I've gone mad. I am also speaking in what I firmly believe is a confident and relaxed tone:

'I happen to know this man personally. Ed. We play badminton together most Monday evenings. In Battersea, actually. Close to where I live. At our club. The Athleticus. And we usually have a couple of beers together after the game. Obviously I'm happy to help in any way I can.'

Then I must have sat down too abruptly and lost my bearings in the process, because the next thing I remember is Guy Brammel suggesting we all take a short natural break.

16

I'll never know how long they kept me waiting in that little room, but it can't have been short of an hour with nothing to read and just a blank, pastel-painted yellow wall to stare at because they had taken away my Office mobile. And to this day I can't fathom whether I had been sitting or standing in the Operations room or just wandering around when a janitor touched my arm and said 'If you'd kindly follow me, sir' without completing the sentence.

But I do remember that there was a second janitor waiting at the door, and that it took the two of them to walk me to the lift while we chatted about the shocking heat we were having to put up with and was it going to be like this every summer from now on? And I know the word *friendless* kept going through my mind like an accusation: not because I blamed myself for being Ed's friend, but because it seemed I was the only one he had, which placed a larger responsibility on me – but for what? And of course with those unmarked lifts your stomach never knows whether you're going up or down, particularly when its churning away on its own account, which mine was now that I had been escorted from the confinement of the Operations room and released into captivity.

But call it an hour before the janitor who had been standing the other side of the glass door all this time – Andy, his name was, fond of his cricket – popped his head round and said 'You're on, Nat,' then in the same cheery spirit led me to another much larger room, again with no windows, not even fake ones, and a ring of nice padded chairs with no distinction between them because we're a Service of equals, and told me to sit in whichever chair I wanted because *the others* would be here in a jiffy.

So I picked a chair and sat on it and cupped the ends of the arms with my hands and fell to wondering who *the others* would be. And I believe I have a memory from somewhere at the start of my escorted passage out of the Operations room of a cluster of top-floor grandees murmuring in a corner and Dom Trench trying to get his nose under the wire as usual, and being told 'No, not you, Dom' rather firmly by Guy Brammel.

And sure enough when my *chers collègues* filed in, Dom was not one of the party, which caused me briefly to speculate again about his concern that I should speak up for him regarding the chauffeured car he'd ordered for me. First into the room came Ghita Marsden who gave me a kindly smile and a 'hullo again, Nat' that was supposed to put me at my ease, but what did she mean by *again*, as if we'd been reborn? Then glowering Marion from our sister Service and just one of her spear-carriers, the bigger, gloomier one, who said we hadn't met and his name was Anthony, then held out his hand and nearly broke mine.

'I like a game of badminton myself,' he told me, as if that made everything all right. So I said, 'Great, Anthony, where do you play?' – but he didn't seem to hear me.

Then Percy Price, keen churchman, rugged face in lockdown. And that shook me, not so much because Percy cut me dead but because he must have handed over temporary command of Stardust to his many lieutenants so that he could be present for the meeting. Then, close on Percy's heels, carrying a plastic cup of tea reminiscent of the one on Ed's tray from the self-service café, Guy Brammel, conspicuously at ease in the company of the diminutive Joe Lavender, grey-man of the Office's secretive internal security section. Joe was carrying a box file and I remember facetiously asking him, just for the human connection, whether the janitors had checked its contents at the door, and getting a dirty look in response.

While they trooped in I was also trying to work out what they all had in common apart from their grim expressions because groups like these don't form by accident. Ed, as we all now know, is a member of our sister Service, which means that in any hardball inter-Service shoot-out he's our find and their mistake, so live with it. Therefore assume a lot of inter-Service haggling about who gets what part of the cake. And when all that's been done and dusted, there will have been one of those last-minute rushes to make sure the audiovisual system in the room we're sitting in is up and running, because we don't need another fuck-up like last time, whatever last time was.

Then, just as everyone is finally sitting down comfortably, enter my same two janitors bearing the same coffee urn, water jugs and sandwiches that nobody had got around to eating at the film show, and Andy the cricketing one winks at me. And when they've gone, in drifts the spectral figure of Gloria Foxton, the Office's *über*-shrink, looking as if she's been hauled out of bed which she may well have been, and three paces behind her my own Moira of Human Resources bearing a thick green file that I suspect is about me, since she's carrying it very deliberately blank side outward.

'You haven't heard from *Florence*, by any chance, have you, Nat?' she asks me in a worried way, pulling up beside me.

'Not sight nor sound, alas, Moira,' I reply boldly.

Why did I lie? To this day I can't tell you. I wasn't practising. I had not set out to lie. I had nothing to lie about. Then a second look at her tells me that she knew the answer before she asked the question and she was testing my veracity, which made me feel an even bigger fool.

'*Nat,*' says Gloria Foxton, with urgent psychotherapeutical sympathy, 'how *are* we?'

'Bloody awful, thanks, Gloria. How about *you*?' I reply cheerfully, and get an icy smile to remind me that people in my position, whatever that is, don't ask shrinks how they are.

'And dear *Prue*?' she enquires for extra fondness.

'Marvellous. Firing on all cylinders. Got Big Pharma in her sights.'

But what I'm really feeling is a surge of unjustified anger for certain hurtful wisdoms Gloria uttered five years back when I unwisely sought her free advice on matters Steff, such as 'Might it just be *possible*, Nat, that by throwing herself at every boy in her class, Stephanie is making a statement about her absent father?' – her gravest offence being that she was probably right.

We are settled at last and high time too. Gloria in the meantime has been joined by two *Unter*-shrinks, Leo and Franzeska, who both look about sixteen. In aggregate I therefore have a cool dozen of my *chers collègues* sitting in a half-circle, each with their unobstructed view of me, because somehow the formation of the chairs has reshaped itself and I'm stuck out on my own like the boy in the painting being asked when he last saw his father, except it isn't my poor father they're here to ask about, it's Ed.

*

Guy Brammel has decided to open the bowling, as he would say, which makes a certain sense because he is by training a barrister and at his stately home in St Albans he runs his own cricket team. Over the years he has frequently roped me in to play.

'So, Nat,' he begins, in his cheery port-and-pheasant voice, 'pretty bloody bad luck is what you're telling us, I think. You play an honest game of badminton with a fellow and he turns out to be a member of our sister Service and a bloody Russian spy. Why don't we take it from the top and go from there? How did the two of you meet, what did you get up to when, omitting no details however slight.'

We take it from the top. Or I do. Saturday evening at the Athleticus. I'm enjoying a post-match beer with my Indian opponent from across the river in Chelsea. Enter Alice with Ed. Ed challenges me to a game. Our first fixture. His unfriendly references to his employers, closely observed by Marion and her spear-carrier. Our first post-badminton pint at the *Stammtisch*. Ed heaps scorn on Brexit and Donald Trump as components of a single evil.

'And you went along with that stuff, Nat?' Brammel enquires amiably enough.

'In moderation, yes, I did. He was anti-Brexit. So was I. Still am. Like most of the people in this room, I suspect,' I retort stoutly.

'And Trump?' Brammel enquires. 'You went along with him on Trump too?'

'Well, Christ, Guy. Trump's not exactly flavour of the month in this place, is he? Man's a bloody wrecking ball.'

I look round for support. None is forthcoming, but I refuse to be ruffled. Never mind my misstep with Moira just now. I'm an old hand. I've been trained in this stuff. Taught it to my agents.

'When Trump and Putin bond, it's a devils' pact as far as Shannon's concerned,' I go on boldly. 'Everyone's ganging up on Europe and he doesn't like it. He's got this German bee in his bonnet.'

'So he challenges you to a game,' Guy Brammel persists, waving aside my blathering. 'In plain sight of everyone. He's gone to a lot of trouble to seek you out, and here he is.'

'I happen to be Club singles champion. He'd heard about me and fancied his chances,' I said, standing on my dignity.

'Sought you out, ridden across London on his pushbike, studied your game?'

'He may well have done.'

'And he challenged *you*. He didn't challenge anyone else. Not your Chelsea opponent that you'd just played, which he might have done. It had to be you.'

'If my Chelsea opponent as you call him had beaten me, for all I know Shannon would have challenged him instead,' I declare, not entirely truthfully, but there was something in Guy's tone that I was beginning to dislike.

Marion hands him a piece of paper. He puts on his reading spectacles and studies it at his leisure.

'According to your receptionist at the Athleticus, from the day Shannon challenged you, he was the only chap you played. You became a couple. Fair description?'

'A *pair*, if you don't mind.'

'All right. Pair.'

'We were well matched. He played fair and won or lost with grace. Decent players with manners are hard to find.'

'I'm sure. You also palled up with him. You were drinking partners.'

'Overstated, Guy. We got a regular game going and had a beer afterwards.'

'Every week, sometimes even twice a week, which is going it, even for an exercise freak like you. And you *chatted*, you say.'

'I do.'

'How long did you *chat* for? Over your lagers?'

'Half an hour. An hour maybe. Depends how we felt.'

'Sixteen, eighteen hours, totted up? Twenty? Or is twenty too many?'

'It could have been twenty. What's the difference?'

'Self-educated sort of chap, is he?'

'Not at all. Grammar school.'

'Did you tell him what you do for a living?'

'Don't be bloody silly.'

'What *did* you tell him?'

'Fobbed him off. Businessman home from abroad, looking around for an opening.'

'And he bought that, you reckon?'

'Not curious, and equally vague about his own job in return. Media stuff, didn't elaborate. Neither of us did.'

'Do you normally spend twenty hours talking politics with badminton partners half your age?'

'If they play a good game and they've got something to say for themselves, why not?'

'I said, *do you?* Not why. I'm trying to establish – simple question – whether in the past you have talked politics at length with any other opponent of similar age?'

'I've played them. And had a drink with them afterwards.'

'But not with the regularity with which you played, drank and talked with Edward Shannon?'

'Probably not.'

'And you've no son of your own. Or not as far as we know, given your prolonged periods of foreign exile.'

'No.'

'And none off the record?'

'No.'

'Joe,' says Brammel, turning to Joe Lavender, star of internal security, 'you had a couple of questions.'

*

Joe Lavender has to wait his turn. A Shakespearean messenger has popped up in the person of Marion's second spear-carrier.

With Guy's permission he would like to ask me a question that has just come in from his Service's investigative team. It is inscribed on a thin strip of paper that he holds between the fingertips of each huge hand.

'Nat. Were you *personally* or were you at any point *aware*,' he enquires with aggressive clarity, 'during the course of your many *conversations* with Edward Stanley Shannon, that his mother Eliza is on record as a serial *marcher*, protester and *rights activist* on a wide range of *peace* and similar *issues*?'

'No, I was *not so aware*,' I retort, feeling the bile rise in me despite my best intentions.

'And your lady *wife*, we are being told, is also a robust defender of our basic *human rights*, no disrespect. Am I correct?'

'Yes. Very robust.'

'Which I'm sure we would all agree is only to be applauded. May I then *enquire*, has there been to the best of your knowledge any *interaction or communication* between Eliza Mary Shannon and your lady wife?'

'To the best of my knowledge, there has been no such interaction or communication.'

'Thank you.'

'My pleasure.'

Exit messenger left.

*

A period of random questions and answers follows, a kind of free-for-all that remains foggy in my memory, while my *chers collègues* take it in turns to 'tighten up the nuts and bolts' of Nat's story, as Brammel kindly puts it. A silence falls and Joe Lavender finally takes the floor. His voice leaves no prints. It has no social or regional origin. It is a homeless, plaintive, nasal drawl.

'I want to stay with that first moment when Shannon picked you up at the Athleticus,' he says.

'Can we say *challenged*, if you don't mind?'

'And you, in order to save his face, which is what you said, thereupon accepted his challenge. Did you observe, as a trained member of this Service, or do you recall now, any casual strangers at the bar – new members, male or female, guests of Club members – taking a more than normally close interest in the proceedings?'

'No.'

'I am told the Club is open to the public. Members may bring guests. Guests may buy drinks at the bar, provided they're accompanied by a member. Are you telling me as a matter of certainty that Shannon's approach to you—'

'Challenge.'

'—that Shannon's *challenge* was not covered or observed in some manner by interested parties? Obviously we'll be getting on to the Club under a pretext and digging out whatever video footage they've got.'

'I did not observe at the time, and nor do I recall now, anyone taking a more than normally close interest.'

'They wouldn't though, would they, not that you'd notice, not if they were professionals?'

'There was a group at the bar having a bit of fun, but they were familiar faces. And don't bother hunting for footage. We haven't installed any video.'

Joe's eyes open wide in theatrical surprise.

'Oh? No video? Dear me. That's a bit strange, isn't it, these days? Big place, lot of comings and goings, money changing hands, but no video.'

'It was a committee decision.'

'You yourself being on the committee, we're told. Did you support the decision not to instal video?'

'Yes, I did.'

'Would that be because, in common with your wife, you do not approve of the surveillance state?'

'Do you mind keeping my wife out of this?'

Did he hear me? Apparently not. He's busy.

'So why didn't you register him?' he enquires, not bothering to lift his head from the open box file on his lap.

'Register who?'

'Edward Shannon. Your weekly and sometimes biweekly badminton date. Service regulations require you to inform Human Resources of all regular contacts of either sex regardless of the nature of the activity. The records of your Athleticus Club tell us that you have encountered Shannon on no fewer than fourteen separate occasions over a highly consecutive period of time. I'm wondering why you didn't register him at all.'

I manage an easy smile. Just. 'Well, Joe, I should think over the years I have played a couple of hundred opponents. Some of them – what? – twenty, thirty times? I don't imagine you'd want them all registered on my personal file.'

'Did you take a *decision* not to register Shannon?'

'It wasn't a case of deciding. The thought didn't enter my head.'

'I'll put it slightly differently if you permit. Then perhaps I'll get a sensible answer out of you. Was it or was it not, yes or no, a conscious decision on your part *not* to register Edward Shannon as a regular acquaintance and playmate?'

'Opponent, if you don't mind. No, it was not a conscious decision not to register him.'

'Turns out, you see, that you have been consorting over a period of months with an identified Russian spy whom you failed to register. Didn't-enter-my-head doesn't quite cover it.'

'I didn't *know* he was a bloody Russian spy, Joe. Right? And neither presumably did you. And neither did his employing

Service. Or am I wrong about that, Marion? Maybe your Service knew all along he was a Russian spy and didn't think to tell us,' I suggest.

My riposte goes unheard. Seated in their half-circle round me, my *chers collègues* are peering at their laptops or into space.

'Ever take Shannon home at all, Nat?' Joe enquires casually.

'Why on earth should I?'

'Why shouldn't you? Didn't you want to introduce him to your wife? A nice radical lady like her, I'd have thought he was just up her street.'

'My wife is a busy lawyer of some distinction and she hasn't the time or interest to be introduced to everyone I play badminton with,' I retort hotly. 'She's not *radical* in your terms, and she plays no part in this story, so once again: kindly leave her alone.'

'Did Shannon ever take *you* home?'

I'd had enough.

'Between you and me, Joe, we contented ourselves with blow-jobs in the park. Is that what you want to hear?' I turn to Brammel. 'Guy, for Christ's sake.'

'Yes, old boy?'

'If Shannon is a Russian spy – which, all right, on the face of it he appears to be – tell me what we're all doing sitting on our backsides in this room talking about *me*? Let's assume he fooled me. He did, right? To hell and back. Just as he fooled his Service and everybody else. Why aren't we asking ourselves questions like who talent-spotted him, who recruited him, here or in Germany or wherever? And who's *Maria* who kept popping up? Maria who only pretended to give him the bum's rush?'

With no more than a perfunctory nod, Guy Brammel resumes his own line of enquiry.

'Surly sort of bugger, is he, your fellow?' he remarks.

'My fellow?'

'Shannon.'

'He can be surly now and then, like most of us. He soon perks up.'

'But why so surly with the Gamma woman, of all people?' he complains. 'He'd gone to no end of trouble to make contact with the Russians. Moscow Centre's first thought – only my guess – was that he was a dangle. Nobody can fault them for *that*. Then they had a second think about him and decided he was a gold mine. Tadzio flags him down in the street, gives him the good news and in no time enter Gamma, apologizing for Maria's behaviour and busting to do business with him. So why the long face? He should be over the moon. Pretending he didn't know what *epiphany* meant. What's that about? Everybody has an epiphany these days. You can't cross the bloody road without hearing about somebody's epiphany.'

'Maybe he doesn't like what he's doing,' I suggest. 'From everything he said to me, maybe he still has ethical expectations of the West.'

'Hell's that got to do with anything?'

'It merely crossed my mind that the puritanical side of him might think the West needs punishing. That's all.'

'Let me get this right. You're telling me the West pisses him off for not coming up to his ethical expectations?'

'I said maybe.'

'So off he hops to Putin who wouldn't know an ethic if it bit him in the arse. Am I reading you correctly? Funny sort of puritanism, if you ask me. Not that I'm an expert.'

'It was a passing thought. I don't believe that's what he's doing.'

'Then what the fuck *do* you believe?'

'All I can tell you is, that's not the man I know. Knew.'

'He never *is* the man we know, for Christ's sake!' Brammel explodes in outrage. 'If a traitor doesn't surprise the shit out of us, he's no bloody good at his job. Well, is he? You should know that if anyone does. *You've* run a few traitors in your day. *They* didn't go round advertising their subversive opinions to every Tom, Dick and Harry. Or if they did, they didn't bloody well last. Well, did they?'

It was at this point – call it frustration or bewilderment or the involuntary awakening of a protective instinct – that I felt compelled to make an appeal on Ed's behalf which, had my head been that much cooler, I might have thought twice about.

I select Marion.

'I was just wondering, Marion,' I say, adopting the speculative tone of one of Prue's more academic fellow lawyers, 'whether Shannon in any *legal* sense has committed a crime. All this talk about top-secret codeword material that he claims to have *glimpsed*. Is that reality speaking out of him, or is it his own fantasy? The other stuff he's offering seems to be all about establishing his credentials. It may not even be classified, or not in any sense that matters. So I mean, might it not be better for you people to pull him in, read him the riot act, turn him over to the psychiatrists and save yourselves a lot of bother?'

Marion turns to the spear-carrier who had shaken my hand and nearly broken it. He peers at me in a kind of marvel.

'Are you being serious at all?' he enquires.

I reply stoutly that I have never been more serious in my life.

'Then allow me to quote to you, *if* I may, Section 3 of the Official Secrets Act of 1989, which provides as follows: A person who is or has been a Crown servant or government contractor is guilty of an offence if *without lawful authority he makes a damaging disclosure of* any *information*, document *or* other article *relating to international relations*. We also have Shannon's solemn oath *in writing* that he will not divulge state secrets, plus his awareness of what will happen to him if he does. Put together, I'd say we're looking at a very short trial in a secret court, terminating in a prison sentence of ten to twelve years, six with remission if he owns up, plus free psychiatric attention if he requires it, which frankly I'd have thought was a no-brainer.'

*

I had vowed to myself sitting alone in the empty waiting room for an hour and more that I would remain composed and above the fray. Accept the premise, I kept telling myself. Live with it. It's not going to go away when you wake up. Ed Shannon, the blushing new member of the Athleticus who's so shy he needs Alice to introduce him, is an established member of our sister Service and a walk-in Russian spy. Along the road, for reasons yet to be explained, he picked you up. Fine. Classic. All honour. A really neat job. He cultivated you, schmoozed you, led you by the nose. And obviously he *knew*. Knew that I was a veteran officer with a potential chip on my shoulder, and therefore ripe for cultivation.

Then blandish me, for God's sake! Cultivate me as a future source! And when you've cultivated me, either take the plunge and make a pass at me, or hand me over to your Russian controllers for development! So why didn't you? *What about the basic mating signals of agent acquisition?* Where were *they* ever? How is your rocky marriage getting along, Nat? You never asked me. Are you in debt, Nat? Do you feel under-appreciated, Nat? Passed over for promotion? Have they chiselled you out of your gratuity, your pension, at all? You know what the trainers preach. *Everyone has something. The job of the recruiter is to find it!* But you didn't even bloody look for it! Never probed, never went anywhere near the brink. Never chanced your arm.

And how *could* you chance your arm when all you did from the moment we sat down together was pontificate about your political beefs, and I barely got a word in even if I'd wanted to?

*

My plea of mitigation for Ed has not gone down well with my *chers collègues*. Never mind. I've recovered. I am composed. Guy Brammel gives a perfunctory nod to Marion who has signified that she has questions for the accused.

'Nat.'

'Marion.'

'You implied earlier that neither you nor Shannon had the smallest idea how the other was employed. Am I correct?'

'Not correct at all, Marion, I'm afraid,' I reply jauntily. 'We had very *clear* ideas. Ed was working for some media empire that he loathed, and I was scouting for business opportunities while I helped out an old business friend.'

'Did Shannon specifically *tell* you it was a media empire he was working for?'

'In as many words, no. He *implied* to me that he was filtering news stories and getting them out to customers. And his employers were – well – they were insensitive to his needs,' I add with a smile, ever aware of the importance of smooth relations between our two Services.

'So it's fair to say, taking your story as it stands, that the bond between the two of you depended on mutually false assumptions about each other's identity?' she goes on.

'If you want to put it that way, Marion. Basically, it was a non-issue.'

'Because each of you blindly accepted the other one's cover story, you mean?'

'Blindly is putting it too strongly. Both of us had sound reasons not to be inquisitive.'

'We are hearing from our in-house investigators that you and Edward Shannon rent separate lockers in the men's changing area at the Athleticus. Is that correct?' she demands, without pause or apology.

'Well, you don't expect us to *share* one, do you?' – no answer, and certainly not the laugh I was hoping for. 'Ed has a locker, I have a locker. Correct,' I continue, as I picture poor Alice being shaken out of bed and made to open up her books at this ungodly hour.

'With keys?' Marion demands. 'I asked you whether the lockers have *keys* as opposed to combinations?'

'Keys, Marion. All keys,' I agree – recovering from a brief lapse in concentration. 'Small, flat – about the size of a postage stamp.'

'Keys that you keep in your pockets while you play?'

'They come with ribbons,' I reply, as the image of Ed in the changing room arming himself for our first-ever encounter comes rushing back to me. 'Either take off the ribbon and put the key in your pocket, or keep the ribbon and wear the key around your neck. It's a fashion choice. Ed and I took our ribbons off.'

'And kept the keys in your trouser pockets?'

'In my case, in the *side* pocket. My rear pocket was reserved for my credit card when we got to the bar, and a twenty pound note in case I felt like paying cash and collecting some parking money. Does that answer your question?'

Evidently it didn't. 'According to your operational record, you have in the past used your skills at badminton as a means of recruiting at least one Russian agent and covertly communicating with him by exchanging identical racquets. And you have received commendations for so doing. Am I correct?'

'You are so correct, Marion.'

'So it would not be an *unreasonable hypothesis*,' she continues, 'that, were you so minded, you would be ideally placed to provide Shannon with secret intelligence from your own Service by the same covert means.'

I take a slow look round the half-circle. Percy Price's normally kindly features still in lockdown. Ditto Brammel, Lavender and Marion's two spear-carriers. Gloria's head tipped sideways as if she's given up listening. Her two *Unter*-shrinks sitting tensely forward, hands locked on their laps in some kind of biological interaction. Ghita poker-backed, like a good little girl at the dinner table. Moira peering out of the window, except there isn't one.

'Anyone second that happy motion?' I enquire, as the sweat of anger runs down my ribs. 'I'm Ed's sub-agent, according to Marion. I slip him secrets for onward transmission to Moscow. Have we all gone fucking mad, or is it just me?'

No takers. None expected. We're paid to think outside the box, so that's what we're doing. Maybe Marion's theory isn't so way out after all. God knows, the Service has had its share of bad apples in its time. Maybe Nat's another.

But Nat isn't another. And Nat needs to tell them that in plain English.

'All right, everyone. Tell me this if you can. *Why* does a dyed-in-the-wool pro-European civil servant make a free offer of British secrets to Russia of all places, a country that, in his judgement, is run by a fully developed anti-European despot named Vladimir Putin? And for as long as you can't answer *that* question for yourselves, why the fuck do you pick on *me* as your punchball, merely because Shannon and I play decent badminton and talk political bullshit over a beer or two?'

And as an afterthought, albeit misjudged:

'Oh, and by the way, can anyone here tell me what Jericho's about? I know it's password-protected and never to be discussed, and I haven't been cleared for it. But neither was Maria, neither was Gamma and neither presumably is Moscow Centre. And certainly Shannon isn't. So maybe we can make an exception in this particular case, since from all we heard it was Jericho that tripped Ed's switch, and Jericho that drove him into the arms of Maria, then Gamma. Yet we're all still sitting here, even *now*, pretending nobody spoke the bloody word!'

They know, I'm thinking. Everyone in the room is Jericho-indoctrinated except me. Forget it. They're as ignorant as I am and they're in shock because I've mentioned the unmentionable.

Brammel is the first to recover the power of speech.

'We need to hear it from you one more time, Nat,' he announces.

'Hear *what*?' I demand.

'Shannon's world view. A précis of his motivation. All the shit he spouted at you about Trump, Europe and the universe, which you appear to have swallowed wholesale.'

*

I am hearing myself at a distance, the way I seem to be hearing everything. I am being careful to say *Shannon*, not *Ed*, although now and then I slip up. I am doing Ed on Brexit. I am doing Ed on Trump and not sure any more how I got from one to the other. Out of prudence, I heap everything on to Ed's shoulders. It's his world view they want after all, not mine.

'As far as *Shannon* is concerned, Trump is devil's advocate for every tinpot demagogue and kleptocrat across the globe,' I declare in my best offhand voice. 'Trump the man is a total nothing in Shannon's view. A mob orator. But as a symptom of what's out there in the world's undergrowth, waiting to be stirred up, he's the devil incarnate. A simplistic view, you may say, not everyone's by any means. But deeply felt all the same.

Particularly if you're by way of being an obsessive pro-European. Which *Shannon* is,' I add firmly, lest I have not made the distinction between us sufficiently clear.

I give a reminiscent laugh that chimes quaintly in the silence of the room. I choose Ghita. She's the safest.

'You'll never believe this, Ghita, but Shannon actually *said* to me one evening that it was a crying shame that all American assassins seem to come from the far right. High time the left got itself a shooter!'

Can the silence get any deeper? This one can.

'And you went along with that?' Ghita enquires for all the room.

'Humorously, casually, over a beer, in the sense that I didn't contradict him, inferentially, as one does, I agreed that the world would be a damned sight better off if Trump wasn't in it. I'm not even sure he said *assassinated*. Maybe *topped* or *offed*.'

I hadn't noticed the bottled water beside me. Now I do. The Office does tap water as a matter of principle. If it's bottled it has come down from the top floor. I pour myself a glass, take a good swallow, and appeal to Guy Brammel as the last reasonable man standing.

'Guy, for fuck's sake.'

He doesn't hear me. He is deep in his iPad. At last he raises his head:

'All right, everybody. Orders from on high. Nat, you go home to Battersea *now* and stay there. Expect a call six p.m. this evening as ever is. Until then, you're gated. Ghita, you take over the Haven with immediate effect: agents, ops, the team, the whole mess. The Haven as of now no longer in the maw of London General but assimilated on a *pro tem* basis into Russia department. Signed Bryn Jordan, head down in Washington, poor bastard. Anyone got anything else on their minds – nobody? Then let's get back to work.'

They troop out. Last to leave is Percy Price, who hasn't breathed one word in four hours.

'Funny friends you've got then,' he remarks without a glance.

*

There's a greasy spoon café just up the road from our house. It serves breakfast from five in the morning. And I can't tell you today, any more than I could have told you at the time, what thoughts were washing through my head as I sat drinking coffee after coffee and listening mindlessly to the workmen's chatter which, being in Hungarian, was as incomprehensible to me as my own feelings. It was gone six a.m. when I paid my bill and stole into the house by the back door, then up the stairs, and into bed beside the sleeping Prue.

17

I ask myself from time to time how that Saturday would have unfolded if Prue and I hadn't had a longstanding lunch date with Larry and Amy in Great Missenden. Prue and Amy had been at school together and friends ever since. Larry was a worthy family lawyer a bit older than me, loved his golf and his dog. The couple had no children to their regret and were celebrating their twenty-fifth anniversary. It was to be just the four of us at lunch, and a walk in the Chilterns afterwards. Prue had bought them a quilted Victorian bedspread and got it all wrapped and ready, and some sort of comic chew for their boxer dog. What with the seemingly eternal heatwave and the Saturday traffic, we'd reckoned two hours, so leave at eleven latest.

At ten I was still in bed asleep, so Prue sweetly brought me up a cup of tea. I'd no idea how long she'd been up and about since she'd dressed without waking me. But, knowing her, she'd put in a couple of hours at her desk grappling with Big Pharma. It was therefore all the more gratifying that she had interrupted her labours. I am being pompous with a reason. The ensuing conversation between us begins predictably enough with a 'whatever hour did you get in last night, Nat?' to which I reply, God knows, Prue, just bloody late, or whatever. But something in my voice or face gets through to her. Moreover, as I now know, the divergence of our supposedly parallel lives since my homecoming has begun to tell on her. She has a fear, only later confided to me, that her war on Big Pharma, and mine on whatever target the Office in its wisdom has assigned to me, far from complementing each other, are pitching us into opposing camps. And it is this anxiety coupled with my physical appearance that triggers our seemingly humble but momentous exchange.

'We are *going*, aren't we, Nat?' she asks me, with what I continue to regard as unnerving intuition.

'Going where?' I reply evasively, though I know perfectly well.

'To Larry and Amy's. For their twenty-fifth. Where else?'

'Well, not *both* of us actually, Prue, I'm afraid. I can't. You'll have to go alone. Or why not try Phoebe? *She'd* go with you like a shot.'

Phoebe, our next-door neighbour, not necessarily the brightest of company but perhaps better than an empty seat.

'Nat, are you ill?' Prue asks.

'Not to my knowledge. I'm on standby,' I reply as stoutly as I can.

'For what?'

'For the Office.'

'Can't you be on standby and still come?'

'No. I've got to be here. Physically. In the house.'

'Why? What's happening in the house?'

'Nothing.'

'You can't be waiting for *nothing*. Are you in some sort of danger?'

'It's not like that. Larry and Amy know I'm a spook. Look, I'll ring him,' I suggest gallantly. '*Larry* won't ask questions' – with the tacit subtext: *unlike you*.

'How about theatre tonight? We've got two tickets for Simon Russell Beale, if you remember. Stalls.'

'I can't do that either.'

'Because you'll be on standby.'

'I'm getting a call at six. It's anyone's guess what happens after that.'

'So we're waiting all day for a call at six.'

'I guess so. Well *I* am, anyway,' I say.

'And before that?'

'I can't leave the house. Bryn's orders. I'm gated.'

'Bryn's?'

'Himself. Direct from Washington.'

'Then I think it's better if I ring Amy,' she says, after a moment's consideration. 'Perhaps they'd like the tickets too. I'll call her from the kitchen.'

At which juncture Prue does what Prue always does, just when I think she has finally run out of patience with me: steps back, takes a second reading of the situation and sets about fixing it. By the time she comes back, she has changed into an old pair of jeans and the silly Edelweiss jacket we bought on our skiing holiday, and she's smiling.

'Did you sleep?' she asks, making me budge over, then sitting down on the bed.

'Not a lot.'

She feels my brow, testing it for heat.

'I'm *really* not ill, Prue,' I repeat.

'No. But I *am* wondering whether by any chance the Office has chucked you out,' she says, contriving to make the question more a confession of her own concerns than mine.

'Well, pretty much, yes. I think it probably has,' I concede.

'Unfairly?'

'No. Not really, no.'

'Did *you* fuck up, or did they?'

'Bit of both really. I just got mixed up with the wrong people.'

'Anyone we know?'

'No.'

'They're not coming to get you in some way?'

'No. It's not like that,' I assure her, realizing as I say this that I am not quite as much in command of myself as I had thought.

'What's happened to your Office mobile? You always keep it by the bed.'

'Must be in my suit,' I say, still in some kind of deceptive mode.

'It's not. I looked. Has the Office confiscated it?'

'Yes.'

'As of when?'

'Last night. This morning. It was an all-night session.'

'Are you angry with them?'

'I don't know. I'm trying to find out.'

'Then stay in bed and find out. The call you're expecting at six p.m. will presumably be on the house line.'

'It will have to be, yes.'

'I'll email Steff and make sure she doesn't plan to Skype at the same time. You'll need all your concentration.' Then reaching the door she changes her mind, turns round and resumes her place on the bed. 'Can I say something, Nat? Non-invasive? Just a small mission statement?'

'Of course you can.'

She has taken my hand back, this time not to feel my pulse.

'*If* the Office is buggering you about,' she says very firmly, 'and *if* you're determined to hang in there nonetheless, you have my unstinted support till death do us part, and fuck boys' clubs. Do I make myself clear?'

'You do. Thank you.'

'Equally, if the Office is buggering you about, and you decide on the spur of the moment to tell them to shove it up their arses and to hell with your pension, we're solvent and we can make do.'

'I'll bear that in mind.'

'And you can tell that to Bryn too, if it's any help,' she adds just as firmly. 'Or *I* will.'

'Safer not,' I say – followed by unforced laughter and relief on both sides.

Mutual expressions of love are seldom impressive to anyone not taking part in them, but the things we said to each other that day – notably Prue to me – ring in my memory like a rallying call. It was as if, in one shove, she had pushed open an invisible door between us. And I like to think that it was by way of this same door that I first started to make vague sense of the scatterbrained theories and bits of half-baked intuition regarding Ed's incomprehensible behaviour that kept springing up at me like fireworks and fizzling out.

*

'My bit of German soul,' Ed liked to say to me with an apologetic grin after he had sounded too earnest for his own blood, or too didactic.

Always his *bit of German soul*.

In order to pull him up on his bicycle Tadzio had spoken *German* to Ed.

Why? Would Ed really have otherwise mistaken him for a street drunk?

And why am I thinking *German, German,* when all the time I should be thinking *Russian, Russian?*

And tell me, please, since I am tone-deaf, why is it that every time my memory replays the dialogue between Ed and Gamma, I have a sensation of listening to the wrong music?

If I have no clear answer to these fumbled questions, if the effect of them is only to intensify my mystification, the fact remains that by six o'clock that evening, thanks to Prue's ministrations, I felt more belligerent, more able and a whole lot more ready than I had been at five that morning to take on whatever the Office had left to throw at me.

*

Six o'clock by the church clock, six o'clock by my wristwatch, six o'clock by Prue's family grandfather clock in the hall. Another sun-baked evening of the great London drought. I'm sitting in my den upstairs wearing shorts and sandals. Prue is in the garden, watering her poor, parched roses. A bell rings, but it's not the house phone. It's the front door.

I leap up, but Prue gets there first. We meet halfway on the stairs.

'I think you'd better change into something more respectable,' she says. 'There's a large man with a car outside who says he's come to fetch you.'

I go to the landing window and peer down. A black Ford Mondeo, two aerials. And Arthur, longtime driver to Bryn Jordan, propped against it enjoying a quiet fag.

*

The church stands at the top of Hampstead hill and that's where Arthur sets me down. Bryn never held with comings and goings outside his house.

'You know your way then,' says Arthur, as a statement not a question. It's the first time he has spoken since 'Hullo, Nat.' Yes, Arthur, know it well, thanks.

Ever since I was the new boy of Moscow Station and Prue my Service spouse, Bryn, his beautiful Chinese wife Ah Chan, their three musical daughters and one difficult son had lived in this massive eighteenth-century hilltop villa overlooking

Hampstead Heath. If we were recalled from Moscow for a brain-storming session, or on spells of home leave, this mellowed brick pile behind high gates with one bell-button was where we would all assemble for jolly family suppers with the daughters playing Schubert lieder and the bravest of us singing along with them; or if Christmas was coming, then madrigals, because the Bryns as we called them were Old Catholics and there was a Christ on the cross lurking in the shadows of the hall to tell you so. How a Welshman of all people becomes a devout Roman Catholic is beyond me, but it was in the nature of the man to be inexplicable.

Bryn and Ah Chan were ten years older than we were. Their talented daughters had long embarked on their stellar careers. Ah Chan, Bryn explained as he greeted me with his customary warmth on the doorstep, was visiting her aged mother in San Francisco:

'The old girl scored a century last week but she's still waiting for her bloody telegram from the Queen, or whatever she sends these days,' he complains boisterously, as he marches me down a corridor as long as a railway carriage. 'We applied for it like good citizens, but Her Maj is not absolutely sure she qualifies if she's Chinese-born and lives in San Francisco. On top of which the dear old Home Office has lost her file. Tip of the iceberg, if you ask me. Whole country in spasm. First thing you notice every time you come home: nothing works, everything's a lash-up. Same feeling we used to have in Moscow, if you remember, back in those days.'

Those days for the Cold War, the one his detractors say he's still fighting. We are approaching the great drawing room.

'*And* we're a laughing stock to our beloved allies and neighbours, in case you haven't noticed,' he goes on merrily. 'A bunch of post-imperial nostalgists who can't run a fruit stall. Your impression too?'

I say, pretty much.

'And your pal Shannon feels the same way, evidently. Maybe that's his motive: *shame*. Thought of that? The *national humiliation*, trickling down, taken personally. I could buy that.'

I say, it's a thought, although I never saw Ed as much of a nationalist.

A high-raftered ceiling, cracked leather armchairs, dark icons, primitives of the old China Trade days, untidy heaps of aged books with slips of paper wedged in them, one broken wooden ski over the fireplace and a vast silver tray for our whisky, soda and cashews.

'Bloody ice machine's on the blink too,' Bryn assures me proudly. 'It would be. Everywhere you go in America, chaps offer you ice. And we Brits can't even make the stuff. Par for the course. Still, you don't do ice, do you?'

He has remembered correctly. He always does. He pours two treble Scotches without asking me to say when, shoves a glass at me and with a twinkly smile waves me to sit. He sits himself and beams mischievous goodwill at me. In Moscow he was older than his years. Now youth has caught up with him in a big way. The watery blue eyes shine their semi-divine light, but it's brighter and more directional. In Moscow, he had lived out his cover as Cultural Attaché with such brio, lecturing his bemused Russian audiences on so many erudite topics, that they were halfway to believing he was a straight diplomat. *Cover, dear boy. Next to Godliness.* Bryn has homilies like other people have small talk.

I ask after the family. The girls are achieving marvellously, he confirms, Annie at the Courtauld, Eliza at the London Philharmonic – yes, cello indeed, how good of me to remember – squads of grandchildren born or expected. All utterly delightful, squeeze of the eyes.

'And Toby?' I enquire cautiously.

'Oh, an *utter* failure,' he replies with the dismissive gusto he applies to all bad news. 'Completely hopeless. We bought him a twenty-two-foot boat with all the trimmings, fixed him up crabbing out of Falmouth, last we heard of him he was in New Zealand getting himself into an absolute *load* of trouble.'

Short silence for commiseration.

'And Washington?' I ask.

'Oh my God, *fucking awful*, Nat' – with an even wider smile – 'civil wars breaking out like measles all over the shop and you never know who's leaning which way for how long and who's for the chop tomorrow. And no Thomas Wolsey to hold the ring. A couple of years ago we were America's man in Europe. All right, spotty, not always easy. But we were *in* there, part of the package, outside the euro, thank God, and no wet dreams about unified foreign policies, defence policies or what have you' – squeeze of the eyes, chortle. 'And *that* was our special relationship with the United States for you. Sucking away merrily on the hind tit of American power. Getting our rocks off. Where are we now? Back of the queue behind the Huns and the Frogs. With a bloody sight less to offer. Total disaster.'

Benign chuckle, and barely a hiatus as he advances to his next amusing topic:

'I *was* rather taken by what your pal Shannon had to say about the Donald, incidentally: the notion that he'd had all the democratic chances and blown them. Not absolutely sure that's true. Point about Trump is, he's a gang boss, born and bred. Brought up to *screw* civil society all ways up, not be part of it. Your Shannon chap got that one wrong. Or am I being unfair?'

Unfair to Trump or unfair to Ed?

'And poor little Vladi Putin never had any democratic potty training at all,' he goes on indulgently. 'I'd agree with him on that one. Born a spy, still a spy, with Stalin's paranoia to boot. Wakes up every morning amazed the West hasn't blown him out of the water with a pre-emptive strike.' Munches cashews.

Washes them down with a thoughtful pull of Scotch. 'He's a dreamer, isn't he?'

'Who?'

'Shannon.'

'I suppose so.'

'What sort?'

'Don't know.'

'Really not?'

'Really not.'

'Guy Brammel has come up with a *grudgefuck* theory,' he runs on, delighting in the term like a naughty boy. 'Ever heard that one before? *Grudgefuck?*'

'I'm afraid not. Cluster only recently, and never grudge. I've been abroad too long.'

'Me neither. Thought I'd heard everything. But Guy's got his teeth into it. A man on a *grudgefuck mission* is saying to the person he's hopped into bed with – in this case Mother Russia – the only reason I'm here screwing you is because I hate my wife even more than I hate you. So it's a grudgefuck. Might that play for your boy? What's your personal take on it?'

'Bryn, my personal take is: I took a hell of a beating last night, first from Shannon, then from my beloved friends and colleagues, so I'm rather wondering why I'm here.'

'Yes, well, they did over-egg it a bit, it's true,' he agrees, open as ever to all points of view. 'But then, nobody knows who they are just now, do they? Whole fucking country in disarray. Maybe that's the clue to him. Britain in pieces on the floor, secret monk in search of an absolute, even if it involves absolute betrayal. But instead of trying to blow up the Houses of Parliament, he sneaks off to the Russians. Possible?'

I say anything is possible. A prolonged squeezing of the eyes and a beguiling smile warn me that he is about to venture into more perilous territory.

'So tell me, Nat. For my ear alone. How did *you personally* respond, you as Shannon's mentor, confessor, proxy daddy, what you will, when you spotted your young protégé, without a word of warning, cosying up to the overweening Gamma?' – topping up my Scotch. 'What went through your private and professional heads as you sat there on your tod, watching and listening in frank amazement? Don't *think* too hard. *Spout.*'

In other times, sitting captive and alone with Bryn, I might indeed have unbared my innermost feelings to him. I might even have told him that, as I sat listening transfixed to Valentina's voice, I imagined that I detected between her Georgian and Russian cadences the presence of an intruder that was neither: a copy, yes, but not the original. And that, at some point during a day of waiting, an answer of sorts had come to me. Not as a blinding revelation, but on tiptoe, like a latecomer to the theatre, edging his way down the row in the half-dark. Somewhere in the most distant rooms of my memory, I was hearing my mother's voice raised to me in anger as she reproached me for some perceived dereliction in a language unknown to her current lover, before as quickly disowning it. But Valentina–Gamma had not *disowned* the German in her voice. Not to my ear. She was *affecting* it. She was imposing German cadences on her spoken English in order to *cleanse* it of its Russian–Georgian stain.

But even as this wild thought comes to me, more fancy than fact, something inside me tells me that it cannot on any account be shared with Bryn. Is this then the germinating moment of a scheme that is forming in my head, but I am not yet cleared for? I have often thought so.

'What I *suppose* I felt, Bryn,' I reply, taking up his question about my two heads, 'was that Shannon must be suffering some sort of mental breakdown in place. Schizophrenia, big-time bipolarity, whatever the shrinks come up with. In which case, we amateurs are wasting our time trying to ascribe rational motives to him. And then of course there was the *trigger*, the final straw' – why am I overreaching? – 'his *epiphany*, for Christ's sake. The one he denied having. The thing that actually made Sammy run, as we used to say.'

Bryn is still smiling but the smile is rock-hard, daring me to venture further.

'Shall we cut to the chase?' he enquires blandly, as if I haven't spoken. 'As of early this morning, Moscow Centre has requested a *second* meeting with Shannon one week hence and Shannon has consented to it. Centre's haste may seem indecent, but to me it spells sound professional judgement. They fear for their source in the long term – who wouldn't? – which means of course that we must be equally fast on our feet.'

A wave of spontaneous resentment comes to my aid.

'You keep saying *we* as if it was a done thing, Bryn,' I complain with our usual determined joviality. 'What I find a bit hard to swallow is that all this stuff is happening over my head. I'm the author of Stardust, in case you've forgotten, so why am I not being kept informed of the progress of my own operation?'

'You *are* being kept informed, dear boy. By me. To the rest of the Service you are history, and rightly so. If I'd had my way you'd never have got the Haven. Times are a-changing. You're at the dangerous age. You always were, but it's showing. Prue well?'

Sends her best, thank you, Bryn.

'Is she conscious? To the Shannon thing?'

No, Bryn.

'Keep it that way.'

Yes, Bryn.

Keep it that way? Meaning keep Prue in the dark about *Ed*? Prue, who only this morning pledged her unconditional loyalty, even if I should feel moved to tell the Office to shove it up their arses? Prue, as good a soldier-spouse as the Office could wish for, who never once by word or whisper betrayed the trust that the Office had invested in her? And now Bryn, of all people, is telling me she is not to be trusted? Fuck him.

'Our sister Service is of course baying loudly for Shannon's blood, which won't come as any surprise to you,' Bryn is saying. 'Arrest him, shake him out, make an example of him, everybody gets a medal. Result: a national scandal that achieves bugger all and makes us look bloody fools bang in the middle of Brexit. So we take that option straight off the table, as far as I'm concerned.'

The 'we' again. He offers me the plate of cashews. I take a handful to satisfy him.

'Olives?'

No thanks, Bryn.

'You used to love them. Kalamata.'

Really not, thanks, Bryn.

'Next option. We haul him into Head Office and make the classic pass at him. Okay, Shannon, you're a fully identified agent of Moscow Centre and henceforth you're under our control or you're for the high jump. Think it would play? You know him. We don't. Neither does his department. They think he's got a girl but they're not even sure about that. Could be a fellow. Could be his interior decorator. He's fixing his flat, they say. Taken out a mortgage on his salary and bought the one upstairs. Did he tell you that?'

No, Bryn. He didn't.

'Did he tell you he's got a girl?'

No, Bryn.

'Then maybe he hasn't. Some chaps can manage without, don't ask me how. Maybe he's one of the few.'

Maybe he is, Bryn.

'So what's your best guess if we make the classic pass at him?'

I give the question the consideration it deserves.

226

'My best guess is, Bryn, that Shannon would tell you to go fuck yourselves.'

'Why so?'

'Try playing badminton with him. He'd rather go down with all guns blazing.'

'We are not playing badminton, however.'

'Ed doesn't *bend*, Bryn. He's not up for flattery or compromise or saving his own skin if he thinks the cause is greater than he is.'

'Then he's out for martyrdom,' Bryn observes with satisfaction, as if recognizing a well-trodden path. 'Meanwhile, we are of course engaged in the usual tug-of-war about who owns his body. We found him, ergo, for as long as we play him he's ours. Once we've no more use for him, it's game over and our sister Service has its wicked way. Now let me ask you this. Do you still *love* him? Not carnally. Love him for real?'

And that's Bryn Jordan for you, the river you only cross once. Charms you, listens to your gripes and suggestions, never raises his voice, never judgemental, always above the fray, walks you round the garden until he owns the air you breathe, then skewers you.

*

'I'm fond of him, Bryn. Or I was, until this blew up,' I say lightly, after a long pull of whisky.

'As he is of you, dear boy. Can you imagine him talking to anyone else the way he talks to you? We can use that.'

'But how, Bryn?' I insist, with an earnest smile, playing the good disciple despite the chorus of conflicted voices resounding in what Bryn was pleased to call my private head. 'I keep asking you, but somehow you don't quite answer. Who's *we* in this equation?'

The Father Christmas eyebrows rise to their extremity as he awards me the broadest of smiles.

'Oh my dear boy. You and I together, who else?'

'Doing *what*, if I may ask?'

'What you've *always* done best! You befriend your man all ways up. You're halfway there already. Judge your moment and go the other half. Tell him who you are, show him the error of his ways, calmly, undramatically, and *turn* him. The moment he says "yes I will, Nat," put a halter round his neck and lead him gently into the paddock.'

'And when I've led him gently in?'

'We play him back. Keep him beavering away at his day job, feed him carefully concocted disinformation which he passes up the pipeline to Moscow. We run him for as long as he lasts, and once we've done with him we let our sister Service wrap up the Gamma network to the sound of trumpets. *You* get a commendation from the Chief, *we* cheer you on your way and you've done the best you can for your young pal. Bravo. Any less would be disloyal, more would be culpable. And now hear *this*,' he goes on vigorously, before I have a chance to object.

*

Bryn has no need of notes. He never did have. He isn't reeling off facts and figures at me from his Office mobile. He's not pausing, frowning, searching his mind for that irritating detail he has mislaid. This is the man who learned fluent Russian in one year flat at the School of Soviet Studies in Rome and added Mandarin to his portfolio in his spare time.

'Over the last nine months, your friend Shannon has formally declared to his employers five visits *in toto* to European diplomatic missions based here in London. *Two* to the French Embassy for cultural events solely. *Three* to the German Embassy, one for their Day of German Unity, one to an award ceremony for British teachers of the German language. And one for social purposes undefined. You said something' – abruptly.

'Just listening, Bryn. Just listening.'

If I had said something, it was only in my head.

'All such visits were approved by his employing department, whether in advance or retrospectively we may not know, but the dates are logged and you have them here' – conjuring a zip-up folder from beside him. 'And one unexplained phone call from a public call box in Hoxton to the German Embassy. He asks for a Frau Brandt from their travel department and is correctly told they haven't got a Frau Brandt.'

He pauses, but only to make sure I am attending. He needn't bother. I'm transfixed.

'We *also* learn, as the street cameras open their hearts to us, that in the course of his cycle ride to Ground Beta yesterday evening, Shannon parked his bike and sat in a *church* for twenty minutes' – an indulgent smile.

'What sort of church?'

'Low. The only sort that leaves its doors open these days. No silver, no sacred paintings, no raiment worth a damn.'

'Who did he talk to?'

'Nobody. There were a couple of rough sleepers, both bona fide, and an old nelly in black across the aisle. And a verger. Shannon didn't kneel, according to the verger. Sat. Then walked out and cycled off again. *So*' – with revived relish – 'what was he up to? Was he committing his soul to his Maker? Pretty bloody odd moment to choose in my judgement, but every man to his own. Or was he making sure his back was clear? I favour the second. What do you reckon he was up to on his visits to the French and German embassies?'

He tops up our glasses yet again, sits impatiently back and

waits for my answer – much as I do, but none immediately occurs to me.

'Well, Bryn. Maybe you go first, for a change,' I suggest, playing his own game at him, which he enjoys.

'For my money, he was *embassy trawling*,' he replies with satisfaction. 'Sniffing out extra morsels of intelligence to feed his Russian addiction. He may have played the ingénu with Gamma but in my view he's in for the long haul, if he doesn't make a horse's arse of himself in the meantime. Back to you. As many questions as you like.'

There is only one question I want to ask, but instinct tells me to kick off with a soft one. I select Dom Trench.

'*Dom!*' he exclaims. 'Oh my dear *Lord!* *Dom!* Outer darkness. Indefinite gardening leave without the option.'

'Why? What's his sin?'

'Being recruited by us in the first place. That's *our* sin. Sometimes our dear Office loves larceny too well. Marrying above his weight is *his* sin. *And* being caught with his pants down by a bunch of muckrakers on the dark web. They got a couple of details wrong, but too many right. Are you bonking that girl who walked out on us by the way? Florence?' – with the most diffident of smiles.

'I'm not bonking Florence, Bryn.'

'Never did?'

'Never did.'

'Then why call her from a public phone box and take her out to dinner?'

'She walked out on the Haven and left her agents in the lurch. She's a mixed-up girl and I felt I should stay in touch with her.' Too many excuses, but never mind.

'Well, be bloody careful from now on. She's out of bounds and so are you. Any more questions? Take your time.'

I take my time. And more time.

'Bryn.'

'Dear boy?'

'What the hell's Operation Jericho?' I ask.

*

To non-believers the sanctity of codeword material is hard to convey. The codewords themselves, regularly altered in midstream to confuse the enemy, are treated with the same secrecy as their content. For a member of the indoctrinated few to utter a codeword within the hearing of those outside the tent would qualify in Bryn's lexicon as mortal sin. Yet here am I, of all people, *demanding* of the iconic head of Russia department: *what the hell's Jericho?*

'I mean, Christ, Bryn,' I insist, undaunted by his rigid smile, 'Shannon took one glance at the stuff as it went through the copier and that was it. Whatever he saw, or *thinks* he saw, that did it. What do I say if he calls me on it? Tell him I've no idea what he's talking about? That's not showing him the error of his ways. That's not putting a halter round his neck and leading him gently in.' And more forcefully: '*Shannon* knows what Jericho is all about—'

'Thinks he does.'

'—and *Moscow* knows. Gamma is apparently so excited by Jericho that she takes on the job herself, with Moscow providing a full supporting cast.'

The smile widens in seeming assent but the lips remain tight shut as if resolved that no word shall pass them.

'A dialogue,' he says at last. 'A dialogue between adults.'

'Which adults?'

He ignores the question.

'We are a divided nation, Nat, as you will have noticed. The divisions between us across the country are neatly reflected in the divisions between our masters. No two ministers think the same way on the same day. It would not therefore be surprising if the intelligence requirements they hand down to us fluctuate with the moment, even to the point of contradicting each other. After all, part of our remit is to think the unthinkable. How many times have we old Russian hands done just that, sitting here in this very room, thinking the unthinkable?'

He is reaching for an aphorism. As usual, he finds one: 'Signposts don't *walk* in the direction they *point*, Nat. It is we humble mortals who must choose which way to go. The signpost is not responsible for our decision. Well, is it?'

No, Bryn, it isn't. Or it is. Either way, you're pulling a lot of wool across my eyes.

'But I am allowed to assume that you are KIM/1?' I suggest. 'As head of our mission to Washington. Or is that an assumption too far?'

'My dear boy. Assume what you will.'

'But that's all you're proposing to tell me?'

'What more can you possibly need to know? Here's a snippet for you, and it's all you get. The top-secret dialogue in question is taking place between our American cousins and ourselves. Its purpose is exploratory, a feeling-out. It is being conducted at the highest level. The Service is the intermediary, everything under discussion is theoretical, nothing is written in stone. Shannon by his own testimony saw one piddling section of a fifty-four-page document, memorized it, probably inaccurately, and drew his own misguided conclusions, which he then conveyed to Moscow. We have no idea which piddling section. He has been caught *in flagrante* – thanks, one may add, to your endeavours, even if that was not your aim. You have no need to engage him in any sort of dialectic. You show him the whip. You tell him you won't use it unless you have to.'

'And that's all I can know?'

'And more than you need. For a moment I allowed sentiment

to get the better of me. Take this. It's one-to-one only. I'm shuttling back and forth to DC, so you won't get me while I'm airborne.'

The abrupt 'take this' is accompanied by the clatter of a metallic object tossed on to the drinks table between us. It is a silver-grey smartphone, the self-same model I used to give my agents. I look at it, then at Bryn, then again at the smartphone. With a show of reluctance I pick it up and, with Bryn's eyes still upon me, consign it to my jacket pocket. His face softens and his voice resumes its geniality.

'You'll be Shannon's saviour, Nat,' he tells me for my consolation. 'Nobody else is going to be half as gentle with him as you are. If you find yourself havering, think of the alternatives. Want me to hand him over to Guy Brammel?'

I think of the alternatives, if not quite the ones he has in mind. He stands, I stand with him. He takes my arm. He often did. He prides himself on being touchy-feely. We embark on the long march back along the railway carriage, past portraits of ancestral Jordans in lace.

'Family all well otherwise?'

I tell him that Steff is engaged to be married.

'My goodness, Nat, she's only about *nine*!'

Mutual chuckles.

'And Ah Chan has taken up painting in a big way,' he informs me. 'Mega exhibition coming up in Cork Street, no less. No more bloody pastel. No more bloody watercolour. No more bloody gouache. It's oils or bust. Your Prue used to be quite complimentary about her work, as I remember.'

'And still is,' I reply loyally, although this is news to me.

We stand facing each other on the doorstep. Perhaps we share a premonition that we shan't see each other again. I ransack my mind for an extraneous topic. Bryn as usual is ahead of me:

'And don't you worry your head about Dom,' he urges me with a chuckle. 'The man's fucked up everything he's touched in life, so he'll be in great demand. Probably got a safe parliamentary seat waiting for him right now.'

We laugh wisely at the world's wicked ways. As we shake hands, he pats me on the shoulder American-style, and follows me the statutory halfway down the steps. The Mondeo pulls up in front of me. Arthur drives me home.

*

Prue is sitting at her laptop. One glance at my face, she rises and without a word unlocks the conservatory door to the garden.

'Bryn wants me to recruit Ed,' I tell her under the apple tree. 'The boy I told you about. My regular badminton date. The big talker.'

'Recruit him for what on earth?'

'As a double agent.'

'Directed against whom or what?'

'The Russia target.'

'Well, doesn't he have to be a *single* agent first?'

'Technically, that's what he already is. He's an upscale clerical assistant in our sister Service. He's been caught red-handed passing secrets to the Russians, but he doesn't know yet.'

A long silence before she takes refuge in her professionalism: 'In that case the Office must collect *all* the evidence, for *and* against, hand it over to the Crown Prosecution Service and see him *fairly* tried by his peers in *open* court. And not go preying on his friends to bully and blackmail him. You told Bryn no, I trust.'

'I told him I'd do it.'

'Because?'

'I think Ed pressed the wrong bell.'

18

Renate was always an early riser.

It's seven on a Sunday morning, the sun is up and the heat-wave shows no sign of relenting as I stride northward over the burned tundra of Regent's Park to Primrose village. According to my researches – conducted on Prue's laptop not my own, with Prue looking on in a state of half-enlightenment, since a residual loyalty to my Service coupled with a pardonable reticence about my past transgressions forbids me to indoctrinate her fully – I am looking for a block of *superbly restored Victorian mansion apartments with resident porterage*, which ought to have surprised me because diplomatic staff like to cluster round their mother ship, which in Renate's case would have meant the German Embassy in Belgrave Square. But even in Helsinki, where she had been the number two in their Station to my number two in ours, she had insisted on living as far – and she would say as free – from the diplomatic ratpack – *Diplomatengesindel* – as she could decently get.

I enter Primrose village. A holy stillness reigns over the pastel-painted Edwardian villas. Somewhere a church bell tolls, but only timidly. A brave Italian coffee-bar owner is cranking down his striped awning and its groans rhyme with the echo of my footsteps. I turn right, then left. Belisha Court is a grey-brick pile on six floors and occupies the dark side of a cul-de-sac. Stone steps lead to an arched Wagnerian portico. Its black double doors are closed against all comers. The superbly restored apartments have numbers but no names. The only bell-button is marked 'Porter' but a saucy handwritten note wedged behind it reads 'Never on Sundays'. Entry is by keyholders only and the lock, surprisingly, is of the pipe-stem variety. Any Office burglar would have it open in seconds. I would take a little longer but I have no pick. Its fascia is scratched from constant use.

I cross to the sunny side of the cul-de-sac and pretend an interest in a display of children's clothes while I watch the reflection of the double doors. Even in Belisha Court some tenant must need an early-morning jog. Half the double door opens. Not for a jogger but for an elderly couple in black. I surmise they are on their way to church. I let out a cry of relief and hasten across the road to them: my saviours. Like an utter fool I have left my keys upstairs, I explain. They laugh. Well now, they did it to themselves only – when was it, darling? By the time we part they are hurrying down the steps still chuckling to each other and I am heading along a windowless passage to the last door on the left before you get to the garden door because, as in Helsinki so in London, Renate likes a large ground-floor apartment with a good back exit.

The door of number eight has a polished brass flap for letters. The envelope in my hand is addressed *For Reni only* and marked private. She knows my handwriting. Reni was what she liked me to call her. I slip the envelope through the flap, crash the flap open and shut a couple of times, press the buzzer and hurry back along the corridor into the cul-de-sac, left and right into the High Street, pass the coffee shop with a wave and a 'hi' for its Italian owner, across the street, through an iron gateway and up on to Primrose Hill, which rises before me like a parched, tobacco-coloured dome. At the top of it an Indian family in bright colours is trying to fly a four-sided giant kite but there's hardly

wind enough to stir the arid leaves that lie around the solitary
bench I select.

*

For fully fifteen minutes I wait, and by the sixteenth I have all
but given up. She's not there. She's out running, she's with an
agent, a lover, she's off on one of her cultural jaunts to Edinburgh
or Glyndebourne or wherever her cover requires her to show
her face and press the flesh. She's frolicking on one of her beloved
beaches on Sylt. Then a second wave of possibility, potentially
a lot more embarrassing: she has her husband or a lover in residence, he snatched my letter from her hand and he's coming up
the hill to get me: except at this point it isn't the vengeful husband and lover, it's Renate herself marching up the hill, fists
punching across her stocky little body, short blonde hair boun-
cing to her stride, blue eyes blazing, a miniature Valkyrie come
to tell me I'm about to die in battle.

She sees me, switches course, kicking up puffs of dust in her
wake. As she approaches, I stand up out of courtesy but she
sweeps past me, plonks herself on the bench and waits, glowering, for me to sit beside her. In Helsinki she had spoken
reasonable English and better Russian, but when passion seized
her she would throw both aside and claim the comfort of her
own north German. From her opening salvo it is apparent that
her English has greatly improved since I last heard it during our
stolen weekends eight years ago in a rattly cottage on the Baltic
seashore with a double bed and a wood stove.

'Are you absolutely out of your *tiny mind*, Nat?' she demands
idiomatically, glaring up at me. 'What the hell d'you mean:
private – ears-only – off-the-record conversation? Are you trying to
recruit me or fuck me? Since I am not interested in either proposal, you can tell that to whoever sent you, because you are

totally out of court and *off the wall* and embarrassing in all respects. Yes?'

'Yes,' I agree, and wait for her to settle because the woman in Renate was always more impulsive than the spy.

'Stephanie is okay?' she enquires, momentarily appeased.

'More than okay, thanks. Landed on her feet at last, engaged to be married, if you can believe it. Paul?'

Paul is not her son. Renate to her sadness has no children. Paul is her husband, or was; part mid-life playboy, part Berlin publisher.

'Thank you, Paul is also excellent. His women get younger and more stupid and the books on his list get lousier. So life is normal. Have you had other little loves since me?'

'I'm fine. I've calmed down.'

'And you are still with Prue, I hope?'

'Very much.'

'So. Are you going to tell me why you have summoned me here, or do I have to call my Ambassador and tell him our British friends are making inappropriate proposals to his head of Station in a London park?'

'Maybe you should tell him I've been slung out of my Service and I'm on a rescue mission,' I suggest, and wait while she gathers in her body: elbows and knees tightly together, hands linked on her lap.

'Is that true? They fired you?' she demands. 'This is not some stupid ploy? When?'

'Yesterday, as far as I remember.'

'Because of some imprudent *amour*?'

'No.'

'And whom have you come to rescue, may I ask?'

'You. Not just you singular. You plural. You, your staff, your Station, your Ambassador and a bunch of people in Berlin.'

When Renate listens with her large blue eyes, you would never imagine they could blink.

'You are serious, Nat?'

'As never before.'

She reflects on this.

'And you are recording our conversation for posterity, no doubt?'

'Actually not. How about you?'

'Also actually not,' she replies. 'Now please rescue us quickly, if that is what you have come to do.'

'If I told you that my ex-Service had information that a member of the British intelligence community here in London has been offering you information concerning a top-secret dialogue we are having with our American partners, how would you reply to that?'

Her answer comes even faster than I'd expected. Was she preparing it as she came up the hill? Or had she taken advice from above by the time she left her flat?

'I would reply that maybe you British are on a ridiculous fishing expedition.'

'Of what sort?'

'Maybe you are attempting a crude test of our professional loyalty in the light of impending Brexit. Nothing is beyond your so-called government in the present absurd crisis.'

'But you're not saying that such an offer wasn't made to you?'

'You asked me a hypothetical question. I have given you a hypothetical answer.'

At which her mouth snaps shut to indicate that the meeting is over; except that, far from stomping off, she is sitting dead still, waiting for more without wishing to show it. The Indian family, tired of trying to fly the kite, descends the hill. At its foot, platoons of joggers run left to right.

'Let's imagine his name is Edward Shannon,' I suggest.

Dismissive shrug.

'And, still hypothetically, that Shannon is a former member of our inter-service liaison team based in Berlin. Also that he is enraptured by Germany and has the German bug. His motivation is complex and for our mutual purposes irrelevant. But it is not malign. It is actually well intentioned.'

'Naturally, I never heard of this man.'

'Naturally you haven't. Nevertheless, he made a number of visits to your Embassy over the last few months.' I spell out the dates for her, courtesy of Bryn. 'Since his work in London didn't provide him with a link to your Station here, he didn't know who to turn to with his offer of secrets. So he buttonholed anyone in your Embassy he could find until he got handed over to a member of your Station. Shannon is an intelligent man but in terms of conspiracy he is what you would call a *Vollidiot*. Is that a plausible scenario – hypothetically?'

'Of course it is plausible. As a fairy tale, everything is plausible.'

'Maybe it would help if I mentioned that Shannon was received by a member of your staff named Maria Brandt.'

'We have no Maria Brandt.'

'I'm sure you haven't. But it took your Station ten days to decide you hadn't. Ten days of frantic deliberation before you told him you had no interest in his offer.'

'If we told him that we had no interest – which obviously I deny – why are we sitting here? You know his name. You know he is trying to sell secrets. You know he is a *Vollidiot*. You have only to produce a fake buyer and arrest him. In such a hypothetical eventuality, my Embassy behaved correctly in all respects.'

'*Fake buyer*, Reni?' I exclaim in disbelief. 'Are you telling me that Ed *named his price*? I find that hard to believe.'

The stare again, but softer, closer.

'*Ed?*' she repeats. 'Is this what you call him? Your hypothetical traitor? *Ed?*'

'It's what other people call him.'

'But you too?'

'It's catching. It means nothing,' I retort, momentarily on the defensive. 'You said just now that Shannon was trying to *sell* his secrets.'

Now it is her turn to retreat:

'I said no such thing. We were discussing your absurd hypothesis. Intelligence peddlers do not automatically name their price. First they demonstrate their wares in order to obtain the confidence of the purchaser. Only afterwards are terms discussed. As you and I know very well, do we not?'

We do indeed know. It was a German-born intelligence peddler in Helsinki who brought us together. Bryn Jordan smelt a rat and instructed me to crosscheck with our German friends. They gave me Reni.

'So, ten long days and nights before Berlin finally ordered you to turn him off,' I muse.

'You are talking total nonsense.'

'No, Reni. I'm trying to share your pain. Ten days, ten nights of waiting for Berlin to lay its egg. There you are, head of your London Station, a glittering prize within your grasp. Shannon is offering you raw intelligence to dream of. But, oh shit, what happens if he's blown? Think of the diplomatic fallout, our dear British press: a five-star German spy-scare slap in the middle of Brexit!'

She starts to protest but I allow her no respite, since I am allowing myself none.

'Did you sleep? Not you. Did your Station sleep? Did your Ambassador? Did Berlin? Ten days and nights before they inform you that Shannon must be told that his offer is unacceptable. If he approaches you again, you will report him to the appropriate

British authorities. And that's what Maria tells him before she disappears herself in a cloud of green smoke.'

'There *are* no such ten days,' she retorts. 'You are fantasizing as usual. If such an offer was made to us, which it was not, then it was rejected immediately and irrevocably and out of hand by my Embassy. If your Service or former Service thinks otherwise, it is deluded. Am I a liar suddenly?'

'No, Reni. You're doing your job.'

She is angry. With me and with herself.

'Are you trying to charm me into submission again?'

'Is that what I did in Helsinki?'

'Of course you did. You charm everyone. You are known for it. That is what they hired you for. As a Romeo. For your universal homoerotic charm. You were insistent, I was young. *Voilà.*'

'We were both young. And we were both insistent, if you remember.'

'I remember no such thing. We have totally different recollections of the same unfortunate event. Let us agree that for once and for always.'

She is a woman. I am being overbearing and I am imposing on her. She is a professional intelligence officer in high standing. She's cornered and doesn't like it. I am a former lover and I belong on the cutting-room floor with the rest of us. I am a small but precious part of her life and she will never let me go.

'All I'm trying to do, Reni,' I insist, not bothering any longer to quell the urgency that has entered my voice, 'is work out as objectively as I know the *procedure*, inside your Service *and* outside it, over a period of ten days and nights, for handling Edward Shannon's unsolicited offer of *prime-quality* intelligence on the British target. How many hastily convened meetings? How many people handled the papers, telephoned each other, emailed each other, signalled each other, maybe not always on the most secure lines? How many whispered conversations in corridors between panicked politicians and civil servants desperate to cover their backsides? I mean *Jesus*, Reni!' I break out. 'A young man who has lived and worked among you in Berlin, loves your language and your people and considers he has a German heart. Not some lowlife mercenary, but a real thinking man with a crazy mission to save Europe singlehanded. Didn't you *sense* that about him when you played Maria Brandt for him?'

'*I* played Maria Brandt suddenly? What on earth gave you *that* stupid impression?'

'Don't tell me you handed him to your number two. Not you, Reni. A walk-in from British intelligence with a shopping list of top secrets?'

I am expecting her to protest again, to deny, deny, as we have both been taught to do. Instead of which, some kind of softening or resignation overcomes her and she turns away from me and consults the morning sky.

'Is this why they fired you, Nat?' she asks. 'For the boy?'

'In part.'

'And now you have come to rescue us from him.'

'Not from Ed. From yourselves. What I'm trying to tell you is that somewhere along the line between London, Berlin, Munich, Frankfurt and wherever else your masters confer, Shannon's offer to you wasn't just blown. It was intercepted and taken up by a rival firm.'

A flock of gulls has settled beneath us in a single swoop.

'An *American* firm?'

'Russian,' I say, and wait while she continues with great intensity to observe the gulls.

'Posing as *our* Service? Under *our* false flag? Moscow has recruited Shannon?' she demands for verification.

Only her small fists, clenched on her knees for combat, betray her outrage.

'They told him that Maria's refusal to accept his offer was a delaying tactic while they got their act together.'

'And he *believed* that shit? Dear God.'

Again we sit in silence. But the protective hostility in her has drained away. Just as in Helsinki, we are comrades in a cause, even if we don't admit it.

'What's Jericho?' I ask. 'The mega-secret codeword material that made him flip. Shannon only read a small part of it but that seems to have been enough for him to come running to you.'

Her eyes are wide on mine all the time, as they were when we made love. Her voice has lost its official edge.

'You don't know *Jericho*?'

'Not cleared for it. Never was, and by the look of it, never will be.'

She has dropped off. She is meditating. She has entered a trance. Slowly her eyes open. I'm still here.

'Do you swear to me, Nat – as a man, as who you are – that you are telling me the truth? The whole truth?'

'If I knew the whole truth I would tell it to you. What I've told you is all I know.'

'And the Russians have *convinced* him?'

'They've convinced my Service too. They made a pretty good job of it. What's Jericho?' I ask her again.

'From what Shannon told me? I am to tell you your own country's dirty secrets?'

'If that's what they are. I heard *dialogue*. That was the nearest I could get. A super-sensitive, high-level Anglo-American dialogue conducted through intelligence channels.'

She takes a breath, closes her eyes again, opens them and fixes her gaze on mine.

'According to Shannon, what he read was clear proof of an Anglo-American covert operation already in the planning stage with the dual aim of undermining the social democratic institutions of the European Union and dismantling our international trading tariffs.' She takes another deep breath and continues. 'In the post-Brexit era Britain will be desperate for increased trade with America. America will accommodate Britain's needs, but only on terms. One such term will be a joint covert operation to obtain by persuasion – bribery and blackmail not excluded – officials, parliamentarians and opinion-makers of the European Establishment. Also to disseminate fake news on a large scale in order to aggravate existing differences between member states of the Union.'

'Are you quoting Shannon, by any chance?'

'I am quoting near enough what he claimed was the introductory foreword to the Jericho document. He claimed to have memorized three hundred words of it. I wrote them down. At first I didn't believe him.'

'Do you now?'

'Yes I do. So did my Service. So did my government. It seems we possess collateral intelligence that supports his story. Not all Americans are Europhobes. Not all Brits are passionate for a trade alliance with Trump's America at any price.'

'But you turned him down nevertheless.'

'My government prefers to believe that the United Kingdom will one day resume her place in the European family and for this reason is unwilling to engage in spying activities against a friendly nation. We thank you for your offer, Mr Shannon, but regret that on those grounds it is unacceptable.'

'And that's what you said to him.'

'That is what I was instructed to say to him, so it is what I said to him.'

'In German?'

'Actually in English. His German is not as good as he would wish it to be.'

Which was why Valentina spoke English and not German

to him, I reflect, thus incidentally solving a problem that had been niggling at me all night.

'Did you ask him about his motives?' I enquire.

'Of course I asked him. He quoted Goethe's *Faust* at me. In the beginning was the deed. I asked him whether he had accomplices, he quoted Rilke at me: *Ich bin der Eine.*'

'Meaning what?'

'That he is the *one*. Maybe the lonely one. Or the only one. Maybe both. Ask Rilke. I looked up the quote and couldn't find it.'

'Was that at your first meeting or your second?'

'At our second meeting he was angry with me. We don't weep in our profession, but I was tempted. Will you arrest him?'

A Bryn aphorism comes swimming back at me:

'As we say in the business, he's too good to arrest.'

Her gaze returns to the parched hillside.

'Thank you for coming to our rescue, Nat,' she says at last, as if waking to my presence. 'I regret that we cannot return the favour. I think you should go home to Prue now.'

19

God alone knows what kind of response I was expecting from Ed as he ambled into the dressing room for our fifteenth badminton session at the Athleticus, but surely not the cheery grin and 'Hi, Nat, good weekend, then?' that I received. Traitors who have hours ago crossed their personal Rubicon and know there's no way back do not in my experience radiate sweet contentment. The exultation that comes from believing you are the centre of the universe is more often followed by a plunge into feelings of fear, self-recrimination and profoundest solitude: for who in the world can you trust from now on except the enemy?

And even Ed might have woken by now to the realization that the perfectionist Anette was not necessarily the most reliable of all-weather friends, even if her admiration for Jericho was unbounded. Has he woken to anything else about her, such as the occasional insecurity of her German–English pronunciation as it slid involuntarily into Georgian-flavoured Russian and hastily returned? Her exaggerated German manner, a little too stereotyped, too *yesterday*? Watching him scramble out of his day clothes I look in vain for any indication that could belie my first impression: no darkening of the features when he thinks I'm not looking, no uncertainty in his gestures, none in his voice.

'My weekend was fine, thank you,' I tell him. 'Yours too?'

'Great, Nat, yeah, *really* great,' he assures me.

And since from day one he has never to my knowledge feigned his emotions in the least degree, I can only assume that the initial euphoria of his treachery has yet to wear off and – given he believes he is furthering the greater cause of Britain in Europe rather than betraying it – that he is every bit as pleased with himself as he appears to be.

We progress to court one, Ed stalking ahead, swinging his racquet and chortling to himself. We toss a shuttle for serve. It points to Ed's side of the net. Perhaps one day my Maker will explain to me how it came about that, ever since that black Monday evening when Ed launched himself on his unbroken run of victories, he has won the toss every bloody time.

But I refuse to be daunted. I may not be in the best shape. By *force majeure*, I have been missing my morning runs and my workouts in the gym. But today, for reasons too complex to separate, I have taken it upon myself to beat him if it kills me.

We reach two games all. Ed is showing every sign of entering one of his twilight phases when for a couple of rallies winning won't matter to him. If I can keep him fed with high lobs to the back line he'll begin smashing erratically. I feed him a high lob. But instead of smashing it into the net as I have every right to anticipate, he tosses his racquet in the air, catches it and announces with debonnaire assurance:

'That's it, thanks, Nat. We're both winners today. And thanks for something else while we're about it.'

For *something else*? Such as accidentally exposing him as a bloody Russian spy? Ducking under the net he claps a hand on my shoulder – a first – and marches me through the bar to our *Stammtisch* where he commands me to sit. He returns with two frosted pints of Carlsberg lager, olives, cashews and crisps. He sits down opposite me, passes me my glass, raises his own and delivers a prepared speech in a voice resonant with his northern roots:

'Nat, I have something to tell you of major importance to me and I hope to you. I'm about to get married to a wonderful woman and without you I'd never have met her. So I'm really truly grateful to you, not only for some highly diverting badminton over the past months, but for introducing me to the woman of my dreams. So really, really grateful. Yeah.'

Long before the 'yeah', I had heard it all. There was only one wonderful woman I had introduced him to, and according to the ramshackle cover story that Florence in her fury had resisted sharing, I had met her on precisely two occasions: the first being when I walked into the office of my fictional friend the commodities trader and she was his high-class temporary secretary, and the second when she informed me that she didn't feel like fucking lying any more. Has she in the meantime told her fiancé that his cherished badminton partner is a veteran professional spy? If the uncluttered sweetness of his smile as we raise our glasses to each other is any guide, she hasn't.

'Ed, this is indeed absolutely splendid news,' I protest, 'but who *is* this wonderful woman?'

Will he tell me I'm a liar and a fraud because he knows bloody well that Florence and I worked cheek by jowl for the better part of six months? Or will he do what he now does, which is bestow a conjuror's artful grin on me, pull her name out of his hat and dazzle me with it?

'Do you happen to remember *Florence* by any chance?'

I try. Florence? *Florence?* Give me a moment. Must be age. Shake of the head. Can't get there, I'm afraid.

'The girl we played *badminton* with, for Christ's sake, Nat,' he bursts out. 'Right *here*. With Laura. Court three. *You* remember! She was temping for your business pal and you brought her along to make a fourth.'

Allow memory to dawn.

'Of course! *That* Florence. A really super girl. My hearty congratulations. How could I be so stupid? My dear man—'

As we grasp hands, I grapple with two more irreconcilable pieces of intelligence. Florence has stuck to her Office vows, at least so far as I'm concerned. And Ed, an identified Russian spy, proposes to marry a recently employed member of my Service, thereby multiplying to infinity the opportunity for national scandal. But these are just scattered thoughts wafting through my head as he lays out his plans for 'a quick Register Office job, no bullshit'.

'I called Mum and she was *magic*,' he confides, leaning forward over his beer and grabbing my forearm in his enthusiasm. 'She's into Jesus in a pretty big way, Mum is, same as Laura, always has been. And I *thought* she'd say, you know, if Jesus isn't going to be at the wedding it's a washout.'

I'm hearing Bryn Jordan: *sat in a church for twenty minutes . . . low . . . no silver.*

'Only Mum can't travel, not easily,' he is explaining. 'Not at short notice. Not with her leg and Laura. So what she said was: do it the way you both like. Then when you're ready, not before, we'll do it the proper way in church and have a big spread and everyone can come round. She thinks Florence is the cat's whiskers – who wouldn't? – same as Laura does. So we're all fixed for this Friday, as ever is, twelve o'clock prompt at the Register Office in Holborn because there's a queue, specially with the weekend coming up. They reckon fifteen minutes maximum to do you, then it's next couple in and round to the pub, if that's all right with you and Prue at short notice, her being a busy hotshot lawyer.'

I am smiling the benign paternal smile that drives Steff round the bend. I have not withdrawn my forearm from his grasp. I give myself time to catch up with the astounding news.

'So you're inviting Prue and me to your wedding, Ed,' I

confirm with appropriately solemn awe. 'You and Florence. We're extremely honoured, is all I can say. I know Prue will feel the same. She's heard so much about you.'

I am still trying to come to terms with this momentous piece of news when he delivers the *coup de grâce*:

'Yeah, well, I thought while you're about it you could – well – sort of be my best man kind of thing, too. If that's all right,' he adds, giving way to his enormous grin, which like his newfound need to grab hold of me at every opportunity has become something of a fixture during this exchange.

Look away. Look down. Clear your head. Lift it. Smile spontaneous disbelief:

'Well of course it's *more* than all right, Ed. But surely you must have someone closer to your own age? An old schoolfriend? Someone from your university?'

He thinks about this, shrugs, shakes his head, grins sheepishly. 'Not really,' he says, by which time I'm at a loss to know the difference between what I feel and what I'm pretending to feel. I recover my forearm and we do another manly handshake, English-style.

'And if it's all right with Prue, we thought she could be the *witness*, because somebody's got to be,' he goes on relentlessly, as if my cup was not by now overflowing. 'They've got one for hire at the Register Office if you're pushed, but we reckoned Prue would be better at it. Only she's a lawyer, isn't she? She'll make it all legal and shipshape.'

'She will indeed, Ed. Just as long as she can get away from her work,' I add cautiously.

'Plus, if it's all right by you I've booked the three of us at the Chinese at eight-thirty,' he goes on, just when I think I've heard everything.

'*Tonight?*' I ask.

'If that's all right,' he says, and peers myopically at the clock behind the bar which is ten minutes fast and reads eight-fifteen. 'Just sorry Prue can't make it,' he adds thoughtfully. 'Florence was really looking forward to meeting her. Still is. Yeah.'

As it happens, Prue has for once cancelled her appointments with *pro bono* clients and is sitting at home waiting for the outcome of this evening's encounter. But for the time being I prefer to keep that knowledge to myself, because by now Operational Man is taking back control.

'Florence is looking forward to meeting *you* too, Nat,' he adds, lest my nose should be out of joint. 'Properly. You being my best man and that. Plus all the games we've had.'

'And I look forward to meeting *her* properly too,' I say, and excuse myself while I pop into the men's room.

On my way I spot a table of two women and two men talking energetically among themselves as I pass. If I am not mistaken, the taller of the two women was last seen pushing a pram on Ground Beta. Amid a hubbub of male voices from the changing-room shower area, I acquaint Prue with the good news in suitably sanitized tones and advise her of my immediate plan of action: to bring them up to the house as soon as we've finished our Chinese meal. Her voice does not alter. She wishes to know whether there is anything in particular that I require of her. I say I shall need a quarter of an hour in my den to make my promised phone call to Steff. She says yes of course, darling, she'll hold the fort, and is there anything else? Nothing I can think of at this moment, I say. I have just taken my first irrevocable step in a plan that, if I am not mistaken, had its unacknowledged genesis in what Bryn would call my other head ever since I sat down with him, and probably before; since the seeds of sedition, according to our in-house shrinks, are sown a great deal earlier than the outward act that results from them.

This said, in my own memory of the short conversation with

Prue that I have just described, I am objectivity itself. In Prue's, I am on the verge of losing it. What is not in doubt is that, immediately upon hearing my voice, she recognized that we were in operational mode and that, although I am never allowed to say it, she remains a great loss to the Office.

*

The Golden Moon is delighted to have us. The Chinese owner-manager is a lifetime member of the Athleticus. He is impressed that Ed is my regular opponent. Florence arrives on time in charming disarray and is at once a hit with the waiters, who remember her from her last visit. She has come straight from coping with builders, and has the paint marks on her jeans to prove it.

By any rational standard I should by now be at my wits' end, but even before we sit down my two most pressing anxieties are laid to rest. Florence has elected to remain loyal to our unlikely cover story: witness our friendly but detached well-hullo-agains. My invitation to a post-prandial coffee with Prue, on which my entire planning rests, meets with hearty exclamations of approval by the bridal couple. All I have to do is whistle up a bottle of spumante in their honour – the best the house can do in the way of champagne – and josh along with them until I can get them up to the house and sneak up alone to my den.

I ask them, as well I might, given that it seems like only yesterday that I introduced the young sweethearts to each other, whether it had been love at first sight. Both were puzzled by my question, not because they couldn't answer it but because they regarded it as gratuitous. Well, there'd been the badminton foursome, hadn't there? – as if that already explained everything, which it scarcely did, since my one abiding memory of that event was of Florence in a fury fit with me after resigning from the Office. Then there was the Chinese dinner that I missed out on – 'at this same table where we're sitting now, right, Flo?' says Ed proudly – and so they are, chopsticks in one hand and caresses with the other. 'And from there on – well, it was pretty much a done thing, wasn't it, Flo?'

Is this really *Flo* I am hearing? *Never call her Flo* – unless you happen to be the man of her life? Their wedding chatter and inability to leave each other alone awaken echoes of Steff and Juno over Sunday lunch. I tell them Steff is engaged to be married and they dissolve in symbiotic merriment. I give them the benefit of what is by now my party piece about giant bats on Barro Colorado. My one problem is that each time Ed joins the conversation, I find myself comparing the cheery love-smitten voice I'm hearing with the grudging version of it that Valentina aka Anette aka Gamma had to put up with three nights previously.

Affecting to have difficulties getting a signal on my mobile, I step into the street and make a second call to Prue, adopting the same airy tone. A white van is parked across the road.

'What's the problem now?' she asks.

'None really. Just checking,' I reply, and feel stupid.

I return to our table and confirm that Prue is back from her law shop and agog to receive us. My announcement is overheard by a male couple at the next table, both slow eaters. Mindful of their tradecraft they keep masticating as we leave.

It is bluntly stated in my personal file at Head Office that while I am capable of first-rate operational thinking on my feet, the same cannot always be said of my paperwork. As the three of us perambulate arm in arm the few hundred yards to my house – Ed, the better for a half-bottle of spumante and insisting that as his best man I suffer the clutch of his bony left hand – it occurs to me that while I may have been doing some first-rate operational thinking, all will now depend on the quality of my paperwork.

*

I have been sparing till now in my portrayal of Prue, but only because I was waiting for the clouds of our enforced estrangement to blow over and our regard for each other to emerge in its rightful colours, which thanks to Prue's life-saving policy statement on the morning following my inquisition by my *chers collègues* it has now done.

If our marriage is not generally understood, neither is Prue. Outspoken, left-leaning lawyer to the poor and oppressed; intrepid champion of class actions; Battersea Bolshevik; none of the easy tag-lines that follow her around does justice to the Prue I know. For all her blue-chip background, she is self-made. Her father the judge was a bastard who hated competition in his children, made life hell for them and refused to support Prue at university or law school. Her mother died of alcohol. Her brother went to the devil. Her humanity and good sense need no underlining as far as I am concerned, but for others, particularly my *chers collègues*, sometimes they do.

*

The ecstatic greetings are over. The four of us are installed in the sunroom of our house in Battersea, talking happy banalities. Prue and Ed have the sofa. Prue has opened the doors to the garden to let in whatever breeze is around. She has set out candles and unearthed a box of fancy chocolates from her gift drawer for the bride and groom to be. She has rustled up a bottle of old Armagnac I didn't know we possessed, and made coffee in the big picnic Thermos. But there is something that, amid all the fun, she needs to get off her mind:

'Nat, darling, forgive me, but *please* don't forget you and Steff have that bit of urgent business to discuss. I think you said nine o'clock' – which is my cue to look at my watch, leap to my feet and, with a hasty 'thank God you reminded me, back in two shakes', hasten upstairs to my den.

Taking from the wall a framed photograph of my late father in ceremonial drag, I place him face upward on my desk, extract a wad of writing paper from a drawer and lay it one sheet at a time on the glass surface in order to leave no imprint. It does not occur to me until later that I am observing ancient Office practice while setting out to break every rule in the Office book.

I write first a summary of the intelligence so far available against Ed. I then set out ten field instructions, one clear paragraph at a time, no bloody adverbs as Florence would say. I top the document with her former Office symbol and tail it with my own. I re-read what I have written, find no fault with it, fold the page twice, insert it in a plain brown envelope and write *Invoice for Mrs. Florence Shannon* on it in an uneducated hand.

I return to the sunroom to discover I am redundant. Prue has already cast Florence as her fellow escapee from the Office's grasp, albeit an undeclared one, and therefore a woman with whom she has an immediate if unspecified rapport. The topic of the moment is builders. Florence, nursing a stiff glass of old Armagnac despite her professed addiction to red burgundy, is holding the floor while Ed dozes next to her on the sofa and periodically opens his eyes to adore her.

'I mean *honestly*, Prue, dealing with Polish masons and Bulgarian carpenters and a Scottish foreman, I'm thinking, give me bloody *subtitles*!' Florence announces to hoots of her own laughter.

She needs a pee. Prue shows her the way. Ed watches them out of the room, then bows his head over his knees, puts his hands between them and lapses into one of his reveries. Florence's leather jacket hangs over the back of a chair. Unnoticed by Ed, I pick it up, take it to the hall, slip my brown envelope into the right-hand pocket and hang it beside the front door. Florence and Prue return. Florence notices her jacket is missing and glances at me questioningly. Ed still has his head down.

'Oh. Your jacket,' I say. 'I had a sudden fear you would forget it. There was something jutting out of the pocket. It looked horribly like a bill.'

'Oh shit,' she replies with scarcely a blink. 'Probably the Polish electrician.'

Message received.

Prue delivers herself of a capsule account of her running battle with the barons of Big Pharma. Florence responds with a vigorous 'They're the worst of the worst. Fuck them all.' Ed is half asleep. I suggest it's time for all good children to go to bed. Florence agrees. They live the other side of London, she tells us, as if I didn't know: one mile as the bicycle rides from Ground Beta, to be precise, but she doesn't say that part. Perhaps she doesn't know. Using my family mobile, I order an Uber. It arrives with eerie haste. I help Florence into her leather jacket. Their departure, after the many thank-yous, is mercifully swift.

'Really, really great, Prue,' says Florence.

'Fab,' Ed agrees through a fog of sleep, spumante and old Armagnac.

We stand on the doorstep waving at their departing car. We keep waving till it's out of sight. Prue takes my arm. How about a stroll in the park on this perfect summer's night?

★

There's a bench on the northern edge of the park that is set back from the footpath on its own bit of space between the river and a clump of willow trees. Prue and I call it *our bench* and it's where we like to sit and roost after a dinner party if the weather's right and we've got rid of our guests at a reasonable hour. It's my memory that, by some leftover instinct from our Moscow days, we didn't exchange one compromising word until were sitting on it, our voices drowned by the clatter of the river and the grumble of the night city.

'Do you reckon it's real?' I ask her after a lengthy silence between us that I am the first to break.

'You mean the two of them together?'

Prue, normally so cautious in her judgements, has no doubt on the matter.

'They were a pair of drifting corks and now they've found each other,' she declares in her forthright way. 'That's Florence's view and I'm happy to share it. They were cut from the same cork tree at birth and for as long she believes that they're fine because he'll believe whatever she does. She hopes she's pregnant, but isn't sure. So whatever you've been cooking up for Ed, just remember we'll be doing it for all three of them.'

*

Prue and I may diverge about which of us thought what or said what in the murmured exchange that followed, but I remember very clearly how our two voices sank to Moscow level as if we were sitting on a bench in Gorky Central Park of Culture and Leisure rather than Battersea. I told her everything that Bryn had told me, everything that Reni had told me, and she listened without comment. I scarcely bothered with Valentina and the saga of Ed's unmasking, since that was already in the far past. The issue, as so often with operational planning, was how to use the enemy's resources against him, although I was less eager than Prue to define the Office as enemy.

And I remember that I was filled with simple gratitude, as we embarked on the fine-tuning of what gradually became our master plan, for the way our thoughts and words merged into a single flow where ownership became irrelevant. But Prue, for all the best reasons, doesn't want to hear that. She points to the preparatory steps I had already taken, citing my all-important handwritten letter of instructions to Florence. In her version I am the driving force and she is trailing in my slipstream: just anything, as far as she's concerned, rather than concede that the Office spouse of her youth and the lawyer of her maturity are even distantly related.

What is certain is that by the time I stood up from our bench and strode a few yards along the river path while careful to remain within Prue's hearing, and touched the key for Bryn Jordan on the doctored mobile he had given me, Prue and I were, as she would have it, in full and frank agreement on all matters of substance.

*

Bryn had warned me that he might be on his way between London and Washington, but the background clamour I am hearing in the earpiece tells me that he is on terra firma, has people round him, mostly men, and they're American. My presumption therefore is that he is in Washington DC and I am interrupting a meeting, which means that with any luck I may not have his full attention.

'Yes, Nat. How are we?' – the habitually kindly tone, tinged with impatience.

'Ed's getting himself married, Bryn,' I inform him flatly. 'On Friday. To my former number two at the Haven. The woman we talked about. Florence. At a Register Office in Holborn. They left our house a few moments ago.'

He offers no surprise. He knows already. He knows more than I do. When didn't he? But I am not his to command any more. I'm my own man. He needs me more than I need him. So remember it.

'He wants me to be his best man, if you can believe it,' I add.

'And you accepted?'

'What do you expect me to do?'

Offstage burbles while he dispatches some pressing matter. 'You had a full hour alone with him at the Club,' Bryn reminds me testily. 'Why the hell didn't you go for him?'

'How was I supposed to do that?'

'Tell him that before you accept the job of best man, there are a couple of things he ought to know about himself, and take it from there. I've a bloody good mind to give the job to Guy. He won't piss about.'

'Bryn, will you listen to me please? The wedding is four days away. Shannon's on a different planet. It isn't a question of who approaches him. It's a question of whether we approach him now or wait till he's got himself married.'

I too am being testy. I'm a free man. From our bench five yards along the river path, Prue awards me a silent nod of approval.

'Shannon's as high as a flute, Bryn. If I make a pass at him now, he'll tell me to get lost and to hell with the consequences. Bryn?'

'Wait!'

I wait.

'You listening?'

Yes, Bryn.

'I am *not* allowing Shannon to make another treff with Gamma or anyone else until we own him. Got that?'

260

Treff for clandestine encounter. German spy jargon. And Bryn's.

'And I am seriously supposed to *tell* him that?' I retort indignantly.

'You're supposed to get on with the fucking job and not waste any more time,' he snaps back as the temperature between us rises.

'I'm telling you, Bryn. He's totally unmanageable in his present mood. Period. I'm not going there till he comes down to earth.'

'Then where the hell *are* you going?'

'Let me talk to his bride, Florence. She's the only viable route to him.'

'She'll tip him off.'

'She's Office-trained and she worked for me. She's savvy and she knows the odds. If I spell out the situation to her, she'll spell it out to Shannon.'

Background grumble before he comes back hard.

'Is she *conscious*? The girl. To what her man's up to.'

'I'm not sure it matters what she is, Bryn. Not once I've spelt out the position to her. If she's complicit, she'll know she's for the high jump too.'

His voice eases slightly.

'How do you propose to approach her?'

'I'll invite her to lunch.'

More off-stage clatter. Then a vehement comeback: 'You'll *what*?'

'She's a grown-up, Bryn. She doesn't do hysterics and she likes fish.'

Voices off, but Bryn's not among them.

Finally: 'Where will you take her, for Christ's sake?'

'The same place I took her before.' Time to pull a bit more temperament. 'Look, Bryn, if you don't like what I'm suggesting, fine by me, give the bloody job to Guy. Or come back and do it yourself.'

From our bench, Prue is drawing a finger across her throat as a signal to hang up, but Bryn, with a terse 'Report back to me the moment you've spoken to her,' has beaten me to it.

Heads down, arm in arm, we stroll back to the house.

'I think she may have an *inkling*, all the same,' Prue reflects. 'She may not *know* a lot, but she knows quite enough to worry her.'

'Well, she'll have more than an inkling now,' I reply brutally, as I picture Florence hunched alone amid the builders' debris of their flat in Hoxton, reading my ten-point letter while Ed sleeps the sleep of the just.

20

It didn't surprise me – I would have been a lot more surprised if it hadn't been the case – that I had never seen Florence's face so taut or so devoid of expression: not even when she was sitting across the table from me in this same restaurant reciting the charge sheet against Dom Trench and his charitable baroness.

As to my own face, reflected in the many mirrors, well: operational deadpan best describes it.

The restaurant is L-shaped. In the smaller section there is a bar with padded benches for guests who have been told their tables aren't quite ready, so why not sit and drink champagne at twelve quid a flute. And that's what I am doing now, as I wait for Florence to make her entry. But I am not the only one who is waiting for her. Gone the sleepy-wasp waiters. Today's crew are obliging to a fault, beginning with the maître d'hôtel who can't wait to show me the table I have reserved, or to enquire whether I or Madame will be having any dietary requirements or special needs. Our table is not in the window as I had requested – unfortunately all our window tables were long taken, sir – but he dares to hope that this quiet corner will be acceptable to me. He might have added 'and acceptable to Percy Price's microphones' because according to Percy your windows, when there's heavy background chatter to contend with, can play the very devil with your reception.

But not even Percy's wizards can cover every nook and corner of a crowded bar, hence the maître d's next question of me, couched in the prophetic tense beloved of his trade:

'And will we be thinking come straight to our table and enjoy our aperitif in peace and quiet, or will we be taking our chances at the bar, which *can* get a bit too lively for some?'

Lively being precisely what I need and Percy's microphones don't, I opt for taking our chances at the bar. I choose a plush sofa for two and order a large glass of red burgundy in addition to my twelve-pound flute of champagne. A group of diners enters, as like as not supplied by Percy. Florence must have attached herself to them because the first thing I know she is sitting beside me with scarcely an acknowledgement. I indicate her glass of red burgundy. She shakes her head. I order water with ice and lemon. In place of Office fatigues, she wears her smart trouser suit. In place of the scruffy silver ring on her wedding finger, nothing.

For my part, I am sporting a navy-blue blazer and grey flannels. In the right pocket of my blazer I am carrying a lipstick in a cylindrical brass holder. It is of Japanese manufacture and Prue's one indulgence. Cut away the bottom half of the lipstick and you have a cavity deep and wide enough to accommodate a generous strip of microfilm or, in my case, a handwritten message on pared-down typing paper.

Florence's demeanour is faux-casual, precisely as it should be. I have invited her to lunch, but my tone was cryptic and in the legend she has yet to learn why: am I inviting her in my capacity as her future husband's best man, or as her former superior? We trade banalities. She is polite, but on her guard. Keeping my voice below the hubbub, I advance to the matter in hand:

'Question one,' I say.

She takes a breath and tilts her head so close to mine that I feel the prickle of her hair.

'Yes, I still want to marry him.'

'Next question?'

'Yes, I told him to do it, but I didn't know what it was.'

'But you encouraged him,' I suggest.

'He said there was something he'd got to do to stop an anti-European conspiracy but it was against regulations.'

'And you?'

'If he felt it, do it and fuck regulations.'

Ignoring my questions, she plunges straight on.

'After he'd done it – that was Friday – he came home and wept and wouldn't say why. I told him that whatever he'd done was all right if he believed in it. He said he believed in it. I said, well you're all right then, aren't you?'

Forgetting her earlier resolve, she takes a pull of her burgundy.

'And if he found out who he's been dealing with?' I prompt.

'He'd turn himself in or kill himself. Is that what you want to hear?'

'It's information.'

Her voice starts to rise. She brings it down.

'He can't lie, Nat. The truth is all he knows. He'd be useless as a double even if he agreed to do it, which he never would.'

'And your wedding plans?' I prompt her again.

'I've invited the whole world and its brother to join us in the pub afterwards, as per your instructions. Ed thinks I'm insane.'

'Where are you going for your honeymoon?'

'We're not.'

'Book a hotel in Torquay as soon as you get home. The Imperial or equivalent. The bridal suite. Two nights. If they want a deposit, pay it. Now find a reason to open your handbag and put it between us.'

She opens her handbag, extracts a tissue, dabs her eye, carelessly leaves the handbag open between us. I take a sip of my champagne and, with my left arm across my body, drop in Prue's lipstick.

'The moment we're in the dining room we're on air,' I tell her. 'The table's wired and the restaurant is crammed with Percy's people. Be as bloody difficult as you always were, then some. Understood?'

Distant nod.

'Say it.'

'*Understood, for fuck's sake,*' she hisses back at me.

The maître d' is waiting for us. We settle to our nice corner table opposite each other. The maître d' assures me I have the best view in the room. Percy must have sent him to charm school. The same enormous menus. I insist we have hors d'oeuvres. Florence demurs. I urge smoked salmon on her and she says all right. We agree on turbot for our main course.

'So it's both the same for us today, sir,' the maître d' exclaims, as if that makes a change from all the other days.

Until now she has managed not to look at me. Now she does.

'Do you mind telling me why the *fuck* you dragged me here?' she demands into my face.

'Very willingly,' I reply in similarly clenched tones. 'The man you are living with and apparently wish to marry has been identified by the Service you once belonged to as a willing asset of Russian intelligence. But perhaps that isn't news to you? Or is it?'

Curtain up. We're on. Shades of Prue and myself faking it for the microphones in Moscow.

*

They had told me at the Haven that Florence had a temper on her but until now I'd only seen it in action on the badminton court. Ask me whether it was real or simulated, I can only reply

266

that she was a natural. This was improvisation on the grand scale: ad lib as art, inspired, spontaneous, merciless.

First she hears me out in deathly stillness, face rigid. I tell her we have unchallengeable visual and aural evidence of Ed's betrayal. I tell her she's welcome to a private view of the footage, a straight lie. I say we have every good reason to believe that by the time she crashed out of the Office she was consumed with hatred for Britain's political elite and it therefore comes as no surprise to me to learn that she has bonded with an embittered loner on a vengeance jag who is offering our hottest secrets to the Russians. I tell her that despite this act of supreme folly or worse I am authorized to offer her a lifeline:

'You first explain to Ed in simple English that he's blown sky-high. You tell him we have cast-iron proof, cooked all ways. You inform him that his own Service is thirsting for his blood, but there's a path to salvation open to him if he agrees to collaborate unreservedly. And in case he doubts it, the alternative to collaboration is prison for a very long time.'

All this quietly spoken, you understand, no dramatics, interrupted once only by the arrival of the smoked salmon. I can tell by her continuing stillness that she is working herself into a froth of righteous anger, but nothing I have seen or heard of her till now prepares me for the scale of the detonation. Ignoring entirely the unequivocal message I have just delivered, she launches a full-frontal assault on its messenger: me.

I think that just because I'm a spy I'm one of God's anointed, the navel of the fucking universe, whereas all I am is another over-controlled public-school wanker. I am a *badminton trawler*. Badminton is how I pull pretty boys. I got the hots for Ed and now I've set him up as a Russian spy because he refused my advances.

Tearing blindly into me like this, she is a wounded animal, a feral protector of her man and her unborn child. If she had spent the whole night dredging up every dark thought she ever had about me, she couldn't have done a better job.

After a needless intervention by the maître d' who insists on knowing that everything is satisfactory, she returns to the charge. Taking a lead straight out of the trainers' manual, she gives me her first tactical fallback:

All right, let's just *suppose* – for argument's sake – that Ed *has* got his loyalties in a twist. Let's suppose he went binge drinking one night and the Russians did a *kompromat* job on him. And that Ed went along with it, which he never would in a thousand years, but let's suppose all the same. Do I then *really* imagine that *on no terms at all* he's going to sign up as a *fucking double agent* in the full knowledge that he will be dropped down a hole any time we feel like it? So in a nutshell, kindly tell her, if I can, what sort of *guarantees* is *my Office* going to offer a double agent without a prayer to his name who's about to put his head in the fucking lion's mouth?

And when I reply that Ed is in no sort of position to bargain and he must either take us on trust or accept the consequences, I am only spared another onslaught by the arrival of the turbot, which she attacks in short, indignant stabs while calculating her second tactical fallback:

'Suppose he *does* work for you,' she concedes in an only slightly more emollient tone. 'Just suppose. Say I talk him into it, which I'd have to. And he screws up, or the Russians rumble him, whichever comes first. *Then* what? He's blown, he's used goods, fuck him, he's on the rubbish heap. Why should he go through all that shit? Why bother? Why not tell you all to take a running jump and just go to jail? Which is worse, finally? Being played by both sides like a fucking marionette and ending up dead in a back street, or paying his debt to society and coming out in one piece?'

Which I take as my cue to bring matters to a head:

'You're deliberately ignoring the scale of his crime and the mountain of hard evidence stacked against him,' I say in my most persuasive and finite tone. 'The rest is sheer speculation. Your husband-to-be is up to his neck in trouble, and we're offering you a chance to dig him out. It's a take-it-or-leave-it, I'm afraid.'

But this only sparks yet another scathing response:

'So you're judge and jury now, are you? Fuck the law courts! Fuck fair trials! Fuck *human rights* and whatever your civil society wife thinks she stands for!'

Only after prolonged thinking time on her part do I secure the grudging breakthrough that she's made me work so hard for. Yet even now she manages to preserve a semblance of dignity:

'I'm not conceding anything, right? Not a bloody thing.'

'Go on.'

'*If*, and only if, Ed says: all right, I got it wrong, I love my country, I'll collaborate, I'll be a double, I'll take the risk. I said *if*. Does he get his amnesty or not?'

I play it long. Promise nothing you can't take back. A Bryn aphorism.

'If he's earned it, and we *decide* he's earned it, and if the Home Secretary signs off on it: yes, in all probability he gets his amnesty.'

'*Then* what? Does he risk his neck for free? Do I? How about a bit of risk money?'

We've done enough. She's spent, I'm spent. Time to call down the curtain.

'Florence, we've come a long way to meet you. We want unconditional compliance. Yours and Ed's. In return we offer expert handling and full support. Bryn needs a clear answer. *Now*. Not tomorrow. It's either a yes, Bryn, I will. Or it's no, Bryn, and accept the consequences. Which is it to be?'

'I need to marry Ed first,' she says, without lifting her head. 'Nothing before.'

'Before you tell him what we've just agreed?'

'Yes.'

'When will you tell him?'

'After Torquay.'

'*Torquay?*'

'Where we're going for our forty-eight-hour fucking honeymoon,' she snaps in an inspired resurgence of anger.

A shared silence, mutually orchestrated.

'Are we friends, Florence?' I ask. 'I think we are.'

I am holding out my hand to her. Still without raising her head she takes it, first hesitantly then clutches it for real as I secretly congratulate her on the performance of a lifetime.

21

The two and a half days of waiting might as well be a hundred and I remember every hour of them. Florence's taunts, however wide of the mark, had been drawn from life, and on the rare occasions when I ceased pondering the operational contingencies that lay ahead of us, her searing performance came back to accuse me of sins I hadn't committed, and quite a few that I had.

Not once since her declaration of solidarity had Prue given the smallest hint of relenting on her commitment. She expressed no pain about my tryst with Reni. She had long ago consigned matters of that sort to the unrecoverable past. When I ventured to remind her of the perils to her legal career she replied a little tartly she was well aware of them, thank you. When I asked her whether a British judge would draw any distinction between passing secrets to the Germans as opposed to the Russians she replied with a grim laugh that in the eyes of many of our dear judges the Germans were worse. And all the while the trained Office spouse in her that she continued to deny went about her covert duties with an efficiency I tactfully took for granted.

For her professional life she had retained her maiden name of Stoneway, and it was in this name that she instructed her assistant to book her a hire car. If the company required licence details, she would supply them when she collected the car.

At my request she twice called Florence, the first time to ask in womanly confidence which hotel the honeymoon couple would be staying at in Torquay because she was dying to send flowers and Nat was equally determined to send Ed a bottle of champagne. Florence said the Imperial as Mr and Mrs Shannon and Prue reported that she sounded focused, and was putting on a good turn as nervous bride-to-be for the benefit of Percy's listeners. Prue sent her flowers. I sent my bottle, each of us ordering online, trusting to the vigilance of Percy's team.

The second time Prue called Florence was to ask whether she could be of any help with organizing the knees-up at the pub after the wedding as her partnership's chambers were just down the road. Florence said she'd booked a big private room, it was okay but smelt of piss. Prue promised to take a look at it, although they agreed it was too late to change. Percy, are you listening there below?

Using Prue's laptop and credit card in preference to my own, we examined flights to various European destinations and noted that in the high holiday season Club Class on regular airlines was still largely available. Shaded by the apple tree, we ran through every last detail of our operational plan one more time. Had I neglected some vital move? Was it conceivable that after a lifetime devoted to stealth I was about to fall at the last fence? Prue said not. She had reviewed our dispositions and found no fault with them. So why don't I, instead of fretting uselessly, give Ed a ring and see if he has time for lunch? And with no further encouragement needed, that is what I do in my role of best man, just twenty-four hours before Ed is due to exchange vows with Florence.

I call Ed.

He is thrilled. What a great idea, Nat! Brilliant! He only gets an hour, but maybe he can stretch it. How about the Dog & Goat saloon bar, be there sharp at one?

The Dog & Goat it is, I say. See you there. Thirteen hundred hours sharp.

*

A dense cluster of civil service suits is packed into the saloon bar of the Dog & Goat that day, not surprisingly since it lies five hundred imperial yards from Downing Street, the Foreign Office and the Treasury. And a good few of the suits are around Ed's age, so it somehow doesn't seem right to me, as he wades towards me through the scrum on the eve of his wedding day, that hardly a head turns to acknowledge him.

There is no *Stammtisch* available, but Ed uses his height and elbows to good effect and soon liberates a couple of bar stools from the mêlée. And somehow I fight my way to the front line and buy us a couple of pints of draught lager, not frosted but near enough, and a couple of ploughman's lunches with Cheddar and pickled onions and crisp bread, handed along the bar in a fireman's chain.

With these essentials we succeed in improvising a watcher's corner of sorts for ourselves, and bellow at each other above the din. I only hope that Percy's people are managing to get an ear in, because everything Ed says is balm to my frayed nerves:

'She's gone completely and totally off the *wall*, Nat! Flo has! Invited all her posh mates to the pub afterwards! Kids and all! *And* booked us a bloody great *hotel* in Torquay with a *swimming pool and massage parlour*! Know what?'

'What?'

'We're skint, Nat! Clean broke! It's all gone on builders! Yeah! We'll have to do the washing-up on the morning after our wedding night!'

Suddenly it's time for him to go back to whatever dark Whitehall hole they've put him in. The bar empties as if on command and we're standing in the relative quiet of the pavement with only Whitehall traffic thundering by.

'I was going to have a bachelor night,' Ed says awkwardly. 'You and me kind of thing. Flo put the kibosh on it, says it's all male bullshit.'

'Florence is right.'

'I took the ring off her,' he says. 'Told her I'd give it her back when she's my wife.'

'Good idea.'

'I'm keeping it on me so I don't forget.'

'You don't want me to look after it till tomorrow?'

'Not really. Great badminton, Nat. Best ever.'

'And a whole lot more when you come back from Torquay.'

'Be great. Yeah. See you tomorrow then.'

On Whitehall's pavements you don't embrace, though I suspect it's in his mind. Instead he makes do with a double handshake, grabbing my right hand in both of his and pumping it up and down.

*

Somehow the hours have slipped by. It's early evening. Prue and I are back under the apple tree, she at her iPad, I with an ecological book Steff wants me to read about the forthcoming apocalypse. I have draped my jacket over the back of my chair and I must have entered some kind of reverie because it takes me a moment to realize that the squawk I'm hearing is coming from Bryn Jordan's doctored smartphone. But for once I'm too slow. Prue has fished it out of my jacket and put it to her ear:

'No, Bryn. His wife,' she says briskly. 'A voice from the past. How are you? Good. And the family? Good. He's in bed, I'm afraid, not feeling his brightest. The whole of Battersea is going down with it in droves. Can I help? Well, that will make him feel *much* better, I'm sure. I'll tell him the moment he wakes up. And to you, Bryn. No, not yet but the post here is haywire. I'm sure we shall come if we possibly can. How very clever of her. I tried oils once but they weren't a success. And goodnight to you, Bryn, wherever you are.'

She rings off.

'He sends his congratulations,' she says. 'And an invitation to Ah Chan's art exhibition in Cork Street. I somehow think we shan't make it.'

*

It's morning. It has been morning for a long time: morning in the hill forests of Karlovy Vary, morning on a rain-drenched Yorkshire hilltop, on Ground Beta and the twin screens in the Operations room; morning on Primrose Hill, in the Haven, on court number one at the Athleticus. I have made the tea and squeezed the orange juice and come back to bed: our best time for taking the decisions we couldn't take yesterday, or discovering what we'll do at the weekend or where we'll go on holiday.

But today we're talking solely about what we'll be wearing for the great event, and what fun it will be, and what a stroke of genius on my part to suggest Torquay because the children seem *quite* incapable of taking *any* practical decisions of their *own* – children being our new shorthand for Ed and Florence, and our conversation being a precautionary return to our Moscow days, because the one thing you know about Percy Price is, friendship comes second when there's a telephone extension right beside your bed.

Until yesterday afternoon I had assumed that all weddings took place at ground level, but I was abruptly corrected on the point when, on my way back from the Dog & Goat, I undertook a discreet photographic reconnaissance of our target area and confirmed that the Register Office of Ed's and Florence's choice was on the fifth floor, and the only reason it had a slot at such short notice was that it boasted eight arduous flights of cold stone staircase before you reached the reception desk, and another half-flight before you entered a cavernous arched waiting room got up like a theatre with no stage, with soft music playing and plush seats and a sea of uneasy people in groups, and a shiny black-lacquered door at the far end marked 'Weddings Only'. There was one minuscule lift, with priority given to the disabled.

I also established in the course of the same reconnaissance that the third floor, which was leased in its entirety to a firm of chartered accountants, gave on to an overhead Venice-style footbridge leading to a similar building across the street; and better still, to a lighthouse-style stairwell that descended all the way to an underground car park. From the insanitary depths of the car park, the staircase was accessible to anyone fool enough to want to climb up it. But to those wishing to descend it by way of the footbridge on the third floor, access was denied to all but certified residents of the block, see the lurid 'NO ENTRY TO PUBLIC' sign plastered across a pair of solid, electronically controlled doors. The chartered accountant's brass plate named six partners. The one at the top was a Mr M. Bailey.

The next morning, in near silence, Prue and I dressed.

*

I will report the events as I would any special operation. We arrive by design early, at 11.15 a.m. On our way up the stone staircase we pause at the third floor, while Prue stands smiling in her flowered hat and I engage the woman receptionist of the firm of chartered accountants in casual conversation. No, she says in answer to my question, her employers do not close their doors early on a Friday. I inform her that I am an old client of

Mr Bailey. She says robotically that he is in meetings all morning. I say we are old school friends, but not to disturb him, and I will make a formal appointment for next week some time. I hand her a printed name card left over from my last posting: *Commercial Counsellor, H.M. Embassy, Tallinn*, and wait till she consents to read it.

'Where's Tallinn?' she asks pertly.

'Estonia.'

'Where's Estonia?' – giggle.

'The Baltic,' I tell her. 'North of Latvia.'

She doesn't ask me where the Baltic is, but the giggle tells me I have made my mark. I have also blown my cover, but who's counting? We ascend two more floors to the cavernous waiting room and take up a position close to the entrance. A large woman in a green uniform with a major general's epaulettes is sorting wedding groups in line ahead. Jingle bells play over loudspeakers each time a wedding ends, upon which the group nearest the shiny black door is ushered in. The door closes and the jingle bells resume fifteen minutes later.

At 11.51 Florence and Ed emerge arm in arm from the stairwell, looking like an advertisement for a building society: Ed in a new grey suit that fits him as poorly as his old one, and Florence in the same trouser suit that she had sported one sunny spring day a thousand years ago when, as a promising young intelligence officer, she presented Rosebud to the wise elders of Operations Directorate. She is clutching a bunch of red roses. Ed must have bought them for her.

We kiss each other: Prue to Florence, Prue to Ed; after which, as best man, I plant my own kiss on Florence's cheek, our first.

'No pulling back now,' I whisper loudly into her ear in my most jocular tone.

We have barely disentangled ourselves before Ed's long arms enfold me in a botched manly embrace – I doubt he's ever tried it before – and the next thing I know he has lifted me to his own height and is holding me chest to chest, half suffocating me in the process.

'Prue,' he announces. 'This man plays bloody awful badminton, but he's all right otherwise.'

He sets me down, panting and laughing in his excitement while I scan the latest arrivals for a face, gesture or silhouette that will confirm to me what I already know: Prue will not by any means be the only witness to this wedding.

'*Edward and Florence party*, please! *Edward and Florence party*, thank you. Over here, please. That's the way.'

The major general in her green uniform is marshalling us, but the shiny black door is still closed. Jingle bells rise to a crescendo and fade away.

'Hey, Nat, I've gone and forgotten the ring,' Ed murmurs to me with a smirk.

'Then you're an arsehole,' I retort, as he pushes my shoulder to tell me he's only teasing.

Has Florence looked inside Prue's expensive Japanese lipstick that I planted in her handbag? Has she read the address it contains? Has she looked up the address on Google Earth and identified the remote guesthouse high in the Transylvanian Alps owned by an elderly Catalan couple who were once my agents? No, she won't have done, she's too smart, she knows her counter-surveillance. But has she at least read my accompanying letter to them, written small on rolled-up typing paper in our best tradition? *Dear Pauli and Francesc, please do your best for these good people, Adam.*

The Registrar is a munificent lady, stern in a good cause. She has a pile of blonde hair and marries for a living, year in year out, you can tell by the patient rhythm of her voice. When she goes home to her husband in the evening he says, 'How many today then, darling?' and she says 'Round the clock, Ted' or George, or whatever his name is, and they settle to the television.

We have reached the high point of the wedding ceremony. There are two sorts of bride in my experience: those who whisper their lines inaudibly and those who belt them out for all the world to hear. Florence belongs to the latter school. Ed takes his cue from her and blurts too, clutching her hand and staring straight into her face in close-up.

Hiatus.

The Registrar is displeased. Her eye is on the clock above the door. Ed is fumbling. He can't remember which pocket of his new suit he put the ring in and he's muttering 'shit'. The Registrar's displeasure turns to an understanding smile. Got it! – right-hand pocket of his new trousers, same place he keeps his locker key while he's beating me at badminton, yeah.

They're exchanging rings. Prue moves to Florence's left side. The Registrar is adding her very personal well-wishes. She adds them twenty times a day. Jingle bells are ringing out the glad news of their joining. A second door opens before us. We're done.

A corridor to our left, another to our right. We are descending the stairwell to the third floor, everyone at a gallop except Florence who is hanging back. Has she changed her mind? The chartered accountants' receptionist grins at our approach.

'I looked it up,' she says proudly. 'It's got red roofs. Tallinn has.'

'It has indeed, and Mr Bailey assured me we were welcome to use the footbridge any time,' I tell her.

'No problem,' she sings, and presses a yellow button at her side. The electric doors judder and swing slowly apart, and as slowly close behind us.

'Where are we going?' Ed asks.

'Short-cut, dear,' says Prue as we scamper across the Venice-style footbridge with Prue leading and cars passing beneath us.

I'm jogging ahead down the lighthouse stairwell, two steps

at a time. Ed and Florence are level behind me, Prue is bringing up the tail. But what I still don't know as we enter the underground car park is whether Percy's people are coming after us, or is it just the clatter of our footsteps following us down? The hire car is a black hybrid VW Golf. Prue parked it here an hour ago. She has unlocked it and is sitting in the driver's seat. I am holding the back door open for the bride and groom.

'Come on, Ed dear. Surprise,' says Prue smartly.

Ed is uncertain, looks at Florence. Florence skips past me on to the back seat and slaps the empty place beside her.

'Come on, husband. Don't spoil it. We're off.'

Ed clambers in beside her, I into the front passenger seat. Ed is sitting sideways with his long legs. Prue touches the central locking, drives us as far as the exit and feeds her parking ticket into the machine. The boom shudders upwards. The wing mirrors are so far clear: no car, no motorbike. But none of that means much if Percy's people have marked Ed's shoes, or his new suit, or whatever else they mark.

Prue has pre-entered London City Airport into the satnav and it's showing as our destination. Damn. Should have thought of it. Didn't. Florence and Ed are busy necking, but it's not long before Ed cranes forward and stares at the satnav, then back at Florence:

'What goes on?' he asks. And when nobody answers: 'What's up, Flo? Tell me. Don't muck me about. I don't want you to.'

'We're going abroad,' she says.

'We can't. We haven't got any luggage. What about all the people we've asked to the pub? We haven't got our bloody passports. It's crazy.'

'I've got our passports. We'll get luggage later. Buy some.'

'What with?'

'Nat and Prue have given us some money.'

'Why?'

Then each with his own silence: Prue beside me, Ed and Florence in the mirror, sitting wide apart and staring at each other.

'Because they know, Ed,' Florence replies at last.

'Know what?' Ed demands.

And again we're just driving along.

'They know you did what your conscience told you to do,' she says. 'They caught you at it and they're pissed off.'

'They *who*?' Ed demands.

'Your own Service. And Nat's.'

'*Nat's* Service? Nat hasn't got a Service. He's Nat.'

'Your sister Service. He's one of them. It's not his fault. So you and me are going abroad for a bit with Nat and Prue's help. Otherwise it's jail for both of us.'

'Is that true about you, Nat?' Ed asks.

'I'm afraid it is, Ed,' I reply.

*

After that, everything went like a dream. Operationally, about as sweet an exfiltration as you could wish for. I'd done a few in my time, just never from my own country. No ructions when Prue bought last-minute Club Class tickets to Vienna using her own credit card. No calling of names over loudspeakers at check-in. No come-this-way-please as Prue and I wave the happy couple through the departure gate into Security. True, they didn't wave back, but then they'd only been married a couple of hours.

True, from the moment Florence blew my cover, Ed didn't speak to me, even to say goodbye. He was fine with Prue, muttered 'Cheers, Prue' and even managed to plant a peck on her cheek. But when my turn came round, he just peered at me through his big spectacles, then looked away as if he'd seen more than he could take. I had wanted to tell him I was a decent man, but it was too late.

Acknowledgements

My sincere thanks to the small band of loyal friends and advance readers, some of whom prefer not to be named, who waded through early drafts of this book and were lavish with their time, advice and encouragement. I may mention Hamish MacGibbon, John Goldsmith, Nicholas Shakespeare, Carrie and Anthony Rowell and Bernhard Docke. For what must be half a century, Marie Ingram, the family's literary doyenne, has never failed us in her erudition or enthusiasm. The author and journalist Misha Glenny gave me unstintingly of his expertise on matters Russian and Czech. Sometimes I wonder whether my novels stumble deliberately into the labyrinth of English legal practice for the sheer pleasure of having Philippe Sands, writer and Queen's Counsel, dig me out. He has done so again this time, while applying his magisterial eye to my textual infelicities. For the poetry of badminton I am indebted to my son, Timothy. To my longstanding assistant, Vicki Phillips, my heartfelt gratitude for her diligence, multiple skills and never-failing smile.

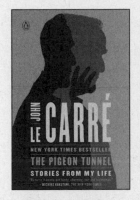